Starr of the Southwest

Starr
of the Southwest
A Western Duo

CHERRY WILSON

SAGEBRUSH
Large Print Westerns

First published in Great Britain by ISIS Publishing
First published in the United States by Five Star

Published in Large Print 2008 by ISIS Publishing Ltd.,
7 Centremead, Osney Mead, Oxford OX2 0ES
United Kingdom
by arrangement with
Golden West Literary Agency

British Library Cataloguing in Publication Data
Wilson, Cherry
    Starr of the southwest: a western duo. –
    Large print ed. – (Sagebrush western series)
    1. Western stories
    2. Large type books
    I. Title II. Wilson, Cherry. Branded sombrero
    813.5'2 [F]

ISBN 978–0–7531–8001–3 (hb)

Printed and bound in Great Britain by
T. J. International Ltd., Padstow, Cornwall

Table of Contents

Foreword

Although Cherry Wilson is virtually unknown today, over the course of her writing career she produced over 200 short stories and short novels, numerous serials, and five hardcover books. Six motion pictures were based on her fiction. Readers of *Western Story Magazine*, the highest paying of the Street & Smith publications where Wilson was a regular contributor, praised her stories in letters to the editors and ranked them with those of Max Brand.

Wilson was born Cherry Rose Burdick on July 12, 1893 in rural Pennsylvania. When she was sixteen, the Burdick family moved to the Pacific Northwest, and Cherry remained a Westerner for the rest of her life. She married Robert Wilson, and for a time the two led a nomadic existence. After Robert fell ill in 1924, they took up a homestead near Republic, Washington.

Prior to Robert's illness, Wilson had written for newspapers and tried her hand at Western fiction. One of her first stories, "Valley of Sinister Blossoms," appeared in Street & Smith's *Western Story Magazine* (8/27/21). Now, to support them, Cherry became a full-time writer. Although Street & Smith would remain her principal publisher over the course of her writing career, around this time she also began contributing stories to Fiction House's *Action Stories*. Her story, "Guns of Painted Buttes", appeared in *Action Stories* (10/25) and was named Third Prize Winner in the Authors' Popularity Contest sponsored by the magazine the year it appeared.

Among her early stories were a series of interconnected tales about the cowhands of the Triangle Z Ranch that emphasized humor and male bonding. She varied the series by borrowing an idea from Peter B. Kyne's *The Three Godfathers* (1913), making her cowpunchers co-operative caretakers of an orphan in seven of the stories. Wilson stressed human relationships in preference to gun play, although action was often supplied by rodeos, horse races, or wild horse chases. Some of her best work can be found in those stories where the focus is on relationships between children and adults, as in her novel, *Stormy* (Chelsea House, 1929), and short stories like "Ghost Town Trail" (1930) — a fascinating tale with an eerie setting and a storyline filled with mystery that can be found in *The Morrow Anthology of Great Western Short Stories* (Morrow, 1997), edited by Jon Tuska and Vicki Piekarski — and "The Swing Man's Trail" (1930) in which a boy doggedly pursues a herd of rustled cattle that has swept up his family's only cow.

In 1936, not long after she was widowed, Wilson gave up the homestead and moved to Hollywood,

California, where she lived until early in 1938 when she moved to Spokane, Washington. She was still living in Spokane when she died on November 18, 1976 at the age of eighty-three.

Buck Jones was a popular movie cowboy in the 1920s and 1930s who made four of the six films based on Cherry Wilson stories, including the first, titled *The Branded Sombrero* (Fox, 1928), based on "The Branded Sombrero" in *Western Story Magazine* (5/14/27), and the last, *Sandflow* (Universal, 1937), based on "Starr of the Southwest", a three-part serial in *Western Story Magazine* (7/25/36–8/8/36). In between came *The Throwback* (Universal, 1935), based on "The Throwback", a three-part serial in *Western Story Magazine* (4/20/29–5/4/29), and *Empty Saddles* (Universal, 1936), based on *Empty Saddles* (Chelsea House, 1929). Jones was also responsible for bringing Wilson's novel, *Stormy*, to the attention of Henry MacRae, a producer at Universal, and it was filmed under this title in 1936, starring Noah Beery, Jr., and Jean Rogers. *The Branded Sombrero* (Fox, 1928) does not survive, but the plot synopsis accompanying the film does indicate that Lambert Hillyer, who wrote the scenario as well as directed, followed the storyline of the short novel rather closely, except for making Starr Hallet, played by Buck Jones, only a stepson to rancher John Hallet while Lane Hallet is his son by birth. *Variety* (3/21/28) in its review complained: "Too much time taken to explain what *The Branded Sombrero* is all about gets this Buck Jones special off to a slow start. Lost time is made up in

3

the last half with the speed of a battler out for the edge in the final round."

In bringing "Starr of the Southwest" to the screen as *Sandflow*, Frances Guinan, an able screenwriter who worked on many of the best Buck Jones Productions at Universal, avoided explaining much at all about the sombrero, although it is prominently displayed, and combined the two stories so that the Hallet brothers have managed to pay off all the ranchers owed money by John Hallet because of his rustling except for the Broken Bell, which turns out to be the ranch in Mexico owned by the father of Rose of Lost Cañada, memorably played in the film by Lita Chevret. Because Jones had established a very definite movie cowboy persona by the 1930s, other elements of the story had to be altered to make it more a Buck Jones vehicle, including changing the name of the character he was playing from Starr Hallet (his character name in *The Branded Sombrero*) to Buck Hallet, and there is no romance between him and Rose of Lost Cañada as in the Cherry Wilson serial. *Sandflow* (Universal, 1937) is available on video and remains one of Buck Jones's finest Westerns. The exteriors were varied and well-chosen, including Red Rock Canyon, Lone Pine, and the Western town at Kernville as well as locations in the surrounding area. Lesley Selander's direction is especially striking, making full use of the locations to create and reflect mood as well as being impressive visually. There is ample use of close-ups and unusual camera set-ups, giving an intimacy to many scenes that require it and providing the entire production with a glamorous sheen expected only in a higher budget Western.

Vicki Piekarski
Portland, Oregon

The Branded
Sombrero

CHAPTER
ONE

"The Heritage"

Folks said he slept with it — that scarred and storied old sombrero. Certainly Clark Hallet of the Flying Dollar was never seen without it. Of Spanish make, and made in a land where a man's hat was considered a very important requisite of dress, it had endured with its owner thirty years of wear and tear and sun and storm. Aging as he aged, graying as he grayed, holding its shape every whit as gallantly, the old sombrero had borne with him for half a lifetime its branded record of — what? From the Río Grande to the San Juan hills, folks asked that question and, encountering the unbreakable wall of Clark Hallet's silence, invented their own reasons for the symbols on the hat. That those brands, burned deeply in every inch of the wide, cupped, silver-conchaed brim and high, peaked crown, were the record of outfits he had worked for they generally agreed, and this despite the insistence of old-timers that Clark Hallet had worked for no man but himself.

Old-timers, too — as old as "Honest" Zain Marsh of the Broken Bell — remembered a time when the hat was new and innocent of brands. It was when Clark

Hallet, no older than were his two sons now, had come into the Black Plains country of New Mexico, and built a cabin on the very spot where his great, adobe ranch house now stood. On a plank over the cabin door he had burned the Flying Dollar brand — a brand now imperishably recorded in the high, stone arch over the ranch house gate. Soon after his coming the first brands were noticed on the big sombrero. But when they first appeared, or when they ceased — from lack of room, or a cessation of whatever motive had caused them to be seared there — were points lost in antiquity, if ever known. In the strenuous life of the frontier, settlers were much too busy to heed the hobbies of other men.

With passing years the branded hat became so much a part of Clark Hallet that neighbors ceased to wonder, and only strangers questioned. Home folks were secretly proud of it, as they were proud of the picturesque and genial cattleman it adorned. He would not have seemed the same to them without it. For always — in the cool patio of the Flying Dollar, on the gray-green plains, in convention at Socorro or Santa Fé, even to Kansas City on annual cattle-shipping jaunts — he wore the big sombrero with its black and flaunting brands. Many knew the hat who did not know the man.

But one mellow, June-sweet day, while riding the Flying Dollar range, Clark Hallet was thrown from his horse and word flashed over the plains that at last he was to part from his old sombrero forever. "At sunset," the doctor said. Nor was man ever paid a more genuine tribute than that given the old rancher in the instinctive way — every eye turned in sorrow and dread to the golden disk high above the Magdalena Mountains.

From his bed at the Flying Dollar, Clark Hallet sought also through the open casement the sun above the distant range, and with that calm with which he met every crisis of life he asked to be left alone with his sons. For them, and them alone, was reserved the true and terrible meaning of the sombrero of many brands.

"Long before you was man-high, an' after," the father labored to speak, his sunken, burning eyes turning from his sons who knelt, pale and tense beside his bed, to the familiar old hat beneath his nerveless hands, "you've asked about these brands. God only knows what I told you, but God knows it wasn't true. But I'm askin' Him to witness the truth I'm tellin' you now! And only He kin know what it's costin' me to tell ... *I must!*" — his fierce enthusiasm silenced their swift protests. "Don't hinder me, boys. I've much to say, an' . . . the sun is settin'."

Yet he paused to search the faces of his sons, and dead must Clark Hallet already have been not to thrill with pride in them. Fine upstanding men — both. Both much like he had been in early youth. It was this likeness to himself that worried the father now. Not so noticeable in Starr — looking at him with his mother's quiet courage and warm, candid eyes of gray — as in Lane, the younger one, who revealed his headlong, impetuous nature even in his grief. Only the father knew how like himself in his own rash youth Lane was, and it was for Lane he worried.

"There ain't time to choose words," he whispered. "I'm givin' it to you straight . . . knowin' you'll stand up to it. For whatever else I've done, thank God I've bred men. My boys," — Clark Hallet closed his eyes, that he might be spared the agony of seeing the horror in theirs — "your father was a thief . . . a rustler! Is still a thief. This old sombrero is the record of my crimes. From every brand burned here, I've stolen cows . . . the dots around each brand tell how many. Most men . . ." — his ghostly smile of self-mockery gave his face a startling resemblance to Lane's — "most men keep their sins under their hat, but I burned 'em deep on mine. Folks think I'm leavin' you the Flyin' Dollar, but all I kin rightly leave you is my ol' sombrero with its record of shame."

He paused, fighting for breath and calm, and scalding tears flowed from under his closed lids down the deep furrows of his face. Comfortingly he felt the warm pressure of their hands on his.

"You know all about my raisin' in Wyomin', an' how my dad was wiped out in the big range wars there. You've heard ol'-timers tell how rustlers got so powerful they made the law. Those operatin' in our section was called the Dagget Gang. Who Dagget was, I don't know. I never saw him . . . few did. Mebbe it's true, as I've heard, that he was only a kid in years, but he shore was a devil in meanness. For they gave my father the same two chances they gave every rancher thereabouts . . . pay tribute to the gang for its protection, or lose every hand on his place, an' mebbe his life to boot. 'Most everyone gave in . . . had to . . .

for the gang controlled the local courts. But a few of the gamest didn't. My dad was one of the few. Inside a year Dagget had cleaned him out, lock, stock, an' barrel, an' Dad died dirt poor. Boys," — pitifully he strove for understanding — "I thought he done wrong . . . then. God forgive me, I used to tell him so. But, all my growin' years, I'd seen the wicked prosper. I'd noticed folks didn't ask how you made your money, but did you *have* it. An' when I was left alone, I made up my mind to git my share, regardless. Boys, I wasn't seein' straight. Every now an' then, I'd catch a rumor of how Dagget was livin' respectable in some fur land . . . livin' high an' fat on his accursed gains, while I was driftin' around the country with nothin' but the cayuse under me an' the duds on my back . . . an' it made my vision crooked."

With the brevity of one on whom each word takes shocking toll in time and strength, he told his sons how, down in Texas, he had heard of the Black Plains country and had come there, of the vast, unfenced, unpeopled land he had found and loved.

"I filed on a homestead, built a cabin, made my iron, an' started up in the cattle business. As a rustler, I was a tinhorn at first. I could be crooked, but I wasn't happy in it, for there was a cross-pull in my blood. So, whenever I worked over a brand on a cow I'd stole, I burned it on my hat, too, easing my conscience with the notion that someday I'd pay it back. I got so expert with the iron, went so far in my raids, that none ever suspicioned, an' the few ranchers in the Black Plains country begun to look up to me a heap. An' then I met

13

your mother. Bein' young an' head over heels in love, I throwed caution to the four winds, an' rustled right an' left. I wanted to be fit for her. Not fit in my heart, but in the way I thought counted . . . cattle, money, lands. I built this house, an' married. An' from then on my life was heaven an' hell in one. For, though I quit rustlin' the day I married, there was never a day but I feared the truth would out, an' your mother would hear. Never a day but I hated myself! She was the soul of honor, an' thought I was. She brought me to see like she did. An' day after day, year in an' out, I'd see myself for the thievin' *hombre* I was . . . unfit for her, not fit for decent folks anywhere. Then the railroad went through, an' I was counted rich for them times. But I had no pleasure in it. All I wanted was to be poor an' honest . . . to pay back what I stole. But I was afraid of bein' found out a-doin' it, an' losin' her respect. I quit lookin' on the Flyin' Dollar as mine, but as a trust for them I robbed."

Spent, he paused to rally strength for what he still must say. Starr Hallet never forgot that moment, the deep, unnatural hush over the Flying Dollar, and, more profound than silence, the muted moaning of the Mexican house servants drifting into the room; once the silvery tinkle of spurs, as the foreman, old Link Jarvis, passed the window, faithfully serving Clark Hallet in his last hour, as he had for the last quarter century.

"That's why I've hung onto this hat," the father whispered. "Folks josh me . . . say I sleep with it. Folks know it by hearsay, who don't know me. All these years

14

I've kept it close, hopin' to make good. It's the only record I made . . . *dared* to make . . . by which I could make good. When *she* died last fall, I swore to do it, but I put it off . . . too late. Now I'm goin' to her, an' I want to go clean."

Frankly, desperately now, his eyes appealed to them. When he spoke, it was in strangling tones, for death had him by the throat. "My sons, I want you to make restitution. No, I ain't askin' you, don't want you to promise. *I'm trustin' you.* An' I want you should think of me, boys, as the man you've allus knowed me. But . . . ," — a rift broke through fog of his eyes and his gaze seemed fairly to leap out at Lane — "but if ever you're tempted, think of me as the miserable, haunted, dishonored human I've really been. In every generation of Hallets, there's been one who's showed yellow. I was the one in mine. I've prayed my sons would escape the taint. I've banked big on your mother's blood. She was strong enough to guide me right, when I had the bit in my teeth an' was runnin' wild. It's a power God gives good women . . . the mothers of men. No spirit so wild but it kin be tamed if the steady, lovin' touch of a good woman is on the reins."

With what hope, what heartache, was Starr to remember that! His father's eyes closed again. Plainly the end was near. It seemed to Starr that the brands on the old sombrero leered at him of sin and anguish past, prophetically spoke to him of worse sin, crueler anguish yet to come. He saw his father's eyes open and fix themselves strangely on the old hat.

"That big brand," he gasped. "What do you make of it?" Clark Hallet couldn't die without assurance that they read his record right.

Quickly Starr counted the dots encircling the most conspicuous brand on the high crown, and his heart almost burst in his breast as he read that brand in the light of its new and shameful meaning.

"It means," he answered steadily, for Lane couldn't speak for sobs, "we owe the Broken Bell . . . Zain Marsh . . . thirty-seven cows."

Peace touched the father's heart at that spontaneous "we". "An' interest," he panted eagerly. "Pay Zain the interest. Of late years . . . my best friend . . . Zain . . . it's shore . . . been hell." A moment later his voice trailed back to them, almost from over the Great Divide. "I can't face *her* till the last brand's vented. Starr, Lane, remember . . . *Lane* . . ."

Could Clark Hallet have known at what awful cost that last brand would be vented, would he have made that frail, broken, frantic appeal to Lane? *¿Quién sabe?* . . . as Black Plains folk would say. Who will ever know? For inexorably, majestically, with a million fiery streamers of light, the sun sank behind the Magdalena Mountains.

CHAPTER
TWO

"The Yellow Hallet"

For one year the branded sombrero was missed from the salt grass plains. It hung on the great buckhorns over the fireplace in the ranch house, an eloquent reminder of Clark Hallet's debt, a debt never alluded to by his sons, a subject on which each thought the other of his own mind. But tonight they would speak of it. They would speak when Starr Hallet finished plowing through the mass of accounts that snowed the living room table under. Opposite his brother, Lane nervously flicked his riding boots with the braided quirt and waited.

For tonight, one year after their father's death — and one month since the last of the red tape surrounding the settling of his estate had been unwound — the Black Plains country was outraged by news that the Flying Dollar had been sold. Those who missed the old sombrero most were the most indignant. Clark Hallet's lifeblood had gone into the development of the ranch. His sons should have kept it, a living, growing monument to him. His friends had taken it for granted that they would keep it, had been loud in their praise of the way Starr had stepped into harness with the old foreman, Link Jarvis, and pulled the ranch through a barren season of drought. Now the place was sold. They did not know that it was sold at Clark Hallet's own personal wish, and his sons were resolved that they never should know.

"Countin' out all debts," Starr cheerfully announced, looking up from his task, "we'll have around twenty thousand dollars. Not bad . . . considerin' the slump, an' that we had to sell for cash. We can pay off most of those brands, then . . ." His heart leaped to his throat at Lane's look of sheer amazement.

"Pay off those brands?" Lane struggled between total incredulity and scorn. "You're crazy, Starr! You sure don't aim to break yourself settlin' them ol' debts!"

Starr Hallet's face went white as the paper under his hand. "Lane, you don't mean that? You . . . you're jokin', Lane. You know you're as keen for it as I am. Why, you couldn't wait till we got everything in cash."

"Sure not," admitted the boy shamelessly. Nor was it shame, but the storm within himself, that now caused him to pace up and down the long room. "Starr," — Lane, turning abruptly, flung out — "I'm sick of ranch life. I *hate* it! I'd go loco if I had to see much more of it. I've found something more to my likin', while you've been pluggin' away here. All my life I've been hobbled. But now the hobbles are off. I'm goin' to stay in town an' kick up my heels a bit."

Stunned, Starr looked at his brother and really saw him for the first time in a year. Saw him with pride, for Lane was a handsome lad, especially now in his defiant pacing with a dare-devil light in his deep, black eyes.

Saw him, too, with nameless fear. What had the past year done to Lane? He'd been too busy with ranch work to pal around with him as he always had done before. But he'd worried about Lane's spending so much time in Mescalero, a rather wild cow town some twenty miles away. He remembered now his many demands for money and guessed, by the expensive clothes he wore, the costly big bay he had brought home last night, that Lane had been drawing on his prospects as well.

"That's why I was wild to sell," the boy went on fiercely. "To get away. Not to turn over my share to pay a lot of whiskered debts I didn't make . . . that were made before I was ever born! Here's one son who doesn't aim to let the sins of his father descend on him. Anyhow, we didn't promise. Dad didn't ask us to . . ."

"He trusted us," Starr said in a shaken tone.

Lane's face flamed, and he looked away. "Dad couldn't see the dry year ahead . . . the cattle slump, with the bottom droppin' out of the beef market," he jerked out defensively, pushing back his black hair with the nervous, irritable gestures so much a part of him. "He wouldn't expect us to do it now . . . when we haven't near the money he figured on. Why, take that Broken Bell brand alone . . . figure the cows worth ten dollars a head when Dad . . . took 'em. The interest on thirty-seven cows would bring it up around fifteen hundred dollars now. But say we paid it out . . . the whole twenty thousand. We couldn't clean the slate, an' we'd be broke. We'd have to go to work punchin' cows at forty per, an' never *could* pay. While, if we put the money to work for us, someday we can square Dad an' never miss it."

There was logic in that, but Starr Hallet didn't hear it. He couldn't hear anything but his father's strangled tones: *I can't face her till the last brand's vented.*

"I reckon you gotta right to do as you like with your share," Starr said slowly. "Dad didn't insist, so I can't. But me . . . I'm goin' to square Dad."

"A regular Honest Zain," Lane bantered.

"I'd rather have a name like Zain Marsh than anything in life," Starr said stoutly. "But don't think I'm settin' myself up for a tin god, Lane. I'm jist made that way." There was an awkward silence, which Starr broke by the appeal: "Lane, change your mind about Mescalero. Come along with me. Keep your half . . . but come. We'll run down those brands an' pay as far as we can with mine. No tellin' how far I'll have to go, or how long I'll be gone. But it won't mean half so far, or so long, with you, Lane."

"No chance!" Lane picked up his hat. "I aim to blaze my own trail now. Anything else on your mind, Starr? If not, I'm ridin' over to the Broken Bell."

There was a queer look on Starr Hallet's face at that. Somehow it hurt, that Lane was continuing his visits to Zain Marsh — to Connie — that the Broken Bell brand on the old sombrero, the fact that his father had stolen from Marsh, wasn't enough to keep him away. Not once since he had learned it, had Starr gone over, although the two families had been always intimate before, although he missed the companionship of

20

pretty, blue-eyed Connie Marsh, more it seemed each day.

But Lane had never thought of it from that angle. Worse, he wrongly interpreted his brother's expression now. Crossing quickly to Starr, he stood over him, his dark eyes earnest. "Sweet on Connie?" he asked gently.

Blankly Starr met his gaze. Was he? He hadn't given a name to his feeling for Connie Marsh. Was it love? Anyhow, it couldn't matter — not now. Slowly he shook his head. "Reckon I'm down in the mouth about leavin' home an' all." He smiled wanly. "It's this break between us, Lane, that hits me hardest. I'd hoped we'd go on together. That's why I held out that cabin and twenty-acre piece mother left me over on Zuñi Creek . . . for our home. I'm sendin' some stuff over from the Flyin' Dollar to make it seem like home. When you get tired of high flyin', Lane, come back there. I'll be back off an' on . . . an' it would make me plumb happy to find you there. You'll come home, Lane?"

"Sure!" Promises came easily to the youngest Hallet. On the way to the door his eyes fell on the old sombrero. "Jist to show I ain't stingy," the boy sang gaily, "I'll give you my share in the family heirloom."

Instantly rising, Starr crossed over to the fireplace, and took the old sombrero from the horns. There was a light of resolution in his gray eyes, a curious pride in the lift of his head, as he put it on. Put on with it, not half but *all* of the cruel burden of shame and debt his father had bequeathed. Till the last brand was marked out he would wear it.

Touched by the act, by all it presaged, Lane in one of his lightning changes took his brother by the shoulders. "Look here, ol' man!" he cried huskily. "You know I'd give you the shirt off my back if you needed it. Don't you, Starr?"

Starr *did* know it! Lane could be cruel and tender, selfish and generous, gay and despondent, all in a breath. Now, as Lane slammed out and his quick, running steps, his merry whistle on his way to the corral, drifted back to Starr, he was strangely tempted to throw off the burden — just for this one night — and ride with him to the Broken Bell. But, no! The Hallets' debt to Zain Marsh was big enough already. Taking off the big sombrero, he looked long at the Broken Bell brand on the crown. Till that was marked out he'd stay away, and, lest he be tempted to pay this debt and forget the rest, he vowed to save it till the last. Until then, the less he saw of Connie Marsh, the better!

One dawn, as the rising sun stained the distant cliffs a blood-red hue, the Hallet boys rode out under the high, stone arch on which was chiseled the Flying Dollar brand. In time they might reënter it, but never again would it be home. This thought clouded even Lane's high spirits, but not for long. He was riding with Starr only as far as the crossroads. He was free, white, and twenty-one. He had $10,000 to his credit in the Mescalero bank. Life loomed like a rainbow of rare and gorgeous tints.

From time to time he stole quick glances at his brother. Starr's face under the old hat looked tired. At

22

the crossroads, he would turn off to hunt the outfits that had suffered from his father's raids. He hadn't enough money to repay half the debts. Then — what? Years of toil, of sacrifice.

"It's a life job, Starr," Lane said.

"I'm needin' a job." The other grinned.

"An' a thankless one," Lane added. "Forgit it, Starr . . . an' come along with me." It comforted him after to remember that he did feel a pang of disappointment when Starr declined.

Now they were at the parting of the ways. Their hands met in a tight clasp, and over them their eyes met, and in their eyes was all the strong, the unusual affection they felt for one another. Strangely, to Starr Hallet in that moment, came the feeling that all was wrong, that he must hold Lane like this always, never let him go. He was too young, too reckless to be thrown into life as it was lived in Mescalero. After all, his first duty was to the living.

"I know what you're thinkin'," Lane startled him by saying, and Starr was no less startled by the sudden change in Lane. "You're thinkin' of what Dad said . . . about there bein' a yellow Hallet in every generation. You're thinkin' I'm the one in mine."

Even as he denied that hotly, Starr saw his way clear. He believed in Lane. He must prove it then by trusting him. So he left his brother to blaze his own trail, and began his long pilgrimage wherever the old sombrero led.

CHAPTER
THREE

"The Trail of Brands"

Far Starr Hallet journeyed, as his father had journeyed so many years ago. Much, too, as his father had journeyed into the Black Plains country — with nothing of his own but the horse under him and the clothes on his back. But Pancho, his stout-hearted, blaze-faced black, was something of home, and in Starr's money belt was £10,000 toward repaying his father's debt, so his heart was as light as it could possibly be without Lane.

To chance travelers, Starr was not merely another dusty, plodding rider, for he wore the sombrero of many brands. It surprised him how many knew the hat, and he was pleased at the respectful attention it drew. Of these wayfarers he made veiled inquiries concerning the brands upon it. Learning that many of them were located in Doña Ana County, he headed Pancho that way.

There is no lonelier land on earth than he traversed after fording the Río Grande and crossing the San Andreas. Now for monotonous days he rode on a high plateau clothed with yellow mesquite grass, black tar brush, and the creamy, waxen loveliness of the

24

blossoming yucca, now over a shimmering desert of glaring white chalk and sand, devoid of life save where, wondrously, an occasional scarlet cactus flamed. Long stretches there were, even more hellish, where the earth beneath Pancho's hoofs was cracked with heat. But at last — sun-dazzled, weary from the blistering miles — he rode up on the skyline of a range and again reached grass and ranches and herds.

Scouting among the cattle, he found many of the brands recorded on the sombrero and decided to make his beginning here. Since he had resolved never to draw on his father's money for his personal needs, he must work his way. That big ranch, looming off there across the plains, was as good as any.

"What ranch?" he asked a *vaquero*, mending fences a half mile out.

"*Señor*, eet ees the Bar Z," was the polite response.

Starr was pleased at his random choice, for that brand, heavily dotted, was on the old sombrero. Briefly and with confidence he made his request for work to the Bar Z rancher who strode out on the porch to greet him. The owner looked over this applicant with interest, for the lean, bronzed, frank-faced, clear-eyed rider before him, in outfit neither too old nor too new, represented the highest type of cowboy obtainable. But there was more than interest in his eyes as he regarded the branded hat.

"That sombrero's all the recommendation I need!" the old cattleman said heartily. "I've heard of it. I've heard a *man* wore it!"

"My father," Starr said with pride.

Warmed by this tribute to his father, he made up his mind to blot the Bar Z first. But here a difficulty arose. He couldn't just count the dots around that brand, figure up the interest, and hand the cash over. It wasn't as simple as that. For, if he was to protect his father's honored name, no one must ever suspect from whom the money came. He decided to return it anonymously and by mail. But he had been a week on the Bar Z before an opportunity came.

Sent to Mesquite one day on an errand for the ranch, he dropped through the mail chute of the little post office an envelope, addressed to his employer containing $700 in bills.

The thrill of satisfaction this act gave him was not to be compared with the thrill that was his on the way back, when, stopping far out on the range, he built a little fire of mesquite twigs, in it heated white-hot a bit of wire he'd brought, and, sitting there cross-legged in the chaparral, burned a thin, straight line through the Bar Z brand on the old sombrero.

"Dad," he whispered to the gathering dusk and boundless solitudes, "I've started. *The first brand's vented.*"

But, as Starr found in his weeks as a Bar Z cowpuncher, it wasn't always so easy to repay. Many of the ranches recorded had changed hands. In some cases the original owners were dead, and there were heirs to look up. Some had left the country and must be traced. But those he could repay, he paid secretly. And to many the money — payment for a few cows stolen long ago and never missed — was heaven-sent. An old loan, they thought. In the open-handed days of the West, most men had made many. But, true to human nature, they didn't delve too deeply into the source of an unexpected windfall.

All that summer Starr pursued his quest. Many localities — the Apache country, the Rolling Mesa, and the Rabbit Ear range — saw the old hat. To him it was Open Sesame. The man who wore it was always certain of a job, and there was now a thin line burned through a full quarter of the brands. But there must come a halt in payments soon, for the money was going fast. Where was more coming from to make the rest?

Always — riding line, standing his lonely watch on the night herd, or trailing the choking dust of the cattle drives — Starr asked himself this question. And always something seemed to pull him back to the Black Plains — an urgent, insistent feeling that he was needed there — that Lane needed him!

"Homesick!" he'd exclaim in self-scorn. "Jist plain homesick for Lane!"

Maybe Lane was waiting for him at the cabin. Maybe that's what this feeling meant. Curious, he remarked to Pancho under the big yellow stars hanging over the high table land where he made his solitary camp, curious how folks had thought Lane had needed him. Lane never *had* needed him as much as he had Lane. Maybe he did steady the kid a bit, but what was that to what Lane did for him? Lane was like a part of him — the dashing, careless, happy part. Why, the kid was so full of ginger, without him there wasn't any spice in life.

Starr missed Link Jarvis, too — good old Link! He'd been foreman of the Flying Dollar since before Lane was born. He'd been a sort of second father to them both. Talked to him like a dad, too, Link had, the night before he left. Told him Lane was running with a wild bunch in town and ought to be checked up a bit. He'd been a little short with Link. Never could bear to have folks pick on the kid. He could trust Lane to the limit and over, he'd told Link. "You kin trust a man to his own undoin', son," Link had said. Had he put too much trust in Lane? With his reckless disposition, and all that money . . . Was the kid in trouble? Was that what this feeling meant?

"Homesick!" he derided himself to Pancho. "Go on . . . make himself miserable thinkin' thataway. You gotta stick!"

But by the middle of August, down in the Pecos Valley of Texas, this feeling had grown so strong that he knew it was what it was. Not homesickness — but a hunch about Lane. He'd felt it a time or two in their kid days, when Lane had come to grief. He'd do what he always had done — go to Lane.

But he'd kill two birds with one stone. The Pecos country had been hard hit by the drought, and cattle were correspondingly cheap. He'd buy up a small band with the money left, drive it home, and turn it on the range back of the cabin on Zuñi Creek. A few months on good grass, and he could sell the cattle at a profit. That way, he'd make enough money to wipe out a few extra brands, just by going home.

Six months after leaving the Black Plains country, Starr Hallet was entering it again, trailing — in stifling dust and heat and with the help of one tatterdemalion Mexican youth, Florencio — fifty head of scrawny two-year-olds.

Although night had come on, they kept the trail. Home was too near to camp short of it. As they wound slowly by the Flying Dollar, Pancho tried to turn in.

"No more, ol' boy!" said Starr, and his eyes smarted.

So they kept on, under a blazing roof of stars, and the cowboy's heart leaped to see far over the plains another star — not a heavenly star, but the light of the Broken Bell. A wave of homesickness swept over him, keener than he had felt for the Flying Dollar. Always, to him and Lane, the Broken Bell had been no less home. When could he go there? Ever? God, but he was lonesome to chin a bit with old Honest Zain! Must be fine to be so respected that folks gave you a label like that! And Connie . . .

Roughly shouldering Pancho against the rest of the flagging, snailing band of steers, Starr climbed the trail along Zuñi Creek. He hoped against hope to see yet another star — lamplight brightening the cabin window, showing Lane was there.

But the cabin was dark, and held no sign that Lane had ever been there. Not having heard from his brother since that dawn when they parted at the crossroads, Starr's anxiety, which had grown with every homing mile, leaped now to panic.

CHAPTER
FOUR

"Folks Talk"

He had to get the herd on the range before seeking Lane, and this took the Mexican and himself most of the next day.

Riding back to the cabin that afternoon, Starr decided to take Lane with him when he left the Black Plains. Likely Lane would want to go, now he'd had his fling. Well, he'd soon know. For he was going into Mescalero as soon as he'd washed up and had supper, and he'd sent Florencio back an hour ago to have it ready. Funny, Starr thought, how he couldn't wait a minute now to see Lane, considering how long he'd . . .

His keen eyes caught a flash above him and, halting, he saw a white mustang tear out along the grassy slope. For an instant it stood there, mane and tail flying against the blue, while its diminutive rider, rising in the stirrups, waved a sombrero wildly and sent a shrill, clear call ringing down to him. Connie!

Unaccountably, as Starr answered hail and wave, his heart leaped in his breast, then fell to pounding madly as the mustang flashed down the slope and vanished in a screen of aspens. Now, as Connie appeared on the level and came toward him, her mustang slowed to a walk, Starr's eyes, sharpened by absence, saw her as might a stranger.

Her beauty amazed him. Beauty to which the old, close intimacy had made him blind — the gold glints in her rich, brown hair where the sun caressed it, her wild-rose skin that no sun or wind could tan, the deeper, violet blue of her eyes, the grace of her in the saddle, her smile, as now, in welcome — was ever anything, he thought, half so sweet and friendly as Connie Marsh's smile? He wondered why he felt like this — as awkward as a schoolboy. It was only Connie. A thousand times he'd met her on the range, but *never* exactly like this! For his heart sang with mad, sweet music, that yet had a sad and tragic undertone.

Why, I . . . I love her! he said to himself, aghast at the thought. *I've given a name to it now. I loved her when I used to tease an' bully her . . . like she was a kid sister of mine. I love her now, when I ain't got no right . . . can't love her!* But he only said, as he leaped from Pancho and took her hands: "Hullo, Connie."

"Hello, stranger." Connie's tone matched his. "When did you get back?"

"Last night."

"And didn't come over?" There was just a hint of reproof.

He was late getting in, he stammered, and had been busy as a beaver all day.

"Were you coming over tonight?" Her blue eyes held his steadily.

Haltingly he told her no. He was framing some excuse.

"Starr," she cut in with that directness that marked her as Zain Marsh's daughter, "it's been more than a year since you've set foot on the Broken Bell. What's wrong? Have you forgotten old friends?"

The truth almost broke from him then — that it wasn't friendship he wanted of Connie Marsh and that he was honor-bound not to say what he did want until the last brand on the old sombrero was burned out. "I've got a hard job ahead, Connie." His slow earnestness brought a deeper glow to the girl's cheeks. "I don't know when I'll see the end of it . . . only that it'll be long. But the minute I'm done, I'm hittin' straight for the Broken Bell."

Somehow talk came easier then. Leaving their horses to graze, they sat down on a boulder, where Connie eagerly told him all that had gone on in his absence. How the new Flying Dollar owners had hired the old crew back — all but Link Jarvis. How the old foreman was now a deputy sheriff in Mescalero. Anything and everything — but of Lane.

"That's good . . . about Link," Starr interrupted. "He'll keep an eye on Lane."

Instantly her face was grave. "If I were you, Starr, I wouldn't depend on Link."

Her gravity chilled him. Connie wouldn't have said that without a reason. He asked calmly: "What's wrong, Connie?"

She rose abruptly. "Let's ride."

Together they rode down the winding trail, but their horses clicked off a mile and still she didn't answer. Her sombrero shaded her face but, in flashing glimpses,

Starr saw that it was troubled. Unable to bear the suspense longer, he quietly prompted her: "What's wrong, Connie?"

"Don't ask me, Starr!" He felt, rather than saw, her keen distress. "All I know is what they say."

"Who's *they?*" he asked quizzically.

"Oh . . . folks."

"Jist what do they say, Connie?"

Then she told him, meeting his look squarely. "They say he's running wild . . . gambling, drinking, squandering the money his father left. They say he's parted with most of it over the tables of the Monterey."

"Yeah?" Starr's tone was as light as his heart was heavy. "What else do folks say?"

His indifference stung her. "They say there's a little *señorita* in the case . . . Rosa Melles. You know, Starr, her father runs the Monterey. They say Lane's stayed there . . . ever since going to Mescalero."

"Folks will talk, Connie." His tone was careless, but his knuckles were white over the reins. Folks mustn't know he was worried by any gossip about Lane. "They don't know Lane like I do, Connie. Me . . . I'm his brother."

"Starr," the girl was doubly serious, "they say Lane's running with Tex Maggart."

At that, Starr Hallet was hard put to hide his fear, but his lean, still face masked it perfectly. Tex Maggart! The worst badman unhung, the worst possible companion for a kid like Lane! Gambling, drinking — what were they to this?

"Folks talk," he reiterated.

"Often with truth, Starr!" she flashed.

"That's so, Connie," he admitted soberly. "Well, I'll look Lane up . . . tomorrow."

And to prove his faith in his brother he postponed their meeting another day. That his was blind, stubborn, fanatical faith, he would learn at bitter cost, bitter regret that he had not rushed from Connie's side to Lane.

Alone that night on the cabin steps in the twilight, with the plaintive strains of Florencio's guitar drifting to him from within, he thought of Lane. Of the heedless, headstrong kid he'd always been. Into one scrape after another, and always sorry as sin when his dad or brother pulled him out. But soon forgetting to be sorry . . .

Out of the dark of the dusk and his thoughts came his father's dying words: *No spirit so wild but it kin be tamed, if the steady, lovin' touch of a good woman is on the reins.*

If only some woman would do for Lane what his mother had done for his father — a woman like Connie! Did Connie love Lane? Was that the cause of her anxiety for him? There was an ache in his heart as he turned the old sombrero around and around in his trembling hands. However he turned it, plain in the dim light was the Broken Bell brand. The day when he could mark it out was far away. The love of a good woman could tame the wildest spirit. And Lane — Lane was running with Tex Maggart! There on the cabin steps, Starr made his decision. While there was any hope of Connie's loving Lane, his own love —

which he knew would endure to his last breath — must be locked tightly in his heart. If he could bring them together, he would. The Broken Bell brand on the old sombrero stood between himself and Connie, but he'd see it didn't stand between Connie and Lane. That debt was his.

Starr Hallet's shoulders drooped, and the ache in his heart was steady and intense, as he went into the cabin.

CHAPTER
FIVE

"Too Late"

Mescalero was coming up for air after a stifling day when Starr rode in. The long street of ugly, squat, reddish adobe structures teemed with swarthy *peónes* and sun-browned cowpunchers, milling aimlessly up and down, or squatting sociably on the curb. Hoping to find Lane among them, Starr tied Pancho to a hitching rail and set out on foot. Before he had gone a block, his arms were clapped tightly to his sides from behind, and someone shook him hard and lovingly.

"Starr Hallet! You ol' hoss thief!" this someone roared, and, recognizing that endearing term, Starr whirled to see old Link Jarvis, grinning from ear to ear. "Waal, I see Zain's answer!" Link said fondly, holding the cowboy off, and hungrily looking him up and down.

"How's that?" Starr grinned, happy as Link at this meeting.

"One day," the old man explained, "I says to Zain as how Clark was luckier'n most . . . leavin' two sons big enough to fill his boots. An' Zain, he says . . . 'What I'm wonderin' is which will be big enough to wear his hat?' An', son, I'd 'a' laid my bets then as how it'd be you who'd blossom out in the old sombrero!"

Uncomfortable at a compliment disparaging to Lane, Starr changed the subject. "How's the world treated you, Link?"

"Tolerable," Link conceded. "But judge for yourself, son." He pulled back his vest with ill-concealed pride to display a silver star.

"Deputy, huh?" Starr couldn't spoil the old man's pleasure by letting him know he'd already heard. "How the Sam Hill did that happen?"

Link glanced quickly around. "Reckon I got rustlers to thank for it, son," he said in a lowered tone. "They've broke out here, for the first time in years, an organized gang of 'em. We've had our suspicions right along who's headin' that gang, but no proof. That's what Sheriff Eph Colter swears me in to git . . . Eph knowin' I savvy the country a mite better'n most."

With naïve pride, he went on to explain how he'd got proof. Trailing some rustled cows, he'd found the hidden cañon in the hills where the gang was bunching the stolen stock till the time came to start it to an abandoned railroad siding near the old Sutter mine, where cars would be waiting. He'd learned when they were starting the cattle, by crawling under cover of night within earshot of their campfire — at the peril of a bullet or knife thrust, a fact Link didn't dwell on. "Kin you keep a secret, son?"

By the old man's manner Starr knew something serious was afoot. "I reckon," he said soberly.

"So do I reckon," endorsed Link, drawing him into the doorway of a vacant building. "Waal, the drive's due to come off tonight," he whispered cautiously, "an' we're pullin' off a raid at moonrise. We aim to trap the whole gang at that cañon, an' make a clean sweep!"

"Where?" by some fortuitous, blessed chance, Starr asked.

"At Carson's Tanks! It's that box cañon right back of the windmill. Better trail along, son. I kin git you deputized. Eph's swore in half the town. The posse's bandin' right now."

"Like to, Link," Starr answered. "Got a herd on the range myself that I'd hate to have rustled. But I come in to see Lane. How is he, Link?"

Instantly Link Jarvis seemed miles removed in spirit. "If you mean, is he in health," he said stiffly, "why, I ain't heard nothin' to the contrary."

Instantly Starr froze up, too. He'd not question anyone hostile to Lane, but it worried him more than his own hunch, or anything Connie had said, that old Link had gone back on Lane. He'd quit this shilly-shallying. He'd go straight to the Monterey and see if Lane was there.

This dive — for he could call it nothing less — was situated in the poorest part of town, a rambling, two-storied affair, part hotel, part gambling hell, but wholly disreputable. It was hard for him to believe that Lane stayed there. He was relieved when a close search of the card rooms failed to reveal him, but a fine-looking Mexican behind the desk in the lobby, who he guessed to be the proprietor, Melles, assured him that Lane would be there soon.

There being nothing else to do, Starr waited. His chair was between the door and a winding staircase, and near the one clean thing in all that room — a caged canary, bursting his little golden throat in song. How could a bird live — in such a place when the atmosphere made even a strong man giddy! How could a kid like Lane — a range kid — stand it? Thirty minutes of it, and the incessant click of chips, the drone of voices, the stagnant air made Starr's nerves raw. But he sat on, one hour, two, for the place was waking up. Any minute that busy door might swing in for Lane.

Three dark-skinned *vaqueros* burst through that door in a high state of excitement, which they seemed to communicate to Melles as they whispered to him before passing on into an inner room. Starr could hear an excited buzz of voices through the half-open door and, looking that way, saw the *vaqueros* in the center of a wildly gesticulating group. Once he caught Tex Maggart's name, and his muscles grew tense. He was looking for Maggart, too, meant to warn that *hombre* to leave Lane alone. But he knew Maggart by sight, and was sure he wasn't present.

Whatever was up, it had set the whole house on its ear. Doors banged, men were running here and there, and whispers, whispers — Melles went upstairs three steps at a time, and, coming down, Starr caught his eyes fixed on him strangely. Often, as men pushed in and out, he saw in their eyes that same look.

A sense of uneasiness grew on him as the moments ticked slowly by — a suffocating, intangible atmosphere of danger. It occurred to him that Lane might have joined the posse, now on its way to apprehend the rustlers at Carson's Tanks. It would be like the kid —

crazy for excitement! But wouldn't Link have said so? Out of all the hints, the whispers, Starr had the sudden, terrible conviction that his sense of danger was for Lane. Unable to bear inaction longer, he was about to rush out to scour the town for him, when his eyes were arrested by a figure on the stair.

Coming down the long, winding staircase was a slim, radiant girl in a vivid, short-skirted frock of poppy hue. He knew, without knowing how he knew, that she was Rosa Melles — the *señorita* with whom Lane's name was linked. Slowly she came, her small, ringed hand sliding along the banister, each high-heeled slipper set very deliberately on the stair. Came thus slowly, Starr was certain, that she might search each face below. Was she, too, looking for Lane?

Reaching for the door, she crossed to the desk, said something in Spanish to her father, who nodded fondly, then moved toward the street door. But, passing Starr, her great dusky eyes flashed to his with a look of desperate appeal. It was only a flash, but more eloquent than words. The look entreated a warning on his part, too, for there was no break in her step. Tingling in every nerve with the certainty that here, at last, was news, *real* news of Lane, Starr curbed his impatience for some moments, then, rising in leisurely fashion, went out.

He found the girl under a spreading cottonwood behind the high adobe wall that skirted the Monterey. He saw at a glance that she was lovely, young — not more than seventeen — and in great distress. He knew instinctively that she was as unaffected by her sordid environs as the little bird that sang.

"*Señor* Hallet . . . Star-r?" she said softly. He was about to express his surprise that she knew him, when she hurriedly explained: "Eet ees the hat! The sombrero of many brands. All my live I have heard about those hat. Have heard my father say there ees in the brandings a brave tale for one with wit to . . . but I have not called you here to converse about those hat! *Señor*," she breathed, stepping closer, "why do you sit there? Tell me! Ees eet that already you have warned your brother?"

Starr stared at her blankly. His face beneath the old hat was hard and cold with a fear he could not name.

"Why do you sit there," she insisted, "when there are whisperings that the posse ees gone? When no man will stir . . . but wait like cows and say eet ees too late! But you are his brother! Why are you here?"

"Lane's with the posse, then?"

"With the posse?" Her eyes were piteous. Queerly Starr felt the pity was for him. "Oh, *Madre de Dios*, do you not understand? Do you not know your brother ees . . . ?" She paused, her carmine lips trembling.

"In God's name *where* is he?" Starr cried in a voice strange to his own ears.

"*Señor*," — and now her soft eyes filled — "he ees in gr-reat danger. He ees . . . you will find him at Carson's Tanks!"

Blindingly, horribly clear everything was now, and the posse had left an hour since! Starr bounded up the walk, but turned back and caught her wrist in a fierce grip.

"Will I find Tex Maggart there?" was his hoarse query.

"Where there ees danger?" cried the Mexican girl with a scornful laugh. "When there are brave men to take the reesk?"

Now it was she who caught and held him as he sprang away. "Hold! One theeng more I tell you. Those Maggart . . . he ees a devil! He have your brother in hees debt . . . the cards. You undeestand? That ees why Lane do thees. But go . . . *prontamente!* Or eet ees . . . too late!"

CHAPTER
SIX

"The Raid"

Out of town, out to the gathering gloom of the Black Plains, on toward the foothills, Starr rode like mad. His one hope, one purpose in life, to reach Carson's Tanks ahead of the posse and save Lane. A vain hope! A vain purpose! For over the way that Pancho's hoofs now thundered, the sheriff's men had ridden an hour ago. They would attack at moonrise, and the moon rose early.

Not even Pancho, good, true Pancho, could do that, could regain that hour he had lost — wasted! But Pancho must do it — for Lane. Suppose he had joined the posse? Suppose they had battled the rustlers, and Lane had been killed! Suppose Rosa Melles hadn't warned him, and he was still cooling his heels at the Monterey, while Lane . . . ?

But he had to quit thinking about Lane, it made him loco, and he couldn't think straight. And he must think straight! Not let Pancho do it all — Pancho, running as if he knew it was for Lane! He could help — pick out the trail, use every short cut, steer him across country when the road knotted in twists and bends. Every yard shortened was a second gained! He felt Pancho's

muscles straining beneath him, his powerful legs
working in lightning rhythm, felt his mighty momentum
in the wind that lashed his face, and could have cried
aloud his gratitude that, in this crisis, he had such a
horse.

Miles fell away, but the night fell faster. Suppose he
lost his way in the dark? But he'd take his chances with
the dark, for when light came, it would be moonlight!
Up there behind Carson's Tanks was Lane, meaning no
wrong — just a high-strung colt, with his blood up and
the bit in his teeth — running wild, not knowing death
was closing in. Lane was game. He'd fight! They'd
never arrest him. Tex Maggart knew that. That's why
Maggart had forced the kid into this to pay his
gambling debt — because he *was* game!

Tex Maggart was a gunman — a killer — worse!
Guilty of every crime under the sun, but too slick for
anyone to hang proof on. Old Link had the proof. But
it wasn't Maggart that Link would trap tonight, but
Lane. Maggart was a devil. There was just one way to
deal with a devil. And he'd sure deal with Maggart if
the kid came to harm!

A groan broke from his lips. He'd let Pancho take
that turn instead of cutting over. He'd lost a second in
which Lane might have been killed or saved! He'd have
to make it up. He'd have to find a short cut, some
nearer way. There must be one, if only he could
remember.

In his extremity a desperate scheme came to him,
and he pulled Pancho up. Off to the left, between him
and Carson's Tanks, a spur of mountain jutted out into

the plains, a hopeless jumble of chasms and crags. Dangerous footing for any horse by daylight, and at night . . . ? The posse would take this road that curved like a horseshoe around the mountain. No man in his senses would cut across.

But he wasn't in his senses, and, if he could scale that crest, he'd save not yards, but the miles the trail wound around the mountain. Could he gain an hour? He knew to his soul's despair that he could not. Pancho couldn't make time there. Pancho and he might die on the way. But what would that matter, when it was Lane's only chance?

"It's for Lane!" he told the straining horse, striking off toward the black wall of that lofty ridge. "For little Lane!"

Strangely, in that hopeless, hideous race, he didn't think of Lane as a grown man, but as the little brother he had protected and loved. A little fire-eater! Always trotting at his heels, mimicking the way he walked and talked, thinking anything Starr did was about right. Cussing him in his baby way one minute, and the next, saying things like — like: "I'd give you the shirt off my back if you needed it, Starr!"

"That's Lane . . . but the posse won't know it!" The strangled cry died under the furious thud of hoofs. "They'll figure him jist like any rustler. They'll treat him like they would Maggart! When he ain't bad . . . Lane ain't! Jist wild."

Now they were beating up that steep and jagged slope, with scant diminution in Pancho's terrific pace, little to show the additional, heart-breaking tax upon him but his convulsive breathing, and the shower of foam borne back by the wind of his running. Starr's heart was nearly breaking under its burden of self-blame. This couldn't have happened if he hadn't left Lane. Who was responsible for a kid, if his own brother wasn't? If only he could get Lane out of this scrape, he'd never leave him again. Never let him do things that would make him miserable and haunted, like his dad when he married a good woman — like Connie.

Up, up they clambered, stumbled, staggered. How many slow and awful miles? Those crags ahead — that was the top. From there, he could look down on Carson's Tanks and the cañon where Lane was working with rustled cattle, while the posse . . . At the sudden, fearful thought his blood ran cold. How could he see those crags ahead unless the moon was rising?

Don't let the moon rise, God, he prayed, *till I git Lane!*

In agony now, as Pancho broke his heart on that last steep pitch, Starr's eyes sought the sky to the east, as they had sought the western sky on that tragic sunset. But with how much more of dread, of horror now! His father had been old, had seen his mistake. While Lane . . .

The first black of night had given way to a pale, ghostly glow, and in it he saw, silhouetted against the whitening sky, a moving blackness, a great cross outstretched in the path of the rising moon — the arms of the windmill over Carson's Tanks. Giant arms, they seemed, raised against his brother. He could hear them groaning in slow revolution. But his taut ears caught no other sound. No faintest echo of shouts, or shots. He plunged down to the cañon rim, and still no sounds.

Pausing to breathe Pancho, and to catch his own breath — for his breathing was as labored as if he, too, had climbed and run — he saw a faint blur far below that he thought was the stolen bands. And he saw, to his right, a black line winding slowly down the slope that he knew was the sheriff's posse. He had won!

But only a moment was his, for now they saw him there against the moonlight and were coming at a gallop. There was no time to circle down to the opening of the cañon. He did not know if the bluff before him was sheer, or possible to descend. He only knew it was the one route by which he could beat the posse to Lane.

Relentlessly Starr sank his spurs in Pancho's sides, and, snorting terror, the horse leaped into space. Sickeningly Pancho dropped beneath him — down, down — struck, with a terrific jar, stumbled to his knees, by desperate struggles regained his feet, and went sliding, slipping down in an avalanche of shale to the cañon's floor.

Across the cañon Starr tore, at the risk of a shot from the rustlers who must have a man on guard, on toward the confused blur of the bunched cattle and men, men busy about their lawless task, unconscious that the law was closing in upon them.

Halfway across the flat, a form rose suddenly before him, and a voice cried: "Halt!"

But he did not halt, for he knew that voice — although a pistol gleamed in the moonlight, leveled, dropped — and Lane flung himself against him, gripping his knee, pistol and all, trembling, shaking, sobbing in his horror: "Oh, Starr, I'd 'a' killed you, but for knowin' . . . Dad's ol' hat!"

In a word Starr told him of his peril. "There's not a second to lose . . . they're here!"

Fortunately Lane's horse was near, and he leaped into the saddle and was shouting a warning to his confederates, when Starr seized his bridle, raking his horse to action.

"Keep close!" he begged. "We'll run for it, Lane!"

For now Eph Colter's men, knowing the rustlers had been warned, stormed into the mouth of the cañon in numbers sufficient to surround and overwhelm them, cutting off retreat. Guns blazed, men cursed, cattle bawled and stampeded in terror. The cañon was a horrible bedlam, would be a shambles soon. But through it Starr fought with Lane at his side. Nothing could stop him, till he got the kid out of this. No old bullet could faze him, now he had Lane! Indeed, the two seemed armored. For bullets crashed around them, a dozen men fought their progress, but they won through. Out of the cañon, and tearing down, down the slope, they saw three riders come in hot pursuit. Thanks to the deceptive light, the broken land, in the course of a mile the pursuers had dwindled to one.

But this one kept to the back trail, now gaining, now losing, but gaining mostly. Implacable, he was not to be shaken off by any ruse, or lost in any devious draw. In this lone pursuer Starr saw the end. Pancho was badly winded, couldn't hold out long. Lane's horse was swift and fresh.

"Beat it, Lane!" he shouted. "Cut an' run!"

His heart bounded with pride and fear at the boy's scornful laugh, his resolute: "Not much!"

Now it seemed, despite their speed, that the sheriff's man bore down on them as if they were standing still. He must not take Lane — to have him classed and punished as a rustler! That he would be judged one, Starr well knew, but that didn't count.

Intent on getting the last ounce of speed out of Pancho, he heard a deafening crash of a rifle and saw Lane's horse pitch headlong and lie without a quiver. As he reined up, Lane gained his feet. There was another roar, and Starr's blood froze as Lane's six-gun jerked up to answer.

"Don't!" he screamed. "Not that!"

Expecting any moment another shot that would end Pancho's life, his own, or Lane's, Starr got his brother up behind him for the last desperate, pitiful attempt at flight. But no shot came. Indeed, in a horror greater than any Starr had yet faced this awful night, he forgot the imminence of a bullet, of capture . . . For Lane was leaning against him too heavily. His arms were gripping his waist too tightly, and something warm, moist, horrible was soaking through his shirt in the back, where Lane's breast rested.

"Hurt, Lane?"

With feeble nonchalance the boy denied this. "Not hurt . . . jist nicked a . . ." His voice trailed off; he became a dead weight.

Heedless of sheriff or deputy on his trail, of all but Lane, Starr dismounted and got his brother in front of him, where he could support him in his arms.

Not till then did he notice with boundless amazement and relief that the back trail was clear. Why had that rider turned back with victory sure? With one horse dropped and the moonlight making their plight, their identity even, day-clear? Why, unless . . . ?

Slowly, holding Lane, Starr headed Pancho home. Exultation pervaded his whole being. He forgot that Lane was wounded, fainting, dying maybe, in his joy that he was taking him home.

Before the cabin, Starr lifted the boy in his arms, quite as if he had been that little Lane of memory. As he carried him through the door, held wide by Florencio, routed from sleep by this tragic return, Lane's eyes opened. They were so big, so black, so full of pain, and his face on Starr's shoulder was so white and young, that when he whispered with a little twisted smile — "No naggin', Starr! No *post mortems* . . . now you got me down!" — Starr's heart and eyes quite overflowed.

As if he could question, reproach Lane now! He told him so, and the boy relaxed in his arms.

"Starr! Good . . . ol' . . . scout . . ."

CHAPTER
SEVEN

"The Penitent"

"Howdy, boys!" Zain Marsh's voice — like himself, big, deep, and hearty — boomed in the cabin door, and, as he and Connie entered, they seemed to bring with them something of the sparkling sunshine of the range.

"How's the prodigal today?" Connie lilted, nearing the couch by the open window on which Lane lay.

"If I felt any better," said the boy weakly, "I'd have to be tied. What you got in that basket today, Connie . . . the fatted calf?"

"For an invalid?" retorted the girl with mock severity. "Not much! But here's jam," — placing the contents of the hamper on the little table at Lane's side — "a custard, and a jar of wild currant jelly, made with my own lily hands, and intended for a better man than you are, Lane Hallet!"

"Meanin' Zain? I sure hate to take the victuals out of your own father's mouth, Connie," said Lane with a flash of his old impudence, "but . . . Starr, trot up a spoon. Stuff another pillow under my head like a good girl, Connie. Starr means well, but his ways ain't sick room ways."

51

As Connie bent over him to adjust the pillow, there was on her face a look of tenderness, womanliness that was new, as beautiful to Starr Hallet and her father, watching, as it was disturbing to them both. A look that had come there in the past two anxious weeks, weeks in which she had helped her father and Starr to nurse Lane through a raging fever brought on by his chest wound and loss of blood. To that look Starr was resigned, as he would resign life itself for Lane's good.

But Zain Marsh, noting it for the first time, frowned. He idolized this daughter of his old age, his only child, and all he had of kin.

"You say you was with him when it happened?" he asked Starr, and his piercing blue eyes under their shaggy brows were troubled.

"Right there, Zain."

The old rancher stroked his beard with a large, slow hand. Starr watched, instantly on the alert. It was the first time Marsh had commented on Lane's injury.

"Waal, it's plumb curious," Marsh said slowly.

"What's curious, Zain?"

"How a man kin be so all-fired keerless as to shoot hisself."

"That's what makes accidents, Zain . . . folks gittin' careless."

"That's so." The rancher nodded, staring fixedly at Starr. "But it's curious it had to happen *that* night . . . the night of the big blow-up at Carson's Tanks."

"Meanin' any connection between the two?" Starr asked steadily.

"Hell, no!" apologetically exploded his friend. "You said you wuz along. I'd take your word, if I knowed better. A lie ain't in you, son."

Shame swept Starr in a hot tide. How little you ever know a man, he thought. Why, a man never knew himself! He'd never dreamed he could lie to Zain Marsh. But he could — he'd lie till he was black in the face — for Lane.

"Took on a new foreman at the Broken Bell," said Marsh. "Bet you can't guess who in a blue moon."

"Who?" asked Starr absently. What was Lane whispering to Connie that made her cheeks more wild rose still? Love words? Well, wasn't that what he wanted?

"Link Jarvis." The quiet words exploded like a bombshell in Starr's ears. "Yeah, Link resigned after that fracas . . . handed in his star that same night. Seems he let two of the rustlers git plumb away . . . after shootin' the hoss from under one, too. Mighty cut up about that, Link was," Zain Marsh mercilessly rambled on, oblivious to the stunning effect of his words on Starr. "Warned me to think twicet about hirin' a *hombre* in his dotage. I told him I'd take a chance on him . . . an' jump at it! Still an' all," Marsh meditated, "that's curious, too. I'd 'a' banked on ol' Link gittin' his man ahead of Eph Colter hisself!"

Still Starr sat speechless, seeing not Zain, or Lane, or Connie, but a lone, implacable rider in the moonlight. That rider had been Link! He'd suspected that, when he turned back. What that must have cost Link — turning back when he recognized Clark Hallet's sons!

Turning his back on a sworn duty, in his quarter century of loyalty to the Flying Dollar. But Starr must say something. Zain was waiting.

"You say there was a horse dropped?" Lane had told him he was riding a borrowed horse and saddle that night. His bay was still at the Monterey stables. "Couldn't they identify it, Zain?"

"Shore. Belonged to a *vaquero*, Blanquez. He says it was swiped that night. Likely was. Anyhow, his alibi is hole-proof. Oh, they'll eventually git the whole gang. With three dead, one in the hospital, an' four in jail . . . they've made a pretty fair start."

"Did they git Tex Maggart?" Starr's supple body seemed to lift and strain as he spoke that name.

Marsh shook his head vigorously. "He skinned out, like allus when things git hot. But there's nothin' to stop his poppin' up here again as bold as ever. They know he headed that gang, but got no proof . . . except Link's bare word as to what he overheard the night he sneaked up on the camp, an' that won't hold in court. Queer how men'll stand by a houn' like Maggart! Not a rustler'd squeal."

A great load was lifted from Starr's mind. For two weeks he'd lived in constant dread lest one of the gang implicate his brother and an officer momentarily appear at the cabin, In his relief, when they were alone, he imparted much of Zain's recital to Lane. How three men had died in the lonely cabin back of Carson's Tanks, four faced long prison terms, and Maggart had skipped.

"The coyote! The yellow coyote!"

Lane's fierce indignation brought even vaster relief to Starr. This was their first mention of Maggart, and he'd been half crazy to know if his dominion over Lane still held.

"But even if the gang doesn't squeal," worried the boy, "that officer that shot me may be wise to who we are, an' make trouble yet."

Then Starr told him it was the old Flying Dollar foreman who had given up the trail that night and that they could safely trust their identity to Link. To his dismay, Lane broke into wild sobs, and turned his face to the wall. It was long before Starr could quiet him. Then he learned how Link had hunted up Lane time and again during the past summer, talking to him like a Dutch uncle, pleading with him to give up that way of living, warning him against Maggart, until Lane got sore, and said things to Link no man could ever forgive!

"I gotta make it up to Link!" cried the boy penitently. "I'll eat dirt . . . do anything . . . to make it up to Link. He just winged me, when he'd oughta killed me! I . . . I ain't fit to live! It was Link I throwed my gun on that night. I'd 'a' killed him . . . but for you stoppin' me. An' now Link done that!"

Long after Starr had talked him out of this wild mood of self-abasement, he noticed how thoughtful the boy was, how his eyes went with him everywhere — "followy" like they had been when Lane was only six. As Starr bent over him to shift the pillows and make him easier, Lane suddenly caught his hand, pulling him down on the couch at his side.

"Starr," he whispered, "want to know how I came to team up with Maggart?"

Remembering his promise, Starr said simply: "I ain't askin', Lane."

"No," was the imperious cry, "I'm tellin' you! I . . . I want to, Starr! You've been so bully. But I don't know how to make you savvy. All my life I've heard what a bad *hombre* Tex Maggart was. I . . . I 'most thought he'd be wearin' horns. But when I saw him . . . he's plumb nice-lookin', Starr."

"I know."

"An' so smooth-tongued. An' when I saw how men kowtowed to him . . . the best of 'em, Starr . . . steppin' mighty easy around him on account of them two guns he packs . . . guns what has snuffed out more lives than folks has count of . . . why, it went to my head . . . his singlin' me out, jist a green kid from the tall grass . . ."

"I know," Starr said again.

"Oh, I know now it was that money, all right! But I was a fool . . . then. I . . . I wanted to pattern after him. I got to drinkin' an' gamblin' . . . jist to stand in with him. An' the hooch an' cards got me, Starr! So when he won all my money, an' staked me, an' won thet, why, somehow it seemed honester to work out my gamblin' debt rustlin' for him, than go on owin' him . . ."

"God knows you've paid him, Lane." Starr was alarmed, so hot was the boy's face to his touch. "Don't worry, Lane. You're through with Maggart. You'll never team up with him again."

"Never again!" Lane vowed fiercely. But he could not rest. Picking up the old sombrero from the floor at his side, he studied it with burning eyes and counted the marked-out brands. "Oh, Starr," he cried brokenly, "you was doin' this for Dad, while I . . . I . . . Starr," he pleaded, "after this, will you . . . kin I help mark out the rest?"

Could he! Starr's soul sang for sheer joy. With Lane to help he could lift a nation's debt. "I'd like that a heap," he said, the pressure of his hand on Lane's making up for his limitations in speech.

"I reckon you can't see how I can be much help . . . broke both ways from the deck," went on Lane eagerly, "but I'll show you! Oncet I git on my feet, I'll work. We'll blot them brands out in no time."

Oh, so happily then in the gathering twilight, Starr told of his trip. Of how he had paid many of the brands, traced most of those unpaid, still had money to settle two of the smaller debts — which Lane could send off himself — and of the cattle on the range, the sale of which would wipe out many more. After that, he said, they'd find a way to make more money.

"I gotta way!" Lane was all enthusiasm. "It come to me all in a flash, while you was talking! We'll catch wild mustangs, Starr . . . right here on the range. We'll break 'em . . . so they'll bring top-notch prices. I've heard there's a big market for them down at El Paso. It'll be better pay, an' heaps more fun than punchin' cows!"

Starr's elation knew no bounds. "That's the difference between us," he admired. "Ideas come hard as pullin' teeth for me, but they come to you all in a flash. We'll make a great team, Lane!"

Dark closed in on the room, and yet Starr sat on by his brother, reluctant to light the lamp, prepare their supper, make any move, lest it break the spell, and he lose Lane. He saw Connie's influence in this change in Lane. If anything could have eased the dull ache in his heart — constant since he had seen that new look in Connie's face — it was this change. He'd give anything to see Lane settled!

"Starr," the boy wondered, "how did you know I was up there . . . at Carson's Tanks?"

With that warm gratitude he felt whenever he thought of Rosa, Starr explained how she had seen him waiting at the Monterey, called him out, and sent him to Lane.

"Sweet kid . . . Rosa," the boy said after a time.

"But not so sweet as Connie," Starr said quickly, and was sure he had won over his own love by his joy at Lane's sincere: "Connie! Oh, she's in a class by herself!"

"It'll be a lucky man that wins her," Starr continued.

"Sure will!"

"He'll have something worth livin' for . . . worth livin' up to. She . . . she was mighty worried about you, Lane. Wanted I should go to Mescalero an' fetch you home."

Starr noticed with what fresh interest Lane regarded Connie when next she came, and that his manner toward her was different. Not so brotherly flippant, but gentle and considerate. And he decided to have a talk with Connie, too. Let her know Lane's wild oats were sown. That he'd seen it didn't pay. That he'd always been clean inside. This — and forever to hide his own hurt — was all he could do for them.

Fate lent a hand. On the Marshs' next visit, Zain left Connie at the cabin and rode on to Mescalero. Florencio, the Mexican boy, who had been guarding the cattle on the range till it was certain all danger from rustling was over, chanced to come in for provisions. So Starr, bent on saying a word for his brother, left Florencio to play nurse in his absence, and rode part way home with Connie.

CHAPTER
EIGHT

"A Jealous Visitor"

Down the trail along Zuñi Creek rode Starr and
Connie, under the white-trunked aspens that showered
their golden leaves in the October breeze, like fairy
coins over the two. Even the fact that he was mounted
on Pancho for the first time since that cruel race
couldn't account for the exhilaration that was Starr's.

One happy mile the blaze-faced black and the white
mustang lazed shamelessly and unrebuked, with neither
girl nor cowboy speaking, nor feeling the need of
speech, till suddenly Starr remembered what he must
say for Lane.

"Connie," he blurted, and this was for himself,
"you're true-blue! I don't know how to thank you for
what you've done for Lane."

She begged him not to — it was nothing.

"That night . . . when I sent Florencio for you an'
Zain" — his gray eyes darkened at memory of that
night — "I . . . I was plumb loco, Connie! I knew you'd
come, though. I knew, somehow, you'd pull him
through. I won't ever forget it, Connie, an' I reckon
Lane won't." Encouraged by how naturally he had
brought up Lane, Starr took the plunge. "He's a mighty

fine kid, Connie. Be a fine man when he settles down. He's home to stay now. Be steady as a rock, once he . . ."

"How's your job coming along, Starr?" she cut in.

"Job?" he echoed blankly.

"The job," she exclaimed tremulously, "that's keeping you from the Broken Bell."

"I . . . I ain't makin' much progress, Connie," he said, feeling his way back to his theme, "but I'll make the dust fly now for Lane's goin' to help me. He's a whirlwind . . . Lane is. Connie," — he looked at her earnestly — "you recollect the kind of man Dad was?"

"Indeed, I do!" she cried warmly. "I honored him above every man I knew."

"You'd never dream Dad was wild, Connie, but he was . . . in his kid days. Wilder than Lane. Lane's like him. Lane's goin' to be a man like Dad. His heart's in the right place, Connie."

The girl's eyes misted, grew wondrously soft and blue. "Starr, it's beautiful, the way you love your brother."

"So would everyone," he said staunchly, "if they knew Lane like I . . ."

This time, it was a rider who interrupted Starr, a dazzling little rider on a spotted pony, trailing a big bay, one who sent Connie into a mental ecstasy of admiration. Such a picture did this rider make in a dashing bolero jacket and riding shirt of black velvet, bordered with tiny, silver *conchas*, and a jaunty little black sombrero edged with the tiniest, silvery bells. Beneath the sombrero flashed the duskiest of eyes, and

61

duskier hair was folded like little shining wings over her ears from which swung slender, glittering hoops of gold.

"Lane's little *señorita?*" asked Connie in a whisper.

"Yeah," Starr said confusedly, "but she ain't Lane's, Connie. She . . . she's bringin' his horse home."

For, although new to his role of matchmaker, he sensed something hostile to his plans in this meeting between Connie and Rosa Melles, and this made him feel more than usually clumsy as he introduced them. But Connie, with her inimitable way of putting all about her at ease, came to his rescue. It was she who presently suggested that Starr ride back with Rosa, and clinching the suggestion by galloping off toward the Broken Bell and turning back to wave farewell to the pair watching in the trail.

"Mees Mar-rsh, she ees ver' dear to you, *señor?*" Rosa guessed.

He took the lead rope from her hand, and swung Pancho up the trail. "A sister couldn't be dearer," he said honestly. "A sister couldn't do more than she's done for Lane." Into her eyes leaped a look Starr would remember when grief and other people's lack of faith in Lane were beating him down. But he misread it now. "Didn't you know," he said hastily, "that Lane got hurt that night?"

"Oh, yes, yes! I have been seeck with worry! You send no word."

There was something piteous in her voice, in her gallant little figure — something that touched Starr deeply.

"I plum forgot!" he exclaimed, ashamed that he could forget. "I'm sorry as sin, Rosa." He leaned in the saddle toward her. "Has Tex Maggart showed up yet?"

"¡Santa Maria!" The girl shuddered. "I theenk not . . . no!"

Starr missed the meeting between her and Lane, for he left her at the cabin door and went to put up the bay. But entering shortly after, he was astounded by her rushing past him, to turn in the doorway, a tempestuous little figure, all tiny flashing *conchas* and bells that her great eyes out-flashed.

"Connie! Connie! Connie!" she mimicked, punctuating each word with a furious stamp of her little boot at Lane. "Ees eet to hear of Connie that I come here! That I so scheme to come! Ees Rosa nozzing? Ah, eet was not of Connie you speak in the waltz, under the deep stars. Connie! A-ah!"

Blindly, then, she ran from the house, and Starr was horrified to see Lane straining to his feet to follow.

"Bring her back!" cried the boy, struggling in Starr's grip. "Don't let her go like that!"

Starr was out of the house in a bound, but Rosa was already in the saddle. Nor would she hear of going back.

"For what?" Her eyes seemed fairly to devour him. "To have those Connie ding-dong in my ears some more . . . the blue-eyed one he love?"

Starr's blood pounded in his temples. "Did Lane tell you that?"

Suddenly Rosa seemed to melt. She seemed very little, very young. "Ah, *señor*," was her hopeless cry, "there was no need!"

Thoroughly upset by this scene, Starr went in to Lane. But the boy was even more disturbed. He'd just been telling her, he said, how Connie had helped take care of him, when all of a sudden she got mad. Yes, all last summer he'd been pals with Rosa. He'd walked, danced, and ridden with her — the same as he would with Connie. She was a good girl. Maybe the Monterey was a wild place, but Rosa was as safe there as Connie was at the Broken Bell. Melles wouldn't stand for any man looking sidewise at her. Not even Maggart, who had some kind of a hold on him. But he and Rosa had been great pals. She'd really taken quite a fancy to him.

"Sure it's jist a fancy?" Starr asked gravely.

"Yes . . . no . . . Oh, for Pete's sake!" cried the boy wildly. "Don't nag me now! Let me alone!"

Such outbursts were frequent in the days that passed. Nothing suited Lane. He was as nervous, as irritable as a stabled colt. That this restlessness was due to confinement Starr felt sure. Once in the collar, he'd work it off. To hasten the day when he and Lane could begin paying off the Hallets' debt of honor, he set to work on a huge corral in the hills in which to hold their wild mustangs.

Connie's visits were discontinued as Lane improved. Then, five weeks after the night he had been brought home, Lane was up and about, and planning to ride next Sunday to the Broken Bell.

That Sunday was memorable for more than Lane's first ride. A cattle buyer looking for feeders happened to come out, and bought Starr's herd. Although Starr could have got better than thirty dollars a head by holding the stock longer, the profit was more than he had anticipated when he had invested his father's money down in Texas, and he was glad to have his mind free for his and Lane's big venture.

"Fifteen hundred dollars!" he exulted that night, showing the roll to Lane. "We'll wipe out a pile of brands with that!"

The boy's eyes glistened. "Better salt it away in a safe place, Starr," Lane said, indicating the door through which Florencio had just passed.

"Shucks!" Starr scorned. "He wouldn't . . ."

"You don't *know* that!" insisted Lane.

Because he wanted Lane to feel that he was an equal partner in this, wanted always to listen to Lane, Starr took down their mother's Bible — one of the home things brought from the Flying Dollar — smoothed the bills, and placed them between the yellowed leaves.

"There!" He replaced the book on the shelf. "Reckon that's safer than a bank!"

Somehow it comforted him, as time went by, to know that it was there. As if his mother's spirit were guarding it! As if she knew that Lane was going to help him now. When those tragic words rang through his mind — *I can't face her till the last brand's vented! Starr, Lane, remember . . . Lane . . ."* — it comforted him that his heart could answer: *It won't be long, Dad . . . now Lane's remembered!* And Starr had need of some such comfort.

CHAPTER
NINE

"Another·Visitor"

In the golden fall days succeeding, Lane was constantly with Connie. He was with her today — on a ride to Dripping Springs — while Starr toiled feverishly on the corral. Seldom in the past few weeks had he seen Connie except with Lane, and in the few talks he'd had with her, their topic had been Lane. He'd held her to it even when she showed a disposition to shy off for he wanted to let her know she wasn't taking any chance with the kid. If he had a single doubt of that, he wouldn't want to see them married even for Lane's good.

Sometimes he felt Connie ought to know about Carson's Tanks, but, not knowing Lane as he did, she might take it too seriously when it didn't mean a thing on earth. But he couldn't help being worried about Lane. Starr's brow was creased as he spiked that length of railing to the post. The kid was as well as ever, the same restless daredevil he'd always been, but he'd lost all interest in trapping mustangs and worried about how long it would take to earn money to mark out the brands, and had black spells, brooding over the money he'd lost to Maggart. But Lane would come out of it, once he buckled down to work. Likely he'd pitch in now the corral was done, or would be done, Starr qualified — picking up his tools and placing them by the nail keg — by tomorrow night sure.

He was a little more tired than usual, as he saddled Pancho and started home that night. But the motion, the crisp air, the miles and miles of tawny plains rolling away to their dull garnet walls, refreshed him body and soul. He took off his sombrero to feel the breeze upon his forehead and, glancing down at the old hat slung over the saddle horn, remembered that two of the brands for which he'd sent money had never been marked out. He'd left it to Lane, wanted Lane to know the thrill of it. But the boy never got around to it. It upset him to mention anything about the old hat.

"Gotta keep Dad's record straight," he told Pancho, and, passing the willow grove by the creek, Starr decided on impulse to stop and do it there.

Again, as on that first day in the chaparral when a Bar Z waddie, and as on many times since, he built a small fire and dropped a short length of wire into the flames. Sitting there, cross-legged, under the willows, his features tense, wholly absorbed in his task, there came to him the uncanny sensation that he was being watched. Quickly he glanced around, and there at arm's length was Connie, and, in the trail behind, her white mustang.

"What on earth!" she cried, her eyes taking in the fire, the glowing wire in Starr's hand, the old sombrero and half-canceled brand. "You scare me, Starr . . . like some medicine man of old."

He made no answer, only looked at her with horror in his gaze — horror that Connie had surprised him in the act. Connie knelt down in the yellow leaves beside him, every bit as grave as he.

"Is this your job, Starr?" she whispered.

Speechless, he nodded.

Tremblingly her finger went out and touched that big, glaring brand on the crown — her father's brand. "When you run a line through this one," she asked with swift divination, "will you be riding to the Broken Bell?"

Again the stricken cowboy could only nod. His heart was in his eyes then for Connie Marsh to see. The moment was perilously sweet, and Connie perilously near.

"When will that be, Starr?"

All his long-repressed, unutterable love for her was in his cry: "I wish to God I knew!"

The sound of his voice recalled him to the barrier between them. He had forgotten that look in Connie's eyes had dawned for Lane, and his own desire that this should be so.

"I . . . I thought you were ridin' with Lane," he said, getting slowly to his feet. "He said you two were goin' up to the springs today."

Suddenly she seemed far away. "We got back an hour ago, Starr."

"Big change in Lane, ain't there, Connie?"

"Yes," she said, and there was little life in her tone.

"He's plumb cured of town life," Starr said as he held her stirrup for her to mount. "Ain't been to Mescalero once since he . . ."

68

"Good bye." Connie gave her mustang a dig. "I'm taking this trail home."

Starr rode on home, happy and blue by turns. That moment — his heart sang with the memory of it! Had Connie any idea of his motive in burning out the brands? He must be more careful. Connie — no one — must ever know that his father . . .

Then he saw something that dashed all else from his mind. A man was riding away from the cabin, a man who didn't want to be seen for at sight of Pancho he had spurred behind the ridge that ran from the cabin into the hills. Who was visiting Lane? At that distance he could recognize neither man nor horse, but, instinctively, he felt that the man was Tex Maggart, and in a burst of fury Starr spurred Pancho to a headlong gallop.

That skunk! Why was he let live to corrupt decent folks? Lane was right — folks, even the best of them, stepped easy around Tex Maggart. Not all because of his nervous trigger finger, either. There was an ugly word whispered about him — blackmail. He snaked his way into folks' black secrets and made them pay for keeping the secret. Most men had some such secret, and feared Maggart. But if Maggart was bothering the kid again . . .

Springing from Pancho, Starr went straight into the cabin and found Lane dressing with more care than he'd taken even on his visits to the Broken Bell.

"Had company, Lane?" It surprised him how stiffly the words jerked out.

69

The boy flushed. His eyes dropped from Starr's, and the hands knotting his silk scarf fumbled. "Yeah . . . Link."

Starr sank on the couch, staring at Lane. He'd have sworn it wasn't Link. Why would Link Jarvis run like a scared rabbit at sight of him? But it must have been Link, if Lane said so.

"Goin' out, Lane?" he asked, fighting a nameless terror that was making him faint and regretting his query as Lane's handsome face darkened.

"I'm goin' to town!" cried the boy pettishly. "Cripe's sake, Starr, do I have to report my moves like a four-year-old?"

But Starr's great love for his brother, never greater than on this night, forced him to one more question: "When can I look for you, Lane?"

"Tomorrow," was the sullen promise, as Lane slammed out.

CHAPTER
TEN

"The Gambling Fever"

Lane Hallet kept his promise. Late on the morrow he rode up to the corral on which Starr and Florencio were putting the finishing touches. It was the first time he had been there but, to Starr's disappointment, he was too strung up to give more than an indifferent glance at the work. While Florencio was snaking in the last rail by the horn of his saddle, Lane took the old sombrero from Starr's head and counted the unmarked brands and the tiny dots around each, swiftly reckoning the amount due in his mind.

"Cripes, Starr!" he complained despondently. "We'll be gray-headed before we pay that off . . . trappin' mustangs."

"You forgot to count in that fifteen hundred at the cabin," Starr tried to cheer him.

But this only drew an irritable gesture, an impatient: "Oh . . . *that!*" Starting home, for he was too restless to wait until all three could ride back together, Lane wheeled abruptly. "Fetched the mail out, Starr," he said, and put a small package in his brother's hands.

While Lane was in sight, Starr watched him. His heart was in his eyes, and in them all his unquenchable love, his heart-breaking anxiety for his brother. Heart and eyes strained after him, as if Lane were riding out of his life forever, as if Starr knew that each headlong leap of the galloping bay was a successive step toward the next terrible sunset.

His eyes were dim at last as he looked at the package. Wonderingly he tore the wrapping from it and turned the contents over in his hand. It was a book — a thin, gilt-edged, leather-bound volume — a little gem of a book. Lifting the cover, his pulses quickened to see inscribed on the flyleaf in a rounded, girlish hand he well knew: **Happy Birthday, Connie**.

Then he remembered that this was his birthday — the Twenty-Sixth. It pleased him that Connie remembered. When they were kids, birthdays had meant big times between the Broken Bell and Flying Dollar. Connie was a great reader, so she'd sent him a book. Likely something she'd enjoyed and wanted to pass on to him. Well, a little reading wouldn't hurt him any, Starr thought sheepishly, remembering how long it had been since he had read a book. But this one — *The Courtship of Miles Standish* — somehow seemed familiar. Yeah, he'd read it in school, although he hadn't the first idea now what it was about.

A little curious about this book Connie had sent, he pulled himself up on the corral fence and dipped into it. Just give it the once over, and save it to read at home. Poetry, huh? When he was a kid, and had time for such things, he'd liked poetry a heap.

Reading at random, a line here and there, his interest was soon fired to such an extent that he turned back to

72

the beginning and read in earnest. Starr forgot time and place, was too absorbed to note Florencio's unholy glee at the spectacle of a cowboy — any cowboy, but particularly this one who he believed as wise as a tree full of owls and consequently above such folly — glued to the sharp edge of a corral fence reading poetry.

It would have taken an earthquake to dislodge Starr. This Captain Standish must be loco — getting another hombre to do his courting! Didn't he savvy he was riding to a fall? No girl wanted a third party horning in! He sure could pity John Alden — loving the girl himself, but feeling bound to praise up the captain to her. Why, a man with half an eye could see it wasn't the captain Priscilla loved, but . . .

Tingling in a most unaccountable way, Starr wound his feet tighter around the lower rail, and pulled the old sombrero over his eyes to shade the page. This book struck pretty close to home. For a month — loving Connie like this hombre, John Alden, did Priscilla — he'd been boosting Lane to her, telling her what a fine man Lane was, just like John did for the captain, and Connie — he meant Priscilla — saw right through him — he meant John . . .

An earthquake dislodged Starr Hallet, a stupendous upheaval of the soul. Picking himself off the ground, he leaned against the fence, dazed, trembling, deaf to Florencio's unfeeling laughter, feverishly seeking the page that had upset him with its glorious revelation and, finding it, reading again in a veritable fever that beautiful passage with its faintly — ever so faintly — underscored line:

**But as he warmed and glowed, in his simple
and elegant tongue,
Quite forgetful of self and full of the praise
of his rival,
A while the maiden smiled, and with lips over-
running with laughter,
Said in a tremulous tone, "Why don't you
speak for yourself, John?"**

In quite a different fever, a deadly, all but incurable fever, Lane galloped home. He was in a frenzy of impatience to reach the cabin, although he couldn't have told why. He hated it! He might as well be in jail as cooped up there, missing everything. Last night, with the old gang, the wild betting, the cards and chips, he'd seen just what he missed — excitement! That was life — the kind of life he wanted. He always had hated ranch life. He hated it a million times more now. Let Starr stick to it; he'd pick something more to his liking.

"But I can't!" he cried with burning resentment, remorselessly spurring the bay. "I'm haltered here!"

He had promised Starr to help pay off that debt. He would have to stick until then. Fat chance they had to pay it, trapping mustangs! It would take years — the best years of his life. If he was an old stick-in-the-mud like Starr, he wouldn't mind, or when he got as ancient as Honest Zain. But now — scrimp and slave, rake and scrape, that's what they'd do. Sweat for every single dollar, when there were many easier ways of making money.

"Gambling!" he cried aloud, his mouth and eyes rebellious.

Wasn't everything a gamble? Take Starr's cattle deal — he'd put money in that herd, risked money. If that wasn't gambling, what was? Starr made a profit, so it was all right. Winning made everything all right. If he had the money Starr had put in that herd . . .

At the cabin this wild mood grew. He built a fire in the kitchen stove and started supper, put the coffee pot on, pared potatoes, and dropped some bacon drippings into the skillet to fry them in. But suddenly he threw the knife and potato from him in disgust. Fine job for a man — slicing spuds! Wiping his hands savagely on his chaps, he fell to pacing. His blazing eyes rested first on this thing, then on that, but longest, oftenest on the little shelf of books. The fever mounted in his blood and he moved as in a dream. If he had money . . . But he didn't, he reminded himself bitterly. He didn't have two-bits to his name. He'd told Tex Maggart so yesterday when he came to the cabin to feel him out about how he got out of that scrap at Carson's Tanks, and how he'd stand in a showdown. Well, he wouldn't squeal on Tex, if they nabbed him. Tex wasn't a bad sort. Not half as black as folks painted him. He was right, too, when he said a man was a fool if he couldn't earn his living with his coat on.

If he had money, just a stake, he'd make it grow mighty quick at the Monterey. He knew he could, tonight, for he felt lucky. A fellow always knew when his luck was in. He'd seen a man win $5,000 in a night — at Pedro's table. If he had money — that money — his eyes were on the Bible, and a chill ran through him that was almost pain. It wasn't any crime to think. If he had it, he'd make enough with it to pay off that debt, square his father, help Starr out, and be free — free! He'd play in Pedro's game, where the sky was the limit, and no limit to what you could win.

But what was the use of thinking — he was broke, and that money belonged to Starr. Suppose — irresistibly, as to a magnet, his pacings drew him to the shelf of books again — suppose he took that money? He'd be back before Starr missed it. He'd just walk in and say: *Here, old man, is that money I borrowed.* It would be fun to see Starr's eyes pop out when he saw the roll. See how it had grown! *Take it all, and blot out all your old brands. Don't say I didn't help!* Starr would be mighty proud of him, he bet.

Lane reached for the Bible. He opened it. His heartbeats filled his ears as his eyes met the bills. He touched them, and the touch burned. In terror, he shut the book to hide them from his eyes, but, through the black cover, they burned out at him — not green against the yellow leaves, but stacks of red and white and blue against the green of Pedro's table. That moment was the most fateful in Lane Hallet's life — when he stood at life's crossroads, with the gambling fever in his blood and his mother's Bible in his hands.

CHAPTER
ELEVEN

"Tex Maggart Schemes"

In a room at the rear of the Monterey a man sat reading a letter. There was nothing ordinary about man, room, or letter. The room — small, dark, and scantily furnished — was notably strategic, for its outer door opened in a blind alley leading to a shrub-concealed break in the adobe wall enclosing the Monterey, an ideal exit in case of alarm. But, tonight, the man expected no alarm. The furor raised by the rustling had died down, making it safe for him to return to this room — always reserved for him — to look after the dozen irons he had in the fire and to plot and dream about this letter. Nevertheless, he was ready for an alarm as the gun on the table at his fingertips suggested. Tex Maggart always *was* ready. It was a principle with him and the chief reason why he was still unhung.

Startlingly like that gun was Tex Maggart, as soulless, ageless, as cold, hard, inflexible as the steel of it, as black in complexion and heart, but many, many times more deadly. He looked it, there in the lamplight, reading that letter, an ink-faded letter, brittle with age, breaking at the creases, but worth a fortune in the right hands. Those womanishly white and slender hands of Maggart were practiced in the handling of such letters. But his were not to be soiled with the grime inevitable to the handling. That was for other hands. Who among his crew had the nerve and brains to help him? Not one! They were a thick-skulled, brainless lot! Not one he could trust. He didn't dare appear in this himself, for there mustn't be anything to give some smart fellow a hold on him when he'd migrated to a new country, built up a reputation, a home. Into his mind's eye leaped a vision of midnight eyes and red, red lips. All his evil being leaped to meet it, to a savage determination to make it real. To do that, he'd find someone, if . . .

His hand twitched to the butt of his gun at a step in the hall outside his door, but relaxed at a single tap of unseen knuckles. The next instant the proprietor of the Monterey burst in.

"Young Hallet ees back!"

"Well?" drawled Maggart sardonically, shielding the letter from the other's eyes. "Don't they always come back?"

"To play . . . yes! But" — and Rosalio Melles leaned tensely across the table — "not to play een Pedro's game."

"In Pedro's game!" Maggart started up. "You're havin' a pipe dream, Melles! The kid's broke!"

"One who ees broke," Melles reminded him quickly, "does not play een Pedro's game . . . weeth a five-hundred-dollar fee to enter! But, I assure you, he ees not broke. He has money. I have seen eet. Bills . . . ver' many, and of beeg denomination. One, two thousand, I . . ."

"So the kid's flashin' a roll?" Maggart's eyes were hawkish. "Where'd he git it?"

"¿Quién sabe?" The Mexican shrugged.

But Maggart wasn't willing to dismiss it with a gesture. If Lane Hallet had money, he had stolen it. Only yesterday at the cabin he had said he was broke. And if he had stolen from anyone, it must be from his brother. The Hallet boys, so Lane had told him, had split fifty-fifty on the Flying Dollar. He knew mighty well where Lane's share was; Starr Hallet wasn't the kind to make any wild plunges. He'd hung on to his half, and it was this . . .

His eyes, narrowed to mere slits, shot a triumphant gleam. Lane Hallet! The very one to help him cash in on this letter. Everything it would take to carry it through the kid had to spare. Yesterday he'd been cocksure he was on the straight and narrow, but now . . . if Lane was gambling with his brother's money *and lost*, he would be desperate — would do anything to get it back!

"Melles," he ordered curtly, "get upstairs on the doublequick. Give Pedro the sign to clean Lane Hallet."

But Melles protested vehemently. He didn't like such dealings. He tried to run straight games. Why did Maggart desire the boy's ruin?

"Because I need him," was the brutal answer, "and I need him broke."

The boy was young, wild, indiscreet. To fleece him of money not his would be dangerous. Melles was silenced by Maggart's ugly look.

"Dangerous!" His tone was uglier still. "I can be a lot more dangerous to you than Lane Hallet . . . don't forget that!" Melles had been getting a little out of hand of late. "But I know the kid . . . he won't squeal. If anyone hollers, it will be Starr Hallet."

"Eet ees of the brother I speak when I say danger!" cried Melles earnestly. "He ees a sleeping dog. I like not to provoke a sleeping dog. He ees a Hallet. I know the blood. Mild as milk in bounds, but rouse those blood, and better you rouse ten thousand devils!"

"It's the Hallet blood I need," said Maggart coldly. "Let the brother come. If Lane's in Pedro's room, he'll have to tear down the building to find him. But git the kid's horse out of sight . . . a long way out of sight! Then see he's cleaned out, an' bring him here. Savvy?"

The Mexican's handsome face had the look of a man who desires battle, but foresees defeat. "Eef I do," he said wearily, "eet ees only that I may have the wherewithal to get out of thees business and set up an establishment of propriety. Always I dream of those place. A nize hotel . . . a nize home for my leetle Rosa."

"Funny how our ambitions run the same." Maggart grinned meaningfully and felt a qualm of terror at Melles's look of hate. "But don't fergit, Melles" — his voice had menace, too — "that you're doin' this because you *have* to! Just bear that in mind. Even if you are memory shy on the day when you was a tramp *vaquero*, without a cent to bless yourself with, and how you've come to be boss of this . . ."

"Of your kindness," Melles said with dignity, "I am not ungrateful." And he left to give the sign to the gamester that spelled Lane Hallet's ruin.

Smiling his thin-lipped, mirthless smile, Maggart waited. The letter and his dream beguiled the time.

Honest Zain Marsh! *he sneered, grinning evilly at the letter.* Well Honest Zain, the time's come when you'll pay for that name. You'll have to dig deep to hang onto it . . . deep enough to stake me to a little respectability myself. Wyomin' was a long way off, Zain, but so's California! If you can shake off your past . . . after running a trail that makes mine look like a piker's . . . reckon I can do the same.

" 'Honest' Tex Maggart." He smacked his lips as if he relished the sound. "Well, why not? I've tried everything else. Ought to be a big kick in that . . . no more dodgin', a home, a pretty, young wife . . ."

And again his mind held a vision of midnight eyes and red, red lips — eyes and lips that had never held for him anything but scorn, a fact that did not dim his vision. He was just on the verge of his fight for Rosa Melles, California, and respectability.

There was another reason, too, why he wanted young Hallet back under his thumb. Once, when the kid was half seas over, he had dropped something about Clark

Hallet's old sombrero. Maggart had a hunch it was right in his line. Small pickings, but still . . .

Hours more Tex Maggart waited. Toward morning, he glided down the dark, musty hall, up three narrow, spiraling flights of stairs, and came to a room unknown and undetectable, save to a favored and initiated few. A room without a window or door, to be entered only by the sliding back of a section of the hall wall that was possible only from within, and never done except in answer to an elaborate signal of raps. But Tex Maggart didn't enter. Silently pushing back a tiny circle of wood, he uncovered a peephole and looked into Pedro's room. Through the thick, blue fog of cigarette smoke, he saw the players, grim and tense — the dealer, Pedro, three house gamblers, a cattleman, who gave every sign of being on the brink of ruin, and — Lane Hallet!

The boy sat facing the peephole and that exultant eye. A half-empty bottle was at his elbow. His face was flushed and haggard, lined with the torture of this night. His black hair was wildly disheveled from constant rumpling by his frenzied hands. His eyes burned feverishly on the cards he held. He discarded one, snatched up the fresh one dealt him, and recklessly pushed the last of his chips into the pot.

Quickly Tex Maggart descended to his room to wait, still smiling, the short while ere Lane Hallet would be brought to him, broken, desperate, and money-mad.

CHAPTER
TWELVE

"Outside the Law"

All this Lane Hallet was, and more, as he flung his arms across the table in Tex Maggart's room and laid his white face on them. The fever had burned out, leaving in its place stark reality with its searing pangs of shame. "I'll die," Lane cried hysterically, "before I'll face Starr again! I didn't aim to steal it. I figured sure I'd win. Something made me do it . . . something I couldn't help. I'm the yellow Hallet. When I think what Starr done for me at Carson's Tanks, an' how this'll look to him . . . how I paid him back . . . Tex, I can't ever face Starr again."

"No," heartlessly Maggart answered the agonized appeal in that tone. "He'd kick you out. I know his kind. They got a lot more respect for a murderer than a thief."

The boy winced as if he had been struck, and Maggart exulted as he saw how his expression hardened.

"No, you can't go home" — he struck another blow at the broken boy — "until you can take that coin you stole."

All this while, with a devilish assumption of sympathy, he had been standing over Lane, patting his shoulder gently. But now he seated himself opposite, lit a cigarette, and seemed lost in reflection.

"I'm your friend, kid," he said at last.

"My only friend!" Lane cried in boyish gratitude. "You've proved it, Tex. I'm down an' out, an' you're stickin' by me."

"But say I give you a chance to go home with that money . . . and *more?*"

Wildly Lane stared into those inscrutable eyes. "Don't kid me, Tex," he begged piteously.

"I'm serious," Maggart assured him slowly. "But I'm wonderin' if you're up to the job. It's outside the law, an' involves some risk."

"Try me, Tex!" pleaded Lane frantically. "Jist try me! I'll do anything to pay Starr back!"

Yet Tex Maggart made a great show of indecision and kept the boy on tenterhooks for age-long, torturing moments. Finally — as dawn crept through the murky window, along with sounds of life, honest life, beyond the thick, gray wall outside — he drew out his wallet and carefully extracted the old, faded letter.

"See this?" he asked, pinning the folded sheets to the table with a soft, white palm.

"Yeah," Lane said curiously.

"There's a fortune in it, for me an' for the one who helps me collect on it."

"I don't see how, Tex."

"You will. Listen. The *hombre* what wrote it is one of the biggest cattlemen in this community. Stands

84

ace-high. Folks swear by him. He's almighty proud of his standin'. See? But this letter will wreck it. For it proves he was a rustler before comin' here. Now! What do you reckon he'll pay for it?"

"His last cent!" Lane was torn between hope and shame.

"That's what we're going to git. Ever hear of the range wars in Wyomin', kid?"

"Who ain't?" There was a strange stirring in Lane's heart.

"Well, this *hombre* was one of a notorious gang up there. The gang was named for him, though he wasn't but a kid at the time, an' never showed his hand much. Few ever saw him. An' this made it easy for him to skin out, go to a new country, an' . . . Why, what's the matter, kid?"

For the boy had risen, trembling. "Go on, Tex!" Lane breathed tensely.

"His playin' shady up there" — Maggart's cold eyes missed no tremor, no shade of expression on Lane's part — "made it easy for him to come here, an' take a new name. He's lived most of his life here . . . straight! Likely forgot when he was anything else. But he made one fool play. Soon after comin' here, he writes back to his pal . . . a *hombre* he trusted like a brother . . . braggin' about what he's been an' what he is, an' advisin' his pal to chuck the gang an' go straight, too. He asks his pal to burn the letter, but his pal didn't. An' when he died, not so long back, his son runs across it . . . I don't mind tellin' you that son was me. Naturally I didn't burn it. For I saw I could follow up that old trail, back what I found with this letter, an' force this *hombre* to . . ."

"His name . . . this *hombre*'s name?" Lane cut in hoarsely.

It was plain the kid knew something, but he wasn't kicking through with that name till the time came to collect. "You're a bit previous," Maggart said coldly. "I ain't given you the job . . . yet! So it ain't likely I'm tellin' you what his name is now."

"I don't give a hang what his name is now!" cried Lane in desperation. "What did they call him in Wyomin'?"

Experimentally Maggart shot it at him. "Dagget!"

The boy gave a violent start. His fingers dug at the table for support. For his brain was playing tricks. Again he knelt at his father's bedside, while the red sun sank in the Magdalena Mountains. Again his very soul was straining for those last gasping words: *I'd catch rumors of how Dagget was livin' respectable in some fur land . . . livin' high an' fat on his accursed gains . . . while I had nothin' but the cayuse under me an' the duds on my back. An' it made my vision crooked!* Back to Lane Hallet surged the hate he had felt for Dagget then.

"You've *got* to give me this job, Tex!" the boy vowed with blazing eyes. "You've got to! It's *mine!*"

His passion amazed Maggart. "Kid, has this *hombre* ever crossed your trail? But that ain't possible . . . he'd run his crooked course before you were born."

"He didn't miss the Hallets!" Lane burst out in a torrent. "He cleaned out my grandfather up there . . .

lock, stock, an' barrel! He started my dad on the wrong . . ." And his lips locked as if they never would open.

"Yeah?" insinuated Maggart in his silkiest voice. "He started your dad . . ."

"Keep your tongue off Dad!" Lane flamed, as furious with himself for the slip as at Maggart. But, cooling a little, he begged fiercely: "Give me the letter, Tex! Tell me where Dagget is. Let me bring that *hombre* to time. Let me show him up . . . tonight!"

"Not so fast, kid. This is a big job. I've been workin' it up too long to go off half-cocked now. I don't want to start anything till them poor fools who let Eph Colter take them at Carson's Tanks have their say in court. Get 'em rattled, an' no tellin' what they'll spill. It won't hurt you any to lay low, either. We'll go up to my hang-out an' make ourselves scarce till this trial's over."

Up at Maggart's stronghold in the hills, Lane looked eagerly forward to the day when he could return to Starr the money he had stolen — money not won by gambling, but money Dagget had stolen from the Hallets long ago. And forcing Dagget to compensate for the crimes of his father seemed not unlawful to Lane, but just and right.

But before he had been at Maggart's a week, a foam lashed horse and rider swooped down on the hidden hut, dashing all hope of an immediate reunion with Starr. For a grand jury investigation of the rustling had been ordered — such was the news Maggart's henchman brought — and a summons was out for Maggart to appear.

"Nothin' for it . . . but duck!" Maggart cursed. "An' you with me, kid. Our deal will have to lay till we git word it's safe to come back."

So Lane Hallet left the Black Plains country with Tex Maggart and, under his evil influence, hit the downgrade at a pace possible only to one of Lane's high-strung nature. Often, when he was sober enough for thought, he wondered what Dagget's name was now. He was well fixed. He'd have to be old. But there were a dozen men in that country who were both. Probably he knew him, for he knew everyone of consequence in the Black Plains. He might even be friends with him. But he vowed that friendship wouldn't matter. He'd show Dagget no more mercy than Dagget had shown the Hallets.

Bitterly, at such times, he missed Starr, and longed to send some word to him. "He's done with you!" Maggart would sneer. "Don't go cringin' back to him. He's let you down!"

Thus day by day Maggart instilled his poison, until Lane's heart grew hard. He might as well go the limit. Nobody cared. And go the limit he did under Maggart's able direction. Lane was putty in those soft, white hands. On one point only was he firm. No amount of liquor or persuasion could draw from him one word concerning the branded sombrero.

"I'd give a heap to know its history," Maggart would wheedle, and could read its value in the way the boy flared up.

The letter and then the hat, Maggart planned. Lane had only taken $1,500, so Starr Hallet must have several thousand left. He'd get the story from Lane in time, get the old sombrero in his hands, and Starr Hallet's money would buy a few feathers for the nest he was planning for little Rosa. Toward this end he fiendishly, systematically dragged Lane down.

But the day would come when Lane Hallet must be told who Dagget was. On that day, a wild, dissolute, and ruined boy would come to manhood. And on that day — so fatal, tragic, and yet sublime — the old sombrero of the salt grass plains would be in Tex Maggart's hands.

CHAPTER
THIRTEEN

"A Cowboy's Cowboy"

Summer smiled again on the Black Plains. Blue summer skies arched overhead. Summer lupine and larkspur flowered the range underfoot, and summer birds sang of summer the livelong day in the green, quivering aspens along Zuñi Creek. But to Starr Hallet it was a barren summer, for he had no joy in life. It was as if he had lived his lifetime of joy in the hour when that glorious revelation had come to him at the corral. "Why don't you speak for yourself, John?" that dimly underscored line had said. And it was as if he had heard Connie whisper: "Why don't you speak for yourself, Starr?" Connie had sent him that book! Had meant him to see it! He had fought down a mad longing to go to her then, knowing that, if he went to Connie with this hope flaming in his heart, his duty to his father would vanish like mist in the sun.

No, he would wait. With Lane's help — so he planned, riding back to the cabin that twilight — he'd wipe out those brands and go to Connie clean. Then he and Connie, together, would look out for Lane. So he came to the cabin, and his hour of joy ended. Lane was gone! The money was gone! How long he sat, head

90

bowed, holding the looted Bible in a grip of intense agony, he never knew. To Starr the money was nothing; that Lane had gone — all.

He scoured Mescalero that night, but found no sign of him, nor at the Monterey. Lane had not been there, Melles assured him, and certainly he would know. Rosa had no knowledge of him, either, or professed none. But, believing her to be the one most likely to hear, Starr gave her a letter to be sent to Lane if she heard from him, in which he begged the boy to come home.

To be home when Lane did come, he stayed on at the cabin. There was an appalling sense of vacancy there now. Even Florencio was gone. Hired by the Broken Bell for the spring roundup, he had been induced to remain on as a regular hand. But as often as his fertile brain could invent excuses he rode to the cabin to see Starr. Often he came upon him staring from window or door, and tears came to the eyes of the devoted youth, for he knew this watch was for Lane. Often spending a night at the cabin, Florencio would hear him start up, and knew he was listening for hoof beats that would spell his brother's return.

Never did Starr leave the cabin without hoping to find Lane there on his return, and each disappointment seemed keener. Daily there grew on him — more insistently than he had felt it on that journey into Dona Aña country — the terrible certainty that Lane needed him. He grew morbid with this feeling. And since all efforts to locate the boy were futile — the range might have swallowed him on that wild gallop from the corral, so completely had he vanished — Starr went to work.

He plunged heart and soul into the work that had been Lane's own idea, the trapping and breaking of wild mustangs. *I'll vent those brands*, he vowed in his heart, *so that when Lane comes home they won't be staring him in the face, discouraging him, and I'll have time to be pals with him again.*

Not once had he seen Connie since the day she had come upon him marking out the brands. Twice he caught far glimpses of her white mustang on the range. He knew she was avoiding him, and he understood. Knowing what Connie must think made his suffering the greater. Small wonder if Starr's restraint was tried to the breaking point, and if at times he was perilously near casting off, as Lane had done, the cruel burden his father had bequeathed. But he did not cast it off. In a desperate attempt to lift it — to hasten the day when he could go to Connie — he devoted every waking moment to his task, riding madly, incessantly like a lost soul the desolate wild mustang range. He roped, trapped, and ran down wild horses until the corral was jammed with fighting brutes that must be broken to the saddle to make room for more. With even more reckless abandon, he plunged into this dangerous work. While engaged in it, Starr conceived a great, a daring idea, one that offered hope of hurrying the day when he would be his own man again. For months Starr tirelessly, alternately trapped and rode.

"Plumb loco!" stormed old Link Jarvis after one of his frequent visits to the mountain corral. "That boy's mad as a hatter! Must have a hundred fuzz tails up there, an' rides a dozen of 'em a day. Ain't content jist to ride 'em! He tries every foolhardy stunt he kin think up. Jumped on one wall-eyed devil today, with a stirrup tied up. Rode him, too! But he don't allus. I've seen him throwed sky-high, an' come back fer more. Rides 'em backwards, sidewise, an' every which way! Zain, I'm plumb worried stiff. Either that boy's tryin' to break his neck, or . . ."

"Ol' Clark . . . his dad . . . was killed thataway," Zain Marsh said gravely.

"Or he's got sumpthin' up his sleeve," completed Link. "Strikes me, Zain, there's a purpose in it. He's so damned systematic'ly loco! Strikes me . . . Starr does . . . as a man who's driv, an' driv hard! Zain, we'd oughta find out that purpose . . . find out what lays behind it. Or, shore as persimmons, Starr Hallet's goin' to go wild . . . wilder'n ever Lane . . ." His harassed old face wreathed into a smile for Connie, who joined them on the vine-shaded verandah of the Broken Bell.

"It's right queer," reflected Marsh, putting a long arm about his daughter and drawing her down on the arm of his chair, "how Lane lit out. Reckon they quarreled, Link?"

"If they did, nobody'll ever know it from Starr," Link opined. Knowing Lane's part in the rustling, he had a hunch that the boy's disappearance was due to the grand jury trial coincident with it, but he wasn't confiding this even to Zain Marsh.

"What's your opinion, lass?" Marsh asked Connie.

She shook her head, but did not lift her eyes.

"But you could find out for us, honey," persisted the old rancher. "We're worried about Starr, an' you an' him was kids together, so he'll tell . . ."

"Don't!" There was a world of distress in her cry. "Please, don't ask me, Dad." She fled into the house, to beat the tears that were very near.

Marsh and Link regarded each other with sage, old eyes.

"Uhn-huh," nodded her father in confirmation of something long suspected. "So *that's* how the land lays. Nothin' but a love spat behind the purpose, Link."

Little they dreamed of Connie's hurt, or the depth of it. She had known, as every woman knows, that Starr Hallet loved her. She knew he had mistaken her pity for Lane in his illness for love. Day after day she saw him sacrificing his own love to his brother, and that day by the willows, seeing the truth in his eyes, she had been moved by womanly compassion and her own great love to give him a sign.

The instant the book was out of her hand, Connie had regretted it, would have given anything to have it back. This regret grew more unbearable with time. She, too, was worried about Starr, but she could never interfere again. What was the job he must do? That he had hoped to do with Lane's help? It was something dreadful; it was connected with his father, for it concerned the old sombrero and its many brands, and she felt sure it vitally concerned the Broken Bell. Often, in her conjectures, Connie hit dangerously near the truth.

To her father it was a lover's quarrel, pure and simple. But Link Jarvis wasn't so sure. He felt that Lane was at the root of it. Starr always had made an idol of the kid. Dangerous business — making idols out of human clay. *And blamed poor clay, in this case*, Link thought. If the boys had had a split and Starr was eating out his heart in secret, there was no telling what might happen. He decided to ask Starr point-blank. With this in mind, he went up to the corral one day, only to find it empty, and Starr Hallet gone.

Miles away over the plains, Starr and Pancho worried a ragged, unkempt band of mustangs over the dusty road, mustangs in every degree of wildness that to trail took all Starr's limitless patience and skill. To prevent their breaking and stampeding back to their native wilds, he had handicapped them in various ways. The most incorrigible were necked three abreast, a more docile one in the middle to hold them from bolting. Others were held in check by tying a front hoof to the long, matted tail, slowing them to a pace no faster than a walk. Others were hobbled by the simple expedient of a rope or hank of hair bound tightly about the hamstring. But once off their home range, the mustangs submitted to handling and, although it was a toilsome and monotonous journey, Starr eventually brought his band to El Paso.

That same day he disposed of them to a speculator at something over twelve hundred dollars for the lot. This sum, for nine months of grueling work that required a lifetime of experience, was little enough, but far more than he could have earned at range work.

Now he was free to try out the idea that had figured so largely in his thoughts all summer — the idea responsible for that summer's riding that had worried Link. Accordingly he headed Pancho up the Río Grande.

Manzana was in the throes of its annual rodeo. Five thousand excited humans packed the grounds. The pack of riders from ranches far and near — professional riders from all sections — swaggered about, gaudily shirted and chapped, or went through dynamics on the track with bucking, sprawling, vicious wild horses and steers fresh from the range. All were cheers and gibes, scrambled color, snaking ropes and dust.

Yet out of all this mad confusion, out of the sea of broad-brimmed hats, emerged an old sombrero, covered crown and brim with brands. Wildly grandstand, track, and infield cheered that hat.

"Why?" asked the stranger of one who applauded most.

"It is of the Old West," explained his neighbor, a little vague himself. "It is Clark Hallet's hat . . . one of our pioneers."

"But this lad . . . ?" gesturing toward the sun-bronzed, lean-faced rider, sticking like pitch to the hurricane deck of a fighting outlaw.

"A Hallet boy . . . his father's own son!"

"Hallet?" repeated the stranger, when he could be heard above the uproar. "It ain't a common name. I run across a Hallet down in Sonora a month back . . . a young fellow, younger than this chap. Dark, good-lookin', looked like he had good blood, but gone bad

. . . all the way. They said he was . . ." — but suddenly recalling that his neighbor might be a family friend — "I ain't repeatin' what they said."

"And kinder not to, by all accounts," was the grave response. "It's his brother."

If it was the old hat the throng cheered first, it was the man who wore it they came to applaud most wildly. Such riding had never been seen on that track, or such nerve, such tenacity. Not as the others rode, with one eye on the grandstand, the other at the grand prize, did Starr Hallet ride. He rode as if his life depended on it. Rode, as he never could have ridden, but for that summer of Spartan training in the hills. Taking four-hoofed demons that had the best riders stumped, and riding them till old rodeo followers were crazily laying bets that the horse didn't live that could throw him. For this gray-eyed, nervy rider in rope-burned chaps and saddle battle-scarred was no fancy grandstand actor, but a ranger, one of themselves — a cowboy's cowboy! And even the defeated and green-eyed professionals joined lustily in the cheers.

"Ride 'im, cowboy!" shrieked one of those, hysterical at the way Starr was sticking to the back of a twisting, man-killing outlaw that had baffled the best riders there. "Ya-ah, hook 'im! Oh, you cowboy in the big sombrero! I'm for you strong!"

And out of three days of terrific toil and strain Starr emerged with the grand prize — $1,000 in gold, $300 more day money, a silver-mounted saddle that was one of the coveted trophies of the event, and the glory of being acclaimed champion rider of the Southwest.

For glory he cared nothing. It was the money he had worked for. This, with what he had realized from the sale of the mustangs, would go — where every cent earned in the last two years, except what was required for the bare necessities of life, had gone — to repay his father's ancient cattle thefts. In one grand sweep he could blot out every brand, except the last, the biggest, the one that stood for the Hallets' debt to the Broken Bell.

He might have sold the silver-mounted saddle, but he didn't. *Lane would like it*, he thought wistfully and, arriving home, hung it up on the cabin wall — for Lane.

CHAPTER
FOURTEEN

"His Brother's Keeper"

Now that he was home again with both objects won, Starr was uncertain how to proceed to the ultimate blotting of that last brand. It would take about $15,000 to repay the Broken Bell in full. How could he hope to earn it? He had drawn so heavily on the mustang stock that it would be years before he could make that pay again and to settle down as a forty-a-month cowpuncher offered even less hope. However, he hadn't the heart to do anything until he heard from Lane.

Starr kept the road hot between Mescalero and neighboring towns, seeking, inquiring, for news of Lane. Melles, polite still, although frostily so, insisted that he had heard nothing. Nor had anyone else as far as Starr could find. But he had one loyal ally. Florencio, still at the Broken Bell, spent every leisure moment hanging around the Monterey, his sharp ears alert for any word his countrymen might drop concerning Lane that he might take it to Starr Hallet who he worshipped. It was he who told Starr that Maggart had been in Mescalero the night Lane had disappeared.

Long ago Starr had learned that it wasn't Link who had visited Lane in the cabin; he was sure now that his intuition then had been correct — that the visitor had been Maggart. The two had gone away together. This he added to the bitter score he would pay Tex Maggart when they met.

Encountering Rosa Melles on the street one day — of late she had shunned him as assiduously as he had hunted her — he asked her if she had sent his letter to Lane.

"Thees many day," she told him. But she steadfastly refused to say where Lane had been. Nevertheless, his heart was relieved, for now Lane knew he was wanted at home.

The change in Rosa shocked him. She was thinner, and her sparkle, her vivacity were gone. Her pale face looked all eyes — shadowy, hungry, beautiful eyes.

"You . . . me . . . ," she whispered sadly, "he have forgotten, *señor*. Ees eet not bes' we, too, forget?"

Forget Lane! As if he could, or wanted to. But there were times when he wished he could forget that Lane was with Tex Maggart. This autumn twilight as he sat on the cabin steps was one of the times.

"Can't you tell an ol' man, son?" Link begged, coming on him there slumped down alone. "Can't you tell ol' Link?"

Because his spirits were at their lowest ebb, because the old foreman of the Flying Dollar was so closely associated with his life and Lane's, because of what Link had done for Lane that night at Carson's Tanks, Starr told him without bitterness — for there was room in his heart for none — under what circumstances Lane had left home — told him all.

100

Long moments the old man turned it over in his mind.

"Son," he said solemnly, "take that leetle gal's advice . . . fergit Lane. Don't let him spoil your life. Folks say he's plumb ornery. They say he's . . ."

"Folks don't know Lane!"

"Mebbe they know him better'n you!" Link replied. "Mebbe you bein' his brother keeps folks from . . ." Abashed, he broke off, but Starr took him up in a flash.

"You've heard something?" he demanded hoarsely. "Don't keep it back! Lane's in trouble?"

Link steeled himself. It was going to be bitter medicine, hard to give, and harder to take, but it was for Starr's good. "I ain't heard he's in trouble," he said firmly. "But, off an' on, fer months I've heard of the trouble he's makin' fer other folks. Like the rest, I've bin keepin' it from you, Starr. But I reckon it's a mistaken kindness. So here goes. Lane's gone to the dogs. He's plumb hit bottom! He's a common drunk. A tinhorn. Eph Colter got word that Maggart was mixed up in the Peyote stage robbery, an' a kid . . ."

"Not Lane!" Starr said fiercely. "He ain't a thief!"

"How about that money of yourn?" Link probed.

"He knew he was welcome to it, Link . . . to anything I got a claim to."

Heartsick with pity, Link saw it would take stronger medicine to effect a cure, and he had the courage to give it: "Son, it's all right an' fine to stick by your brother, but there's limits. All your life you've pulled him outta one scrape after another, rangin' from harmless pranks to that night at Carson's Tanks. Nope, we won't beat around the bush any longer! We both know he was in on that . . . even if I did quit the trail when I made out Clark's ol' hat. Allus you've took blame for deviltry he's done. But there's an end to how far you kin go with Lane. The boy's hell-bent, an' you . . ."

"He's just a kid, Link." Starr's lips quivered. "Jist a wild kid."

"Kid? What are you, son . . . not five years older!" In his warmth Link Jarvis rose from the steps and looked down through the dusk at Starr. "Kid! He's a spoilt brat! He's selfish to the core. Allus was, an' allus will be! He never done one decent thing in his life. He ain't worth two whoops in Hades! He . . . good Lord, son," cried the distraught old man in pity and wrath, "I'm tryin' to tell you *he's yellow!*"

Starr's fists were balled as he rose, his face was strangely white, and in his eyes was a quality that caught and held Link Jarvis. "I'd not take that from any man but you," he said coldly. "I'm rememberin' what you done fer Lane an' me. If the lad's spoiled, I helped. Tex Maggart finished what we . . . all of us at the Flyin' Dollar . . . started. If he's ridin' wild, that's my fault, too. I could 'a' dropped everything an' been pals with him. But whatever he is, he's my kid brother, an I know him better'n you, Eph Colter, or anyone else. An' the man that calls him yellow has me to . . ." Suddenly his voice broke, and he sank down on the steps, silent, shaking.

"Mean that much to you, son?" Link asked huskily. And his arm across Starr's shoulder tightened convulsively at the broken cry.

"Oh, Link, if I could jist git him away from Maggart! Git him home! He'd listen to me, Link. If he'd jist answer my letter, Link!"

"Figger on gittin' an answer, son?"

"Why not?"

"Why not!" mocked Link, although with more tears than mockery in his voice. "I don't claim to be no shark on this here love stuff, but I got sense enough to know that leetle gal never sent your letter. She's sweet on Lane, ain't she? Waal, fer the love of Pete, does it stand to reason she'd want him back out here . . . right next door to the Broken Bell, hobnobbin' with our Connie? With mebbe you a-pullin' ag'in' her, too?"

A blinding light flashed on Starr. He recalled now that look in Rosa's eyes that day on the trail when he had told her of Connie's care for Lane, recalled, too, her outburst in the cabin: *Connie! Ees Rosa nozzing!* Of course, she hadn't sent it! Then — and this thought was much the harder to bear. "Lane thinks I'm through with him!" Starr cried, leaping to his feet. "That's why he doesn't come home. Can't you see? Shame's keepin' him away! He thinks I cared for that ol' money, Link. An' he's with Maggart. Maggart will poison his mind against me to keep his hold on him. But I'll find him, Link. I'll never stop till I find Lane now. I'll bring him home."

He started as if he meant to go that instant, but the old cowman seized his arms, crying insanely: "Here goes nothin'! An' to hell with consequences!" As Starr stood rooted in amazement, Link said quietly: "Lane's at the Monterey. Nope, I ain't loco," he added wearily.

103

"It's true. Florencio seen him last night. I had to lock that young squirt in the tool shed to keep him from scootin' over here an' blabbin' it to you. For he's got you classed jist one notch below his saints. Melles has lied to you all along. He's had tags on Lane. Lane's a wreck. The life's got him. He won't want to come. Maggart won't . . ."

"Then Tex Maggart's with him?" Metallic, that query.

"Maggart's with him," admitted Link, with resignation. "They're layin' low in Maggart's room back in the Monterey. There's something black an' slimy in the wind. I was afeered you'd go a-rarin' into another mess like Carson's Tanks. Maggart ain't takin' any chances on you bustin' into his game. He's got a dozen men posted on the look-out fer you . . . Oh, Christ, why couldn't I a-held my tongue!" Link cried, following Starr into the cabin, where the youth jerked his holster from the wall and strapped it on.

But Link was on his horse when Starr came up with Pancho.

"You'll be killed in that den!" he predicted. "I'm trailin' along, son."

"No, you're not, Link!" Starr would brook no refusal then. "This is my job, an' I'm goin' it alone!"

Alone, he galloped off under the million brilliant stars hanging low over the plain. Pancho's hoofs drummed the refrain of his heart: Going to Lane! Going to Lane! Nothing could stop him now — lies, or a dozen men.

Swerving into the highway, he all but collided with a white mustang. A girl's face, lovelier than ever by moonlight, looked into his. Well did the daughter of the range know what Starr's look and manner meant. More did she know, by the damning phrases Florencio had caught of what Lane had been and was and the danger Starr ran, than Link had even hinted.

"You've heard?" she cried with the cruel anxiety of love.

"I've heard, Connie, an' I'm going for him!"

"Not like this, Starr!" she pleaded in her fear for him. "Wait till morning. Wait till you've cooled down."

"I'm getting Lane out of there . . . tonight," he told her gently. "I'm goin' to bring him home."

Nothing could dissuade him. Suddenly she was faint, as if with a merciless divination of how she next would see him. Suddenly she knew resentment for the loved and worthless brother. Bitterly in this resentment, she cried: "He's not worth it, Starr! Oh, I know I shouldn't say this to you . . . but he's not! Dad . . . Link . . . everyone says it. We can't all be wrong. Starr, can't you give him up?"

"He's my brother."

"You're not your brother's keeper!"

"I am!" he cried with solemn calm. "I'm the only one who believes in Lane. Everyone else has given him up. Even you, Connie!"

And Pancho plunged down the starlit road.

CHAPTER
FIFTEEN

"The Sleeping Dog Provoked"

Slowly the door of the Monterey was pushed in and a man entered, a man wearing the weather-beaten old sombrero of the salt grass plains. To the startled hodge-podge of humanity thronging the lobby, both man and hat were familiar, yet both were now sinisterly strange.

For a long moment he stood there, his eyes passing from face to face. At last they came to rest on Rosalio Melles, behind the desk fenced off by a low railing, and on him gleamed coldly as cracked ice in the glow of the chandelier.

Melles blanched as Starr Hallet strode toward him. The Hallet blood was aroused. The sleeping dog provoked — mad! Yet gentle the voice that made of him, no query now, but low command. "I've come for Lane, Melles. Show me to my brother."

Seeing over Starr's shoulder that his henchmen were inching up, Melles took heart. "*Señor*," he said, and his lips were stiff, "your brother ees not here."

106

"You lie!" was the cold retort. "He's here . . . with Maggart. Show me to Lane!"

With an imploring glance beyond his inquisitor, Melles insisted: "I am ver' sorry, señor, but you have been misinform'."

Like lightning Starr's arms shot out, seized the man who had lied to him for months, and yanked him bodily over the railing, shaking him as if he would shake the truth from him. But, as if this act had been a signal prearranged, a dozen men — the toughest, most vicious lot that land could boast — sprang upon Starr, seeking to separate the two, kicking, clawing, striking blows that made the room rock, but did not drag him down.

Miraculously wrenching free, he pitched Melles, who he still held in his grip, over the railing and, backing to the desk, reached for his gun. It was gone! Nor did he care. His unchained spirit welcomed combat. And he met the rush of that snarling mob with a smashing attack that sent men right and left, but sheer force of numbers bore him down . . .

Down under a seething mass of bodies that thrashed on the floor, seeming not so much like human arms and legs and bodies, as like some hydra-headed monster that had Starr Hallet in its grip. But there was a great rending in that mass, a vast upheaval at its core, and Starr rose to his knees, struggled to his feet, with a fighting human burden on his back. Throwing up his arm, he caught this man in a powerful head hold and sent him crashing over his head, back into the mass.

Before Starr recovered his balance, someone struck him a reeling blow. In reeling, he shot his fist into the face of his attacker, and with teeth clenched, every muscle in his body tight as a steel spring, he fought like a demon, with superhuman strength, these men who were keeping him from Lane. Faces, dark and ugly, hemmed him in. Faces were but obstacles in his way. Send one careening, and another closed the gap. He felt the force of fists upon his head and body, but felt no pain; he was benumbed to all save the one consuming fact that Lane was here, and that he was going to Lane.

Link had said Lane was in a back room with Maggart, so Starr fought toward the hall. Taking blows, giving blows. Faces — and yet more faces. His ears rang to the wild uproar — scraping feet, screams, sharp oaths, the thud of landing fists and bodies. Through it all he had the curious impression that Rosa — white, scared, horrified — gazed down from the balcony above!

Then he was in the hall; it was blocked with men, their faces determined and a little scared. Some of their fists held guns but none dared use one. Once a knife flashed, but he caught the wrist that held it, bent it back, and the knife fell to the floor.

His bare flesh was taking the blows now, for his clothing was stripped off to the waist. At times he must leave his face unguarded and wipe the blood from his eyes. There were fewer faces now. Inch by inch, in a way that struck terror to the depraved souls there — terror and superstitious awe — and bearing a man or two upon his shoulders at every inch, Starr battled through those faces until the hall was clear ahead, and he could see — see the man who stood in an open door at the end of the hall with a leveled gun, a man who brought a furnace of madness blazing to Starr's eyes.

"Stand back!" Tex Maggart yelled to the mob. "Clear out! Let him come!"

Starr felt that this order was to clear the path for Maggart's shot. He felt that Maggart meant to kill him. He knew death was in that room. But so was Lane — whose soul this man had tried to kill — and staggeringly, doggedly he went on. Foot by foot, unarmed, under the threat of Maggart's gun, into the room, as Maggart retreated, step by step, warily, as cold and venomous as the six-gun in his hand. Starr came at last to Lane.

The boy lay on Maggart's bed in a sleep too deep for even this wild uproar to disturb. His black hair fell in disorder and sharp contrast to his white face, a face ravaged of all youth, yet strangely youthful. Never loved more by Starr than now, as he bent over him, crazed by the fear that Lane was dead. But the boy stirred at his touch.

"Drunk! Dead drunk!" groaned Starr, and in insane rage whirled on Maggart. "You devil! You black-haired devil! This is your work!"

Heedless of his battered body, heedless of the hungry mouth of that black gun, Starr sprang. He felt a terrific shock, a deafening roar, thought that the room was reeling, and did not know it was himself. Then he fell, and knew no more.

Disturbed by the explosion, the unconscious boy on the bed whispered in his drunken sleep: "Good ol' scout."

And the room was still for Tex Maggart had fled. He had no wish to be caught there by the officers who would surely come to investigate this fight. But first he sought an old sombrero, somewhere among the ruins.

Rosa Melles, stealing down the dim stair, a part of the shadows in the long black scarf that swathed her, saw that old sombrero lying under the light of the chandelier — blood dyeing the Broken Bell brand on the crown. She saw Maggart snatch it up and duck through the open door into the blackness. She saw her father sitting at his desk, staring into space, his face the face of a man damned. She saw a man grotesquely sprawled in the corner, legs and arms hideously awry, crossed herself, and hurried on.

None there was to stop her. The rats had deserted the sinking ship. For the Monterey would sink. The Black Plains country would draw a line at this thing that had been done to Starr Hallet.

Rosa had always been sheltered from scenes like this by her father's devotion, the respect he forced all to pay her, and by her own deep abhorrence of such scenes. But now she went to that rear room from whence the shot had sounded, driven by fear for the brother of one she dearly loved, by fear for her father lest the officers come and place the blame on him.

The door stood ajar. Lane slept on, unconscious of that still, bleeding form beside him. But over it a boy hung, sobbing wildly in his grief. It was Florencio who had escaped from Link's prison and torn madly after Starr.

"He ees dead," he moaned as Rosa bent over him.

"Hush," she begged in their own tongue, "he is not dead. You must be *muy hombre*. I need your help."

Fiercely he dashed the tears from his eyes. "*Señorita*," he panted, "did you pass a man jack-knifed in a corner? I did that when he would have stabbed my old *jefe*. I ask you, then, am I not *muy hombre?*"

"You are!" Rosa said truly. "You will . . ." Her head lifted, and her eyes dilated at a burst of feet in the lobby, a barked query. "The officers! Quick! Help me move him from this place that his blood may not be on my father's head!"

Together the youthful pair carried Starr through that strategic door, down the blind alley, through the secret break in the adobe wall, and laid him gently beneath the shrubs where Rosa guarded him while Florencio went to get a buckboard from the stables of the Monterey.

Together, when it was brought, they lifted Starr to the floor of the vehicle and started slowly off. Florencio held the reins, and Rosa crouched in the back, with Starr's head pillowed in her lap.

Rosa's heart was heavy. Lane Hallet must always hate the name of Melles, when he was himself again and learned of this thing that had happened at the Monterey. She scarcely realized that it was not at the cabin on Zuñi Creek where Florencio stopped, but at the Broken Bell. Link and Zain Marsh were called, quietly, not to arouse Connie, who they believed to be asleep — not knowing she shared their fear. They bore Starr Hallet over the threshold of the Broken Bell, which he had vowed never to cross till he could do so with honor, which he had not crossed in the two years since Clark Hallet's death. They had him on the white counterpaned bed in the spare room, and their faces went pale and grim as they saw his torn, bruised body, the bullet wound a scant half inch above the heart. But they said nothing in consideration of the poor girl who had accompanied him there.

"The bullet went clean through," Marsh said as they washed and dressed his wound, "but . . . it looks bad!"

Starr looked dead to Connie who — bursting into the room, and throwing herself down at his side — strained that battered head against her heart, covering it with kisses, crying in her anguish: "Starr! Starr!"

There was no mistaking the wild love in that cry. Rosa heard it with numb surprise and shame. Starr heard — and smiled. His eyes opened. He lifted his lips to Connie's but, even in so doing, seemed to withdraw.

"One . . . more . . . brand . . . ," he whispered. "The Broken Bell!" He reached blindly up, groping for something and, not finding it, distractedly cried: "My hat! Dad's old sombrero!"

Where was it? His wanting it was a delirious whim, but it must be humored. Helplessly they gazed at each other, but Rosa darted to his side.

"Lissen, *Señor* Star-r!" she begged softly. "You lose those hat in the fight. Only have patience and trust me, I will breeg eet!" She went to the door, but ran back and, taking Connie's hand, tugged at it, panting: "Quick! I mus' speak to you! Come!"

"Tell me," she implored in the dark of the verandah, "ees eet not Lane you love?"

112

In Connie's surprise she read confirmation of that grief-stricken cry.

"Oh, what have I done!" moaned Rosa. "Since that first day we met, I have hate you! I have let go on that which I might have stopped. Because I am jealous! Because I theenk you love Lane! Eet has been like a knife . . . here!" — pressing her hand to the silken scarf over her heart.

Quick to sympathize, even in her own grief, Connie asked pityingly: "You love Lane so much?"

"Oh, yes, yes!"

"And Lane?" Connie asked gently. "Does he love you?"

The girl shrugged with that graceful, hopeless gesture of her race. "*¿Quién sabe?* Sometimes I theenk so, and eet make me ver' happy. Sometimes no, and I am ver' seeck . . . here. I theenk if I were not the daughter of Rosalio Melles, he would love me. But . . . oh, believe me, Mees Mar-rsh, my father ees a good man!"

That plea was more than Connie could withstand. Impulsively she flung her arms about Rosa. A gesture, spontaneous, natural, that would pay her bigger dividends than any conscious act. For a moment the two girls stood thus.

"And me . . . I am a good girl!" Rosa wept.

"Oh, Rosa, we all know that," said Connie.

As Rosa drove off in the buckboard, Connie went back to Starr, sat down beside him, and took one of his limp hands.

"A good woman . . . can tame . . . the wildest blood," he muttered. "A gift . . . God gives . . . the mothers . . . of men."

"Ramblin'," said old Link to Zain.

But to the listening girl every word was a revelation.

"Jist wild . . . ," he fretted. "Me an' Connie . . . we'll look out for Lane."

CHAPTER
SIXTEEN

"A Man at large"

A timid, little, black-draped ghost glided into the Monterey by the rear, and down the long hall. So still the place, and silent, like a tomb. The better so, the better to bury all hope of happiness in such a tomb. For this she must do. She, Rosa Melles, had in her short life accomplished much of evil. She could still do much of good. If she must be sad always, she could make others, more deserving, always glad. If only she could keep her heart strong — like now. If only — please God — she did not meet her father first.

But though it was mid-forenoon, there was no one in the hall. In the lobby, only old Esteban, sweeping valiantly at the débris, as foolishly, Rosa thought, as the old woman who sought to sweep back the sea. Last night she had been too scared to note how completely this room was wrecked. Shattered glass from broken bottles and showcases strewed the floor. Every chair was broken, and the hall door, splintered, hung only by one hinge. That sad, tiny chirp? Even the little bird's home had not escaped, but swung crazily. Mechanically she righted the cage, thinking, perhaps, if she stayed in this room, the great courage of the one who had fought here would be a help.

"Where is my father, Esteban?" she asked in Spanish of the old retainer, who was regarding her with mute wonder and awe.

"He sleeps, *señorita*. He sought his bed at daybreak."

That was good. Her father had believed her in her room, ignorant of all that had transpired.

"Tell me . . . what did the officers do?"

"But little." The old man was doubtful how much to tell her, how much she already knew. "They asked sharp questions, *señorita*, as is their way. But few there were to answer. The conflict" — with a gesture about the devastated room — "speaks for itself. Unluckily they found one *peón* incapacitated for this world, and instructed that the Monterey be closed until they have more fully investigated."

"Is *Señor* Hallet still here?"

"But surely. Even the police could see he had no part in this trouble. He still sleeps, *señorita*."

That, too, was good. She was to be given no excuse.

"Wake him, Esteban. Bring him here . . . then leave us alone. Tell him it is of the most terrible import."

Daintily she picked her way through the mess, and sank down on a low couch by the window to wait for Lane. Although she had passed a sleepless night and had driven forty slow miles, she could not rest, eat, or sleep, until she had made confession. But even in her misery she had the feminine wish to change her attire, smooth her hair, make herself beautiful for the man she loved. But what did it matter? Such things were over — or would be soon?

It was long ere Lane came, stumbling, through the unhinged door. Haggard, unkempt, in the clothes he had slept in, he was pitifully bewildered and unnerved.

"Looks like a cyclone hit here." Confusedly he stared about, sitting there beside her. "What happened?" He dropped his hot forehead in his palms. "Rosa," the boy shuddered, "there was blood by my bed!"

She shuddered, also. There had been a fight, she told him. Oh, such a fight! "Your brother Star-r . . . he came for you!"

That brought Lane up with a jolt. "Starr came for me! Was Starr in that fight? Quick! Rosa, was Starr hurt?"

The girl burst into a wild fit of weeping that sent a chill along his fevered veins. Frantically he tried to drag down the hands she held before her face.

"Starr . . . ," he whispered thickly, "he's dead."

Chokingly she denied that. Of course, she knew. Did she not help convey him to the Broken Bell? But he was injured — shot!

"Shot?" he echoed. "Who shot him, Rosa?"

Through her sobs Lane heard that name. Drugged as he was, it seemed to have the power to turn him to stone. "Tex shot Starr! I dreamed a shot!" Over and over, with slow and awful distinctness as if this were a point he must get straight, he repeated: "Tex shot Starr!" Then suddenly he closed his eyes as if to hide something dreadful from his sight. "An' *that* . . . Rosa, that was Starr's blood?"

"Oh, *Madre de Dios!*" cried Rosa, springing up and facing him, a broken, tragic little figure. "Who ees to blame for . . . *that?* Who but me! I do eet! But for the mercy of God, I keel *Señor* Star-r!"

"Not you, Rosa . . . Tex!"

"No, me, Rosa!" Passionately she struck her breast. "But for me he would not have come here las' night. There would be no need! But for me you would not be wreck' . . . like thees awful place! Always your brother have come here . . . everywhere . . . for seek you. We lie! We do not know where you are, we say! But to me . . . even to wicked, deceitful me . . . he give a letter, which I am to send to you. Which I tell heem I have send! But which I do not send!"

"Starr wrote me?" Lane cried in anger and despair. "He gave you a letter for me? Why didn't you send it? I'm askin' you . . . why?"

"Why?" — with a regal gesture she drew the scarf tighter about her slender form. Proudly, fiercely, she lifted her tear-stained face. There was in it a primitive glory that thrilled him, even in the great change he was undergoing. "Because I loved you! I am jealous of that blue-eyed one. I do not want you near her! I fear if you come back to her, I lose you sure. Until tonight I do not know eet ees the *Señor* Starr she love!"

Lane's brain was clear now, but things were coming too fast. Tex had shot Starr! Starr hadn't thrown him down! Starr had written to him! Rosa had kept the letter through jealousy of him. But Starr had written! Oh, how he clung to that, with flaming hatred for

118

Maggart, who had shot his brother, and a revival of all his old love for Starr. Magically the bitterness of the past year was washed from his heart as if it had never been.

"You theenk thees ees easy for Rosa?" The girl was stung by his silence. "Easy to tell you thees, and make you hate me. You wonder I do not die of shame! Then lissen . . . thees ees my penance. I do eet for them . . . for your brother and the blue-eyed one, who caress me like a sister. What I have done, I have done. I cannot undo eet. But I can stop those devil Maggart from spoiling their happiness. For I tell you, Maggart ees hatching evil for the father of those girl!"

"Evil for Zain Marsh?" Lane's soul shrank from a sudden, black suspicion.

"He has an evil letter!"

Letter! The only letter Lane could associate with Maggart was the one written by Dagget long ago. Soon he was to learn who Dagget was, for yesterday Maggart had sent a message to Dagget, naming a lonely rendezvous, and demanding his appearance on threat of exposure. Lane was to put the screws to Dagget this very night. What was Rosa saying?

"Long ago I have seen heem study those letter. I have heard heem whisper . . . 'Honest Zain.' . . . and curl hees lip up in a sneer. Only las' night I meet heem in my walk, and he was foolish with liquor, and he say . . . 'When you are Mees Maggart,' . . . and he snap my earring . . . 'I will buy you many trinkets such as these. And you will be a fine lady, my leetle Rosa!' I am ver' angry. I ask heem how eet ees he knows so much, and he weenk to me, and say in a way that have two meanings . . . 'Eet ees written in a letter.' And I know eet ees of *that* letter he speak!"

So did Lane know of it. She saw him change before her eyes, saw his mouth set firmly, and blood glow through the gray pallor of his cheeks. Saw in his eyes an upflaring of the fire that had been there when he — a dashing, young *caballero* — had ridden into her heart. But she stood in tremulous awe of him as he leaped up, and caught her arms.

"Rosa, are you sure?"

"*Santa María*, yes!"

"And are you dead sure Starr an' Connie are in love?"

"In many theengs," she assured him wistfully, her eyes following him in his fierce, impatient stride, "I may be deceive, but not in the ways of love. I see her rush to heem, take hees head upon her breast, and kees heem . . . oh! And eet call heem back. He have such a happy look. I theenk he will kees her then. But, no! He whisper crazy talk . . . 'One . . . more . . . brand . . . ' . . . like that, and he do not kees her!"

One more brand! What was delirium to Rosa was like a written page to Lane. Those brands had stood between Starr and Connie. This, then, was why he'd quit riding to the Broken Bell. Somehow Starr had paid off all the brands but one. Which one? Did Rosa hear?

" 'The Broken Bell,' he whisper. Then he feel for hees hat . . . you know, those sombrero of many brands. But

120

eet ees not there. He ees distract'. I tell heem he lose eet in the fight. That I will breeng eet. For I know who has those hat!"

Stern and cold, Lane swung on her. "Rosa, who has that hat?"

"Maggart."

She told him how she had seen Maggart pick it up, after leaving Starr for dead, and still he stared at her with that strange look. She gloried in his anger, although it filled her heart with dread. Bravely she met his look, as he took her by the shoulders and held her back.

"Is Starr hurt bad?" His eyes burned into hers soul deep.

"He will not die," she said steadily, praying it was true. "But you must go to heem. Return hees horse, which ees here in the chaparral saddled since las' night. I, myself, will breeng the hat."

"No, I'm takin' that hat back!" Lane's voice rang with deadly purpose. "I'll get Dad's old sombrero, an' I'll get that letter, or I'll get Maggart!"

Seeing too late the pitch to which her disclosures had roused him, knowing too well the risk he ran in meeting Maggart while this mood was on him, Rosa flung herself upon him, clung, in her terror, to him, as if with her own puny weight to hold him back.

"Oh, no, no, no!" she protested wildly. "Oh, what have I done? He ees a gunman! What chance have you? See. How you shake. How you tremble. He will keel you!"

Firmly, but not roughly, he disengaged her arms. "Better let him kill me like a man," he said with awful bitterness, "than kill me . . . like this!"

And as Rosa flew up the staircase, for what mad purpose she only knew, Lane rushed out to Pancho.

CHAPTER
SEVENTEEN

"The Last Brand"

Again Pancho tore out of Mescalero, bearing a Hallet to a brother's aid. Again his direction was Carson's Tanks. For up in the red, broken hills behind the windmill was Maggart's hidden hang-out, to which he had fled last night. Much as Starr had thought of Lane on that fateful ride, so now did Lane think of Starr. His life swept by, swifter than the landscape skimming under Pancho's hoofs — his aimless, sordid, sinful life, and gold against that black pageant, the countless devoted acts of Starr for him. Desperately he searched for one such act on his own part, but found none. He'd used, abused Starr's faith and love and trust, then thrown it in the discard. He'd wanted to blaze his own trail. Well, he'd blazed it — a selfish, wicked trail that led to Maggart!

But Starr had stuck by him to the last, had come for him last night, had cleaned out the Monterey — fighting through to him. Starr — and his reawakened soul recoiled in shame — Starr had seen him — like that! Too drunk to lift a hand to help his brother! Too drunk to know when his brother was shot down at his side! Too drunk to keep Maggart from stealing the old hat, so that he could fleece Starr when he was through with Zain! "I'll go to pieces thinkin' thataway!" he cried to Pancho.

Why hadn't he guessed that Dagget was Zain Marsh? But how could he? Maggart hadn't hinted. He hadn't been on the look-out for hints, on the look-out for anything — all that year, ramming around, till Melles sent word it was safe to come back — but for something crooked. He'd patterned after Maggart. Went him one better, drinking, gambling, helping hold up that stage . . .

"Oh, what ain't I done?" he groaned as Pancho took the mountain trail at a gallop.

What if Zain Marsh *was* Dagget? He'd have to have been almighty young then. He'd been square for forty years. He'd helped more folks than he'd ever hurt. Nobody could count up the good old Zain had done. Surely that ought to make up for a wild year or two when he was just a kid. It was what a man did when he had man sense that counted — not while he was climbing up fools' hill.

The West was a heap different forty years ago. Most men were a little wild. The land was wild. Marsh's rustling then — like his dad's — wasn't in the same class with Maggart's rustling now. And he'd helped Maggart rustle! He wanted to go straight now, if he could. Suppose he did go straight for forty years? Would folks hold the last year against him? Zain's kind wouldn't, but Maggart's would. They'd try to drag him down.

Funny how clearly he was seeing now. Why, he could see right through Maggart. All Maggart wanted of him was what he could get out of him. Wanted him now, so that if Zain Marsh ran in a whizzer, it would be Lane Hallet who would be caught and sent up for blackmail, while Tex Maggart, as usual, went scotfree. *A tool!* A humiliating thought for one of Lane's high pride. *A tool . . . blunted of all decency to hit old Zain! But you turned this tool on yourself, Maggart, when you shot Starr!* Anger steeled his nerves better than any stimulant could have done, as Pancho burst out on the rim trail, and Lane saw the warped-board hut huddled in the cañon below, and Tex Maggart in the door.

Confident of his ability to handle Lane in any mood, Maggart calmly watched the whirlwind approach. The boy was riding his brother's blaze-faced black, and that looked like trouble. It was an awkward time for trouble, and he was in pretty deep already. Better try to talk him out of it.

"You're early, kid!" Maggart called, with his deceitful grin, as Lane pulled Pancho to a rearing halt a few yards away. But his smile faded as the boy slid from his horse and advanced a step, his face set, determined, as Maggart had never seen it.

"Maggart, I want that letter!" Lane demanded in a tone Melles had heard in another Hallet's voice last night.

"Yeah? Come on in, kid."

"I want that letter," repeated Lane quietly, for all his emotion crackled in his eyes, "an' I want Dad's ol' hat."

"Yeah?" Maggart drawled again with slow and maddening insolence. "Jist how do you aim to get 'em?"

Lane's right hand dropped to his hip. "Jist like you got that hat, if I have to . . . kill you an' take 'em! Maggart, I got your number now. You're a sneak! A low-down, yellow sneak!"

Malevolence shot through Maggart's narrowed eyes. His face twitched. "Why, you half-baked brat!" he snarled. "I've killed men . . . get that? Men! . . . for a blamed sight less. I could drill you before you got that gun half out." Then, ingratiatingly, his smile came back. "But I don't want trouble, kid," he said in his silkiest tone. "We can't afford to fall out now. Forget the hat . . . you're drunk! Listen. I'll tell you how I . . ."

"Will you give me that hat an' letter?" The boy's gun hand trembled — fatally!

"No, you fool!" yelled Maggart, his hand arching down in a flash and in the same instant a streak of flame spurted from his hip.

As Lane fell back against Pancho, his gun still leveled, a ghastly pallor overspreading over his face, Maggart taunted: "You asked for it! You asked . . ."

Lane's gun belched! With a horrible look of surprise, of unbelief, Maggart rocked back on his heels, teetered slowly forward, and fell face downward.

The smoking gun slid from Lane's hand. Maggart was dead! Nothing to prevent his taking hat and letter now, nothing but this funny, all-gone feeling, and he wouldn't be licked by that. But he wished things would stay hitched. This wasn't any old merry-go-round.

126

He took a stumbling step toward the door, fell, at terrible cost in strength rose to his knees, and dragged himself on — on, over Maggart's prostrate body, and through the darkened door.

"Gotta git . . . ol' hat first," he kept repeating, to fix the thought in his swimming brain.

But it was a Herculean task to locate it — moving on his hands and knees when every movement caused pain unspeakable — although Maggart's chest was the one place in that room where it could be hid. When he found it, it handicapped him — kept doubling up in his way.

Jist one place to pack a hat, he decided, and, pushing off his own sombrero, he put his father's ancient, branded one on his head. Then, holding fast to the next thought: *All set . . . but the letter*. Lane crept back into the sunlight.

It saved precious energy that he knew where to look. Fumbling in Maggart's pockets, he drew out the wallet, took the letter out of it, and pushed it into the pocket of his shirt.

He'd go home now — Starr was hurt! But it was a million miles to Pancho, and he was tired. Never had been so tired before.

Somehow he reached the horse and drew himself up till he could twine his fingers in Pancho's mane. Pancho, a little terrified by the scene and smell of Lane, shied off a step and the movement helped to pull the boy to his feet. He had to rest a little against Pancho's shoulder till the world swung back his way. Couldn't rest long, though. Had two jobs to do before he could rest — destroy that letter for Connie and Zain, and take the old hat to Starr. Starr loved Connie, but the Broken Bell brand stood between.

Exerting all his will, he lifted his foot to the stirrup, missed, and, exhausted by the effort, swayed back against the horse. Just a minute — he'd take another whack at it. He had to get back to Starr. Wanted to help Starr settle that Broken Bell brand. A tremendous idea came to him. Maybe he *had* settled it! That letter would have cost Zain Marsh his fortune. He'd saved Zain that money, and his good name. Maybe the Hallets' debt to Zain was paid!

"Gotta ask Starr . . . about that," he mumbled. "Starr will know. Gotta hurry home an' ask Starr."

But he couldn't seem to find the stirrup. Awkward as the bird they called the elephant, he was. Always had been able to find a stirrup, on the darkest night. Just one place for a stirrup. Setting his teeth to bear the pain, nerving himself for one more try.

If at first . . . you don't succeed . . . , grinned the yellow Hallet, lifting his foot again. But again he missed, lost his balance, and fell . . .

Fell into a pair of little arms that slipped up out of nowhere and eased him to the ground.

"Rosa!" he groaned up at the swimming, tragic little face under the gay, belled sombrero. "You game . . . little girl . . . you tagged! Glad you did . . . Rosa. Gotta go to Starr . . . he's hurt. Tex shot him. I killed Tex. Gotta git back . . . see if Starr don't think I settled the ol' bill to Zain. But . . . danged stirrup's . . . hidin' out on me. Help me on Pancho . . . like a good fellow."

He was never to get on Pancho — on any horse again! He saw it in Rosa's wavering face, and, straining to rise, he realized it for himself. But he didn't care. Living, he'd never done one thing worth remembering now. Dying, maybe he'd square that last brand for Starr and Connie. He might be worth that much . . .

"Got your conceit right with you . . . Lane Hallet," he mocked himself. "You . . . ain't worth . . . two-bits!"

Still Zain might think so — he thought a lot of the Hallets! Starr sure would think so. And he'd die right happy doing one good turn for Starr.

"Build a fire by me, Rosa . . . jist little . . . fire."

She made a little moan — cold, already so cold! But mutely she obeyed, caught up a few handfuls of brittle leaves and mesquite faggots, and heaped them by his side. She searched his pockets for a match and was bending to the leaves when he said, holding something toward her:

"Start it . . . with this, Rosa."

It was the old, ink-faded letter, worth a fortune in the right hands, but in Lane's, in Rosa's, only a worthless taper to start a mesquite fire. Pride throbbed with agony in Rosa's heart, as she ignited the letter and held it to the leaves.

Now the fire burned up brightly, and she laid some larger faggots on.

"Unstrap my spur, an' throw it in . . . fire," the boy begged. "Want the rowel hot!"

Wordlessly she obeyed. Dying men had strange fancies. And when the rowel was red, she lifted him at his request. She held him — his back against her little

129

spangled jacket, his father's old sombrero gripped awkwardly between his knees — while with the red-hot rowel he burned a coarse and jagged line through the Broken Bell brand.

Oh, the pity of it! That Clark Hallet couldn't have known how gloriously that last brand would be vented. Or, perhaps, he did know. *¿Quién sabe?* as Black Plains folk would say.

"Want you . . . take hat . . . to Starr!" he entreated next. "Burn . . . breeze . . . Rosa! Take hat to Starr!"

But this she couldn't obey. No, she wouldn't leave him. *¡Nombre de Dios!* Do not ask her that! She would take it . . . soon. But now — he must let her stay! Say she could stay!

"Till sunset," he whispered, and presently: "Always was . . . sweet on you . . . Rosa. But knowed . . . wasn't fit . . . for li'l queen . . . like you."

So the two sat on, in their first and last embrace. Her arms about him, her dusky hair mingled with his, her white cheek pressed to his, and their hearts were not unhappy. Lane had done all any man could do for a brother, and Rosa's heart was answered at last.

The lengthening shadow of the hut crept along Maggart's immobile form. And the sun, with a million fiery streamers of light, sank behind the Magdalena Mountains.

CHAPTER
EIGHTEEN

"Dagget Speaks for Himself"

June, with bright blue glances and fragrant promises, wooed the salt grass plains. As surely, mercifully, as the earth has seasons, the human heart has, too. The frozen winter of Starr's grief was over, although its season was more of an April time than June.

Months had passed since Rosa had brought the old sombrero to him. Months since he had been strong enough to be told of Lane. The boy lived on in his heart, as he would live forever — the kid brother, debonair, blameless, and beloved. But years of anxiety, of haunting dread had been laid to rest with Lane. No longer did Starr wear the old sombrero with the black and flaunting brands. The hat, with its last brand cancelled, he had laid away. But he could not lay his thoughts of it to rest.

How had Lane repaid Zain Marsh? He *had* repaid him. His last act had been to vent the Broken Bell brand. But how? This question kept his mind dwelling on the past. Until he knew, he couldn't help but brood.

He had a conviction that Zain Marsh knew, a curious feeling that frequently in their talks it trembled on Zain's tongue. And this June-sweet day, as Pancho loped with him to the Broken Bell, Starr resolved to make a clean breast to Marsh in the hope of settling that point, that he might lay the dead past away and, with Connie, face the future. He found the rancher enjoying his pipe in the cool of the verandah.

"Connie's down to the lower meadow with Link." Zain's honest old face lighted with the affection it always held for Starr Hallet.

Starr sat down on the bench beside him. "Like a word with you first, Zain," he said. Briefly, without preamble, while Zain Marsh made no sound or motion to break the tale, Starr told him of the Hallet's ruin by Dagget in Wyoming, the story of the old sombrero's brands, and of his father's dying wish that they be canceled. He told of his own struggle to pay the debt, and of Lane's venting the Broken Bell brand for a reason now death sealed. "Zain, I can't rest until I know how he done that!" Starr appealed. "He paid our dad's old debt. Won't you tell me how?"

Starr had expected Marsh to be stirred by what he had told him, but he was surprised at the agitation Zain betrayed. For long moments he strode up and down the porch, his hands gripped behind him, watching Starr with something like fear in his eyes.

"Son," he said in a shaken tone, "a dozen times I've been on the point of tellin' you, but lost my nerve. Lovin' Connie like I do has made a coward of me. An' God pity me now, if what I say brings sorrow on my little girl!" Then, as Starr stared at him, speechless: "Son," he said miserably, "I'm Dagget! At least, I'm the man your father meant by Dagget. I was born Zain Marsh, but my folks died when I was mighty young, an' a man named Dagget brought me up. Naturally I was known by his name. Not *well known*, either! For he was a renegade of the worst kind. He joined the Wyomin' rustlers, an' come to head a gang operatin' under his name. He was killed in a raid when I was jist turnin' eighteen, but the name stuck to the gang. My bein' the only Dagget in the country then, folks took me for the leader, an' painted me mighty black . . . with some right, too, for, to my everlastin' shame, I rode with the gang." A pleading note crept into his voice as Starr still stared, trying to reconcile this revelation with his idea of Honest Zain. "Son, I was a heap like Lane . . . crazy for excitement. I was a-ridin' in raids afore I was out of knee pants, afore I knowed what it was all about. But when I got old enough to know . . . I quit cold. Contrary to what your dad heard, Starr, I pulled out without a cent. I swear it! I've built up the Broken Bell, every stick an' stone of it myself . . . an' honest! An' when your dad drifted here . . . a Wyomin' Hallet . . . an' we was neighbors an' friends, an' me knowin' what I did . . . son, it shore was hell. But this ain't gittin' us to Lane," Marsh said wearily. "Like you, Starr, I've allus been a one-man man. Up there I left a pal I loved, Joe Dixon. An' I couldn't rest till I'd wrote an' told him about the opportunities here, beggin' him to quit the gang an' come here, an' I'd put him on his feet. But I never heard from Joe, an' thought him dead. I tried to put him out of my mind like I'd put out . . . in the years of peace an' happiness with my family here . . . that I ever rode with the Dagget gang.

"Son," he sat down by Starr, and laid a hand on his knee, "the day before Lane died, I got a note. It was addressed to Dagget, an' ordered me to come next night to that old windmill at Carson's Tanks. I knowed then my past had found me out. I knowed I'd have to go. That I'd have to give . . . for Connie's sake . . . whatever they asked. But I couldn't imagine what holt they had on me. They found papers on Maggart that proved that name was an alias, an' he was Joe Dixon's son. So I knowed it was him blackmailin' me, but still I couldn't see how, till that little Melles girl told me Maggart had a letter of mine, an' then I recollected the letter I'd wrote to Joe." Old Zain's hand closed over Starr's with a firm grip, as if what he was now to say would tear open old wounds. "Son, Lane went up there to get that letter an' Clark's ol' hat. He got killed a-doin' it, but he saved his father's name an' mine. If the Hallets ever owed me anything, it's been paid a hundredfold. But they never have, son . . . the debt's all mine!"

After they had silently mulled over the story that had no gaps now. "Son," Zain philosophized, "human nature's a frail bark for a hard journey, an' mighty easy capsized. Clark an' me both done wrong. But we was both mortal sorry for it. A man can't do more. Lane made his mistakes, but he redeemed 'em. We humans ain't nothin' but straws in the wind, an' the power behind that wind is something a heap bigger'n you or me. Lane died so you could be happy . . . don't ever forgit that."

He rose, and Starr rose with him, their hands gripped in a clasp of friendship that no storm of life could break.

"My eyes an' ears ain't what they used to be," Zain said with a twinkle, "but ain't that Connie down there, knee deep in alfalfa, yoo-hooin' to you?"

June came to Starr's heart as he went down the hill to Connie. She came to him through the purpling alfalfa, with her lithe, free step, and the future in her eyes. A one-man man — as Zain had said — Starr Hallet was no less a one-woman man, and Connie Marsh was the one woman. Vast and true enough her love to assuage every loss. Side by side, they walked through the flowering field, in that perfect understanding that needs no words, till . . .

"Guess who I heard from today?" Connie asked suddenly.

But Starr, his heart singing with this new pride in his brother, and his eyes full of Connie, was in no mood to guess.

"Rosa!" Connie exclaimed. "Melles is doing fine in El Paso. He's running a nice hotel . . . nothing like the old Monterey. And I gather that Rosa's quite a belle."

"Fine!" Starr was sincerely glad. "She's a dear kid. I'd like her to be happy. She's young, Connie . . . in time she'll forget Lane."

"She says not," Connie replied with a tremulous smile, "but she mentioned one young *caballero* . . . oh, such a handsome *caballero!*" Seeing in Starr's gray eyes the wistful light that always dawned at mention of Lane, she said softly: "But we'll never forget Lane, Starr."

"Nor that we owe him . . . this!" Starr cried.

And what they said, or did, or thought then doesn't concern in any phase the sad and colorful history of the old sombrero of many brands.

Starr of the Southwest

CHAPTER
ONE

"Trouble in the Wind"

By a sheer and blessed chance the old stone hut — last outpost of the great Loop Loop cattle outfit in the lonely, god-forsaken Sandflow region of the southern Río Grande — was inhabited this hot, starlit September night. Eleven months of the year it was deserted. Eleven months of every year nothing crossed its unbarred threshold but the hissing sand, the fiery wind, the slow-moving rattler. And so it would be tomorrow. For then the Loop Loop men, quartered here the two weeks past, scouring these wastes of sand and cactus for far-straying stock, would have left.

Already their work was done. The brush corrals before the crumbling, one-room structure were filled with cattle. At dawn, the trio limned by lantern light inside the hut would hit the trail. Just now the lanky, grave-faced Texan draped over the rough plank table was playing solitaire. The slim, olive-skinned, white-haired old Mexican, kneeling in the red and fitful flare, laced a broken stirrup leather in his saddle. The big, hard-eyed, disagreeable border drifter, Quayle — latest recruit to the outfit — paced the floor, grumbling, as he always was, about his wages, now two months in arrears.

139

"I earned that money! I earned it by the sweat of my brow. I earned a million, if sweat means anything, poundin' leather in this Sandflow! But I ain't askin' a million. I'm just askin' what's comin' to me. An' by the Lord Harry, I . . ."

"It's been a tough year on cowmen." Wearily the Texan looked up from his game. "A mighty tough year, what with the banks closin', and receivers callin' in loans the banks'd expected to renew and let run for years yet."

"Am I to blame for that?" Quayle snapped, finding here the argument he'd been looking for. "I didn't break the bank, did I? I didn't even borrow from it. I ain't goin' to be beat out of two months' pay just because a bank went flooey! An' I'm tellin' you, Tex . . ."

"Not just one bank" — the Texan's patience was wearing thin — "but seven of them. The whole Valle chain! It's a lucky cowman who can pay his help this year."

"So what?" snarled Quayle. "So the help can whistle! Is that it? Help can whistle because cowmen trusted Jord Valle's banks, an', when they asked for their money, it wasn't there. An' neither was Jord Valle! Where's he gone? Nobody knows. But *I* ain't hidin' him. I never even seen the man! I wouldn't know him from . . ."

The old Mexican, whose hands had been for seconds idle over his lacing, his white head bent, listening, suddenly sprang to his feet, and threw a hand up.

"*¿Qué es?*" he cried sharply. "What is that?"

140

They all heard it then. Startling as rifle shots in the dead quiet of that wild spot — the pound of hoof beats at mad gallop.

"What is that?" the old Mexican cried again.

"Trouble!" swore Quayle, and reached for the six-gun at his belt.

"I reckon so," agreed Tex, but his tone was quiet. "No man rides like that unless he's in trouble, or runnin' from it."

An instant later, all three stood outside the door, straining their eyes into the darkness. By the increasing pounding they could follow the approach of the horse — a horse, indiscernible at first, but rapidly taking form as it broke through the gloom — a trim-limbed sorrel covered with foam. Reeling, swaying on the trim-limbed sorrel's back, hands gripping the saddle horn, was a white-faced rider whose years could not exceed a score.

As the spent and quivering horse stopped fully in the glare from the open door, the cowpunchers saw that the boy's dark shirt was much darker on the side toward them. The wide belt was saturated and blood ran down his winged chaps, dripping onto the ground. His fine eyes — so tragically black, in his drained-white face — burned on them in some desperate appeal that his gray lips vainly tried to form.

The Texan sprang to him. "Boy, you're hurt!"

"Shot through . . . ," he gasped with awful effort. "Bullet here . . ." His hand trailed toward his side, but couldn't make it. Furious at his weakness, he panted imperiously: "Don't want it there! Somebody got . . .

razor . . . knife? Cut it out!" Coming from one in his plight it was astounding. "Don't need . . . no . . . sinker," he assured them with a grin of ghastly humor that haunted them long after his meaning was clear. Then he pitched into the Texan's outstretched arms.

His hat, an ancient, Spanish sombrero, with wide, cupped, silver-*concha*ed brim and high, peaked crown, toppled to the ground. It was a hat to draw the eye, even at such a time, but hardly one to draw such a cry as burst from the throat of Florencio, the Mexican, as he caught it up, and stood staring at it, as if it were a live thing. No! A dead thing one had known long before. The ghost of a friend.

With no thought to Florencio, who was following like a sleepwalker still staring at the old sombrero, the Texan carried the wounded lad into the hut and laid him down upon a bunk. Quayle led the foaming horse around and tied it in the brush behind, for trouble was in the wind. No telling where it was blowing from, and it always paid to take precautions in the lonely Sandflow of the southern Rio Grande.

Regardless of borrowing trouble, the Texan tore the boy's stained shirt away, dropped his belt, and bared the wound — a ghastly hole in his left side, just above the waistline. Feeling around, he found the lump on the other side, where the bullet had lodged deeply under the skin.

"Boy, who done it?" he asked, his lean, bronzed face hard-set.

There was pain in the black eyes staring up — pain not wholly physical. "No matter." The boy's hand

142

tossed in a feeble gesture. "I've been riding . . . toward that bullet. Now, it's done . . . its work. Cut it out."

But the Texan dared not take such a responsibility upon himself. "Boy, you don't know what you ask. An incision there . . . it's dangerous. I'll patch you up the best I can, and send . . ."

"No!" the boy protested fiercely, starting up. "*You* do it!"

"But I ain't no doc . . ."

"You don't have to be! You got a knife, ain't you? You . . . can cut."

"But there's nothin' to give you to ease the pain."

"I can stand it, if you can," the lad insisted with a gameness that thrilled the Texan. Suddenly all his bravado gone, his white face quivering, and looking very helpless, very young, he moaned piteously: "I can't die . . . with the . . . damned thing . . . in me."

Although shaken by the anguish in that plea, the Texan dared not give in. He was still groping for words to say so, when there was no longer any necessity. The boy was gone — or so the Texan thought. But, no — his heart still beat! Slowly, faintly. It could not beat long.

Sitting on the edge of the bunk, fingers pressed to that failing pulse, Tex gazed into the boyish face with interest. It was a fine, passionate young face that had in it — although the boy was unconscious and his fiery eyes shut — something headlong, willful, tameless. Who was he, this nervy lad? Who had fired that shot he'd been riding toward, that sinker he didn't need?

The Texan's gaze rested on the table where Florencio sat bowed over that hat, Quayle leaning over his shoulder, his hard eyes agleam with curiosity. Instantly Tex was on his feet and bending over the hat, hoping it might hold some clue to the boy's identity. One look at the hat here in the light, and he all but forgot its owner. It seemed imbued with a personality peculiarly its own, one that dominated everything else. He saw, then, what had escaped him outside — brand on brand, of every conceivable size and description, burned deeply on every inch of that old sombrero!

"What do you make of them?" he asked Quayle.

"Show-off!" sneered the big rider. "Show-off, pure an' simple. Just a fool kid with a big head, tryin' to draw notice to hisself by messin' up his headgear with the brands of outfits he's worked for, Tex."

"He's a sight too young to have worked for so many," remarked Tex dryly.

Which was undeniable even for Quayle. The hat looked like the tally sheet of every roundup held since Lot had his range dispute with Abram and drove his flock over the Jordan. The Seven Up, the Dagger Hilt, the Broken Bell, the Y Lightning. Half the old outfits in the state.

"An' them other hieroglyphics?" Quayle's interest was blazing. "That line burned deep through every brand? An' them little dots around each one? What do they mean?"

Memory dogged the Texan's mind. He could almost grasp it, but never quite. He said soberly: "That hat's got a history."

"*Si*," murmured the Mexican, "a sad and sinister history."

144

"You know it?" cried Tex eagerly. "You know that history, Florencio?"

A shrug like a shudder convulsed Florencio's taut frame. "It is written," he said strangely.

"What? Where?" insisted Quayle. "You mean them brands?" Harshly he commanded: "Read it, then!"

CHAPTER
TWO

"Branded History"

Like a man in sleep, or deep in a hypnotic spell, wholly subservient to another's will, his eyes frozen on the old sombrero, as if what he recited actually were written there, Florencio began in a queer, strained, disembodied tone that rang weirdly through the room.

"Long ago, when the state was young, this hat was seen on the Black Plains range. Even then men asked, as you ... 'What means the symbols on that sombrero?' And no man knew that the proud old cattleman who wore it had in his rash youth been a rustler, that his vast herds were built on stolen cattle, that those brands were the record of his crimes! But always his conscience had troubled him, and, whenever he stole cattle, he burned the owner's brand upon his hat ... with dots around to indicate how many ... meaning to pay them back someday." Slowly, like a record run down, his voice died away.

There was no sound but the labored breathing of the unconscious boy on the bunk beside them and the soft hiss of wind-flung sand on the windowpane.

"But those marks through every brand?" prompted the Texan.

146

"Yeah?" Quayle challenged. "How do you account for them?"

"That," said the old man, and every word seemed wrung from him, "is the history of the second generation, on whom the sins of the father descended, for he was never to make restitution. Death overtook him. There was only time to summon his sons and tell them the true and terrible meaning of the brands, to pray they make good every theft . . . and his soul might rest. But . . ."

A start ran through him. The Texan thought he was going to stop. After a moment, he went on, dazed still, revealing things no power on earth could have made him tell in circumstances other than here.

"Of his two sons, the younger . . . wild and lawless like his father . . . refused to use his inheritance to pay debts nobody knew existed, debts contracted before he was born. He squandered his share over bars and gambling tables, while the other nobly shouldered the full burden. One by one, he hunted up the outfits branded on the hat, and secretly made good his father's thefts. As he cleared each brand, he burned a line through it . . . to keep his record straight. But the money from his heritage did not go far, and he slaved to make more. By the labor of his hands, his wits . . . every possible way! Yet strive as he did, there was one he could not pay. This" — pointing to it, branded black in the gray nap, on the very peak of the old hat — "the Broken Bell. This was left until the last . . . lest he be tempted to pay it, and forget the rest. This one, which *must* be paid! For it showed his father had stolen many

147

cows from the father of the girl who was all of earth . . . aye, and heaven . . . to him. Until that debt was paid, life held no meaning. But he was never to mark out that brand."

"Yet it's cancelled!" cried the Texan.

"*Si* . . . by a dying hand!" was the tragic answer. "By the hand of the black-sheep brother. Too sad, that is, for tongue to tell! With his life's blood, he paid the debt to the Broken Bell. Thus honoring" — a light almost of personal pride broke the still surface of Florencio's dark face — "the last debt recorded on the old sombrero of many brands."

Close on the hush that followed this, the wind soughed in, as if the very night had caught its breath. With it, through the open door, came the howling of corralled cattle, the shrill, sweet whinny of a horse in the brush out there. A moan broke from the unconscious figure, and the lantern flame flared and fell, with a brighter glow, on those fresh, red stains on the ancient sombrero.

Jarringly Quayle's laugh broke in. "That's quite a story, Florencio. Did you make it up as you went along?"

"It's no story, Quayle!" the Texan cried, memory no longer eluding him. "It's true! Every syllable! That hat belongs to the Hallet family over in the Black Plains country. Why, it's as much a part of New Mexico as the longhorn is to Texas, or the Alamo!" Blind to the look Florencio shot at him — Florencio now alert — the Texan continued: "I've heard that story before, but Florencio didn't tell it all. There's still another chapter.

A third generation of Hallets. Two brothers again, Starr and Lane. Starr, the elder, is a square-shooter like his father, who cancelled these brands. The other is wild as the grandfather who contracted that fatal debt, as the uncle he was named for, who gave his life to square the Broken Bell. But from what I gather, Lane Hallet hasn't the redeeming grace of his uncle. They say he's plumb bad. Always has been. At the rodeo in Lasco last spring, he got into a shooting scrape and killed the sheriff . . . Pat Donovan, a mighty popular man. The county got out a reward for him. A thousand dollars, dead or alive! But last I heard . . ."

"A thousand dollars!" Quayle's greedy soul took fire. A thousand days of slaving at thirty per — and not getting it, what was more! If he had half, a third that sum . . .

"Last I heard," heedlessly the Texan rushed on, "he was still a fugitive, with every officer in the state hunting him, with his brother Starr moving heaven and earth to find him. They say Starr Hallet has a blind, stubborn, fanatical faith in his brother . . . refuses to believe him guilty of murder. He hunts Lane to hear from his own lips what did happen, that he may find the real killer."

"Then this kid" — Quayle's hot eyes slid toward the bed — "is one of the Hallet boys?"

"He must be," admitted the Texan.

Hoarsely Quayle demanded: "*Which* one?"

But the Texan didn't know.

Quayle whirled on Florencio. "You know the Hallets?"

"*Sí*," was the silken, soft response — dangerous as a panther's purr. "I work for the father of these boys when he marked out the brands on that sombrero. One time" — slowly the old Mexican's eyes narrowed on the smile in them — "when he fight to take his brother from a gambling den, I kill a man with my knife to save a Hallet's life. Even yet" — softly, and with a smile, he stated — "I would kill a man to save a Hallet."

There was that in his voice which made the Texan shiver.

Quayle seemed not to notice. "Tell us," he insisted, "which is this . . . Starr or Lane? The Hallet worth a thousand dollars, or the blind fool huntin' him?"

Like a panther Florencio was around the table, between Quayle and the helpless figure on the bunk, his hand slipping beneath his shirt to close on the knife that he always carried there. "It is Lane," he said softly.

"Are you sure?" cried Quayle. "Would he be apt to wear a hat as well known as that? One that would make him a marked man?"

"It is Lane," said the Mexican.

"Dead or alive?" Quayle licked his lips. *Dead or alive?* Hard to tell which. But no matter which! Either way he was worth the same. He stepped toward the bunk as if the still form on it were a roll that he could pocket.

Death hovered in that hut — closer to another than the wounded boy on the bunk. The Texan watched in smothering horror. Was Quayle crazy? Hadn't he understood that threat? Didn't he know the loyalty of Florencio's race? That once they have worked for a

150

family, they are as loyal as if they'd been born in it? Couldn't he see the only way he could collect that reward would be over Florencio's dead body? As that deadly knife was about to flash into action, Quayle froze in his step, his hand dropping to his gun.

But it was never drawn. The thud of galloping hoofs cut in, of many horses this time. To Quayle their coming was a threat of the prize snatched from him, or whittled down by many sharings. He sprang toward the door, the Texan but a step behind.

A dozen riders were galloping up, their horses lunging, snorting, the wet coats evidencing a mad race through heavy sands. The men jerked and swore, trying to get them in hand. All was wild confusion. Faces and forms were indistinguishable in the night. Only one stood out — a rider framed fully in the shaft of light from the open door, a tall, sinewy, young rider on a cream-colored horse of striking size and beauty. He leaned tensely forward in the saddle, his smoldering eyes fixed beyond the two in the doorway to the Mexican inside, holding up, as in the act of donning it, an old sombrero, brands invisible in the gloom, but with contours as familiar as the face of a brother.

It was only a flashing glimpse, then Quayle slammed the door behind him. There was $1,000 in that hut, and you couldn't be too careful in the lonely Sandflow — or any man's land — playing for a stake like that.

CHAPTER
THREE

"An I.O.U."

Flashing as that glimpse had been, the Texan had noticed it. He fixed his eyes on the young rider. Certainly he'd never seen him before, yet he had no doubt as to his identity, so strong was the resemblance to the other tense, young face the Texan had looked into this night. In pity and horror that this rider must see that bullet-riddled form in the hut, he scarcely gave a thought to the other men, scarcely a glance at the man who, as Quayle jerked the door shut, shouldered aside the cream-colored horse and came up, firing questions like a Gatling gun. The newcomer was a stocky, grizzled man whose features were lost in the star's wan light. His voice had the ring of authority, and on his broad breast gleamed an official badge to back it.

"What outfit is this?" he — Tom Garret, Lasco sheriff — demanded.

With no thought of anyone, or anything, but that stake and how he could hold it, Quayle retorted: "Loop Loop."

"Had a caller recent?"

"Yeah. The boss was out to check up on us a coupla days ago."

152

"You call that recent?" flared the officer.

"Mighty recent . . . in the Sandflow."

"I mean *plumb* recent," explained the sheriff, obviously nettled. "An hour ago . . . or less. An' I ain't concerned with folks on legitimate business here. A young hellhound on a sorrel . . . that's the man we're after."

"What's he wanted for?" asked Quayle cautiously.

"Murder!" came the chilling, the terse answer.

It was like a lash in the face of the young rider. The Texan, whose eyes had never left him, saw him flinch and whiten. Then, as the sheriff went on hotly, the youth slowly backed his horse out of the jam, unobtrusively slid into the deeper shadow at the corner of the hut, and disappeared.

"Murder!" flamed the officer. "The murder of my friend and predecessor! The whitest man that ever wore a star. Shot him down like a coyote! But he'll swing for it!" he said sharply.

"You don't mean young Hallet?" asked Quayle. "The kid who killed Pat Donovan?"

"That's who I mean! He's managed to hide out half a year. But we're on his trail. Sighted him a dozen times this afternoon. Right on his heels at Skull Crossing! I'd 'a' swore I winged him!"

"A bounty on him, ain't there?" Quayle was playing *plumb* careful. "A thousand bucks, I hear."

"That's right!" said the sheriff shortly. Damn an *hombre* who thought of money when it came to doing what was the bounden duty of every citizen! "A thousand dollars to the man who produces him."

"Produces him where?" Quayle pressed, like a man just talking to hear himself. "To the Law? You, for instance? Or lands him in jail? Say we'd been lucky, an' he'd come here, an' we turned him over to you, right side up an' handled with care? Would we get the reward?"

"You sure would."

"Dead, or . . . ?"

"Come on, Tom!" an impatient voice from the posse cut in. "We're wastin' time here. I told you that wasn't the sorrel's trail. We lost it in the wash where the cattle crossed. Like the same cattle these boys is drivin'. That yearlin's doubled back on us, an' is hittin' out of the country. Gittin' farther away every . . ."

"Reckon you're right, Joe." Garret was wheeling his horse to direct the manhunt away from that hut, out of the Sandflow, when Quayle seized his bridle.

"Wait!" he cried with a savage exultation that made the Texan's blood boil. "I'm claimin' that thousand! Your man's here!"

They stared, stunned, not believing.

"He's in there" — Quayle pointed toward the door — "dead or dyin'!"

All was a tangle again. An uproar of men, piling out of the saddle and into the hut. Between their shuttling forms, the Texan saw the sheriff approach the bunk, and stop. His square figure stiffened. "What's the big idea?" he cried wrathfully. "Tryin' to make a fool of me?"

Tex saw Quayle go up to the bunk — stop — and his jaw drop. Fighting through the clamoring posse, the

154

Texan, too, went up to it, halting dumfoundedly. The bunk was empty!

The bunk was empty and Quayle was like a man gone suddenly crazy. "He *was* here!" he swore. "He was here when we went to the door! He come rampin' in on a winded sorrel. Shot up! Bleedin' all over the place! The blankets . . . here's where he was layin'! Look!"

The sheriff stooped to examine it, but his eyes fell on something just under the bunk, and he snatched it up. "He was here, all right. Here's his hat!"

He held it out to the lantern light. Eagerly the men crowded about, a strange awe stealing over them. The old sombrero of many brands! Relic of the wild frontier, and familiar, then, on every cattle trail from the San Juan hills to the Río Grande. Its story was whispered in many a version, until, with passing time, everything pertaining to those first years and characters took on glamour and interest. Like the first stagecoach — the great white-topped schooner of the plains — the old sombrero was brought forth to appear at frontier celebrations and help revive some gleam of the virile days that had been. The last such time was six months ago at the Lasco Rodeo.

"He was wearin' it!" Tightly the sheriff gripped that scarred and storied old sombrero. "He had it on when he killed Pat! Lost it makin' his getaway. We've been holdin' it since for evidence, but last night he come out of hidin', broke into jail, an' stole it. Game! Give him credit for that. But this hat will put the noose on his neck. For it will give us his trail." He dropped the

155

sombrero on the table, his eyes raking the dim interior. "How did he get out of here?"

Even as he asked, he saw.

Quayle tremblingly pointed to the one window, tall and narrow, in the stone wall opposite. "It was shut. Now . . . it's open. He opened it!"

"Energetic for a dyin' man," suggested someone.

"Mebbe he was playin' 'possum," another added. "But" — eyes looking shudderingly from that blanket — "that don't look like it."

"He had help. That Mexican" — Quayle glared wildly about him — "where's he?"

"What Mexican?" asked Garret. "Was there another man here?"

"Florencio! He works with us. But he used to work for the Hallets. Said he'd kill for a Hallet. He was goin' to knife me when . . ."

Breaking through the confusion, seeming to come from right under the window they looked from, was the sound of a horse thundering off.

"He's gone!" Quayle screamed. "That greaser! Damn him! Got him on the sorrel, an' . . ." The mad rush for the door drowned the rest of his words.

The hut was empty of everyone but Quayle and the Texan. They stood together at the table, while the posse mounted and galloped away, hoofbeats growing fainter . . . fainter . . .

"Right through my hands!" Quayle was storming. "A thousand bucks . . . right through my hands!"

156

But the Texan was thinking of that young rider he'd seen vanish around the hut. He hadn't shown up again. Where was he? Only one horse had galloped away.

"That greaser won't get a mile," moaned Quayle. "But it might as well be a million. We'll never collect. The posse'll get the . . ." He stopped, staring at the window, his jaw dropping farther than when he'd found the boy gone.

Between him and the outdoors, two booted feet swung. He stared, speechless. The Texan, bewildered, stared at two legs encased in chaps descending into view. Then a man dropped to the ground, and, climbing back on the ridge of earth that banked the hut, reached up with the utmost care and effort, and lowered a heavy object. Tenderly clasping his awkward burden, he looked straight in at them. It was the same rider they'd seen in that shaft of light, but haggard now, as if years had elapsed — years spent on the rack.

"Help me fetch him in," he said in a tortured tone.

The Texan sprang to aid him. Together they bore the unconscious youth back into the hut, gently depositing him on the bunk he had been snatched from so recently, so mysteriously. The Texan stepped back, but the other bent silently over the inert form. His shoulders shook, and his cheek gleamed wet, but he was tensed like a man whose hardest task still lies before him and dares not give up.

Unable to wait longer for an explanation, the Texan asked earnestly: "How in the world did you do it, Hallet?"

Slowly the tired eyes looked up. "You know?"

"Sure. I'd know you were his brother anywhere."

Anyone would have known. Although Starr was older, taller, with gray eyes instead of black, and dark-brown hair, the resemblance was unmistakable. He had the same finely cut, spirited face. There was the same high-bred stamp on it. Only there was a steadiness, a gravity not in the other face, and tragic in a youth of twenty-four, so deeply the experiences of life had bitten there, experiences not his own, but those of the erring, younger brother — hunted like an animal — dying like one.

"I didn't do it alone," he told them gravely. "The instant I rode in, I saw Florencio holding the old sombrero, so I knew Lane was here. I slipped around the cabin, and Florencio was trying to get him out the window. Between us, we got him on the roof. Then Florencio lit out on my horse. Pancho's fast. Nothing in the posse can touch him. Florencio's tryin' to toll them off, till I take Lane . . ."

There was a snarl across the table, the flash of a gun in Quayle's hand. "You'll take him nowhere!"

Starr Hallet stared at that six-gun, completely dazed by such an action. Because they had been with Florencio, because he had seen Quayle close the door and parley with the sheriff, and heard nothing since, in the excitement of getting his brother onto the roof and helping Florencio to get away because of what he believed he'd seen in the eyes of the Texan — he had thought them friends.

158

"You'll take him nowhere," Quayle was vowing over that gun, "till I collect the bounty on him. I'm takin' no more chances on that killer."

Another lash in the face of the brother, a lash that made him flinch, whiten, and storm madly back: "Don't call him that!"

"Why not? He's earned the title! Why not call him a killer? He is one. He killed Pat Donovan! He killed Donovan, an' he's goin' to swing!"

"He may . . . swing," Starr flashed whitely, "but he's not guilty!"

"That's up to the jury."

"But" — voicing the awful fear that had haunted him all this summer when he'd been moving heaven and earth to find his brother — "they may not wait for jury trial."

"That ain't my responsibility."

"You'd see an innocent man hung for a thousand dollars?" cried Starr incredulously.

"What they do with him," was the devilish reply, "ain't my concern."

Sick with horror, Starr turned to the Texan. "Where do you stand?"

Tex wasn't sure. He had no sympathy with murder, but a man wasn't necessarily guilty of murder just because he was accused of it. Suddenly he knew that whether Lane Hallet was guilty or not, he stood with this gray-eyed rider. He said shortly: "Count me on your side."

"Thanks," said Starr. "That's what I thought." It seemed to buck him up, give him courage to fight.

159

Despite the bitter defeat sealed by that gun, he meant to fight — and win. Quick! Before the posse got back. "Listen," he swung to Quayle again, "nobody *saw* Lane kill Donovan. The evidence is all against him, I'll admit. He ran. That looks black. But he had some reason. I've got to talk to him . . . find out why he ran. But first we must get him away from here."

"You don't move him one step."

Starr threw up a hand. "If it's money you want," he promised Quayle, "you'll get it. Only give me time . . . a month . . . two weeks . . . to find the real killer. I'll pay that thousand."

"Not a min . . ."

"Fifteen hundred then!"

The gun wavered in Quayle's hand. Every fiber of his avaricious soul was yearning to reach out and seize this greater sum, but he dared not, lest he lose the thousand already in his grip.

"Two thousand!" Starr raised desperately. "Twice as much as the law will pay. *Six times as much!* For you're not the only one entitled to that reward. There's Florencio! And my friend here! You'd have to split with them. But wait two weeks, and you'll get two thousand for yourself."

Quayle was dripping cold perspiration. "If he dies . . ."

, "Then" — Starr's eyes went to the bunk, and came back wet — "you still collect."

The gun was down, but Quayle was protesting, almost whimperingly: "How do I know you'd pay? I'd have to have some guarantee."

Some guarantee! Desperately the gray eyes swept the hut, as if seeking some guarantee in it. By chance, or fate's grim design, his eyes fell on that old sombrero. He picked it up. His grandfather's hat! Ledger of his youthful crimes! In remorseful years, his crown of thorns, to which he had clung as his only hope of redemption. Sins expiated by the bitter sacrifice of one son, and the lifeblood of the other. Gray eyes dark with the pain of his thoughts, Starr looked at Quayle. "You know the story of this hat?"

"Florencio was tellin' some cock-an'-bull . . ."

"You know a debt on it is sacred to a Hallet?"

In the face of that deadly sincerity, in the almost living, awesome presence of that old sombrero, Quayle could only nod that he knew.

Quickly Starr Hallet reached into the pocket of his black flannel shirt for a cigarette, lighted it, and rapidly smoked it a quarter down. Then, as they mutely watched him with a thrilling glimmer of what he was about, he bent over that hat, seeking a space free of brands. Finding one — beside the fateful Broken Bell, on the high crown — he applied to it the glowing tip of his cigarette.

Not a sound, not even a breath was drawn. The odor of burning felt — the very essence of all the tragedy that had been, and was to be — permeated the hut as the old hat knew again the searing pressure of a new brand furrowed on its aged nap in an awful pact. Nobody saw the wounded boy's eyes open on the grim act. Nobody saw him start in horror from the blanket.

161

As Starr turned the fresh brand to Quayle — Q2000, flanked by the dollar sign, beside the Broken Bell — he said: "There's my I.O.U . . . my promise to pay two thousand, in two weeks' time, if you keep quiet about Lane and give me a chance to find the murderer."

"Two weeks, an' not a day more," Quayle answered hoarsely. "If you ain't here then, I'll turn him in!"

A wild cry filled the hut, echoing back from those walls of rock, seeming to voice the horror of all the dead Hallets: "Don't do it, Starr! Don't make a deal like that!"

CHAPTER
FOUR

"Fox and Geese"

The history of two generations was on that hat, and the third was in the writing. Most sad, most sinister, it would be when written, beautiful, the story of faith unalterable — a brother's fight to save a brother, against the world, against time, against even that brother's will. While the hut still echoed with that cry of protest, Starr Hallet dropped beside the bunk. Throwing his arms about his brother, he tenderly supported him as Lane panted a wild confession: "Let him turn me in. I killed Donovan."

The Texan looked with regret and deep compassion on Starr, who showed no feeling of any kind. There was not the slightest tremor in the hand gently brushing Lane's black hair back, or in his low-toned: "Hush. You're excited, Lane. You don't know what you're sayin'."

"I do!" fiercely the boy insisted. "I was at the dance. Been drinking . . . all day. Was leaving, when the sheriff cornered me. He . . . got tough. An' I . . . I let him have it. I was seeing red, Starr."

Wasting time, when there wasn't a second to spare. Wasting strength, when he shouldn't be talking at all.

"Lane," Starr cut in, "you're lying to me. I was at the dance, too. I went there hunting you. I was right over the wall, when . . . You weren't alone, you and Donovan. I heard a man singing. There was a woman . . . You're shielding someone. Who is it, Lane?"

Starr's heart sank as the boy strained away from him, eyes flashing through all their frightful pain, the stubborn defiance always in them when anyone took issue with him. It wasn't safe to antagonize Lane in his condition, but Starr had to know.

"Lane" — gray eyes probed the very soul of his brother — "who was with you there?"

"Oh, stop quizzing me, Starr," the boy groaned. "I told you I did it."

"Who was that man singing, Lane?"

The white lips locked.

"That woman . . . ?" pressed Starr. "Was that Rose of Lost Cañada?"

Instantly Lane was like a wildcat, struggling to get free, shrilling with hot ferocity: "You keep her out! Do you hear? She . . . you don't know anything about her!"

"Nobody does." There were tears in Starr's eyes, but his grip was like steel. "Nobody knows anything about her . . . except she's a rodeo rider and comes from some place called Lost Cañada. But I know you were seen with her at every rodeo last spring. I know she was in Lasco the night Donovan was . . ."

"You know" — said the distracted youth bitterly, falling back in exhaustion — "a hell . . . of a lot."

But Starr didn't. Not much. Just a few facts, which constant thought had worn to the bone. They stood out

164

in his mind, sharp, glistening as the bones of a desert victim through which white sands stream endlessly. Endlessly a thousand hopes, fears, and conjectures flashed through his mind. There on his knees, his arms about Lane, tensely watched by Quayle and the Texan, Starr's thoughts swept over the network of fancy and fact, which he must fill out — quicken — with the living truth that would save his brother.

That April night when he'd come home from work to find the old sombrero gone, and a note from Lane saying he'd taken it to wear to the Lasco Rodeo, he was hurt because Lane hadn't waited to see him. Somehow he had a feeling that all wasn't well. Whispers and hints that folks had let drop strengthened his apprehensions. Lane had slipped his bridle — was running wild. Mixing in bad company? Crazy over Rose of Lost Canada — a girl without a regular name or habitation that anybody could discover. A girl who appeared out of nowhere to ride in rodeos, then disappeared into nowhere again. Whose beauty was like mescal on men. A dangerous girl for a kid like Lane.

Feeling that he must see Lane, talk to him, he had hurried to Lasco. Somewhere he had learned that Lane was at the dance, and went there — whipped by a nameless fear. Bursting into the hall, he had glimpsed the old sombrero vanishing through a door in the rear. Struggling through the jam of dancers, he had found Lane gone. He was groping around the lot in back — dark, for a high wall shadowed it — and trying to get around the wall. He had heard that song. The song had haunted him ever since. It was an undertone to all the

165

miles he had hunted Lane. The voice, of deep, rich, musical timbre, had held — strangely, for a refrain so tender — a warning note. A man had sung — with a warning note — just over the wall:

> **If I should die and o'er oceans foam,**
> **Softly a white dove on a fair eve should come,**
> **Open thy lattice, dearest, for it will be,**
> **My faithful soul . . .**

The song had broken there, and almost on the same spot, with a scrape of feet on gravel, a sharp command to halt came, an answering cry, inarticulate, scarcely human, then a woman's scream — and a shot. He had stood rooted to the spot, while people rushed from the hall, from among horses and rigs tied in the lot. Plunging after them, he had found Lane standing over the dead body of Pat Donovan, holding the crowd at bay with a gun, seen his brother, still menacing them, dart swiftly back to his horse and gallop off. The old sombrero, swept from his head by heavy shrubs along the wall, had been caught and held as if *it* were the murderer.

Two people must know who was guilty. The man who had sung, and the woman who had screamed. Why hadn't they spoken up for him? Why hadn't the girl . . . ? He'd stake his soul that she was Rose of Lost Cañada! Why hadn't she . . . ?

"Don't try to pin it on somebody else," Lane begged piteously, his voice bringing his brother's wandering thoughts back. "I done it."

166

Donovan shot down, as Garret had put it, like a coyote! Starr thought bitterly. "You *couldn't* do that," he insisted huskily.

"You don't know me," retorted the boy. "Folks don't know each other when they're kin. They don't see each other like . . ."

"You're a Hallet."

Terribly Lane reminded him: "Hallets . . . *do* things! Look at that hat!" His eyes widened on it there, fully in the lantern light on the table. "It shows what the Hallets are! Rustlers . . . *worse!* Uncle Lane . . ."

"He wiped all that out when he cancelled the Broken Bell," said Starr.

"But now" — it was a mere whisper of horror — "my mark's on it."

"You've got to help me wipe it out!" cried Starr. "You've got to tell me who's been hiding you? Who were those people over the wall?"

There was no answer, only a fading light in the black eyes, a laxity in the slight figure like a slow parting of flesh and spirit, for all Starr's grip of steel. In an agony of fear for his brother, with no hope but to clear his name of a charge so horrible, he cried wildly: "Lane, where's Lost Cañada?" The weight in his arms lay, impassive, voiceless. In tones that might have reached a heart long worn away by streaming sand, he cried: "I *know* you didn't do it! Pat Donovan was killed by a Thirty-Eight bullet. I found your Forty-Four in the brush under the wall, where you threw it!"

Sympathetically the Texan bent over him. "Better put him down. He's fainted again."

"It's worse than a faint," protested Starr. "He won't get well."

"I'd 'a' said not, an hour ago," the Texan admitted huskily. "But now . . . well, he's stood so much . . ."

"He's got to stand more!" his brother said vehemently. "I've got to get him away from here."

Instantly Quayle was wary. "Where you takin' him? Wherever it is, I'm goin'!"

Where was he taking Lane? Starr didn't know. He didn't know the Sandflow. In helpless appeal he looked at the Texan, an hour ago a stranger to him, but one he'd known instinctively he could tie to. With what justification, he was to learn later. Now he looked to the Texan for help, and Tex didn't fail him.

"There's an old dugout not far from here," he told Starr. "I run across it hunting cattle. It's drifted over. Nobody'd find it who didn't know it was there before. He'll be safe there."

Quayle making no objection, they set immediately about transferring the desperately wounded boy to the old dugout situated in a deep depression about a mile north of the hut, and further hidden by great, wind-sculptured dunes. Sand had drifted over the roof, and only a door was in sight.

"Like an igloo," Tex put it, halting the procession there in the starlight.

Like a tomb, Starr thought, but he believed Lane would be safe here. He felt a vast relief when they laid Lane on blankets spread on the dugout floor. The Texan and Quayle returned to the hut for what supplies they had left there and such camp equipment in the hut as was necessary to maintain Lane. Florencio came back with them.

The old Mexican was coated with sand and tired from his hard run, but his white teeth flashed in a victorious grin.

"Fox and geese," he described the chase to Starr. "Lost them in the dunes easy, but they'll find their way out at daylight. Maybe they come back. Better they find nothing at the hut. You boys . . ." — addressing Quayle and the Texan — "take the cattle home, like we plan. I will stay with Lane."

"No, you don't!" strongly Quayle objected there. "I ain't leavin' here. You two take the cattle."

"I stay with Lane," said Florencio uncompromisingly.

"I'll take the cattle." Tex settled the question, although it would be a tough job for one man. "I can tell the boss you boys are hunting stock farther on."

"Better, then," Florencio warned, "we cover every track up here. So if the posse comes back to the hut, the only trail they find will lead out of the Sandflow. But we must work fast. Day breaks soon."

While Starr gave Pancho a quick rubdown, turning him loose to forage on the meager grass in the vicinity of the dugout, Tex and Florencio went over the ground, carefully obliterating the trail. When all was done, dawn was streaking the eastern horizon.

CHAPTER
FIVE

"A Wild Plan"

"I feel better about leaving, with Florencio here," Starr told Tex, as they stepped out of the dugout for a last look around. "He'll do everything for Lane that can be done."

"And as quick as I deliver them cows," Tex promised him, "I'll be back to do what *I* can. I'm seein' this through."

Starr's eyes filled. "You're a prince, Tex."

"No, just ordinary," the Texan denied smilingly. "And ornery enough to have a little curiosity. How come you to be with the posse?"

Unhesitatingly Starr told him: "I'd been hanging around Lasco off and on, thinking Lane might come back after that hat. It means a lot to a Hallet. I knew he'd stop at nothing to get it. And he didn't! He slipped into town, held up the jailer, and got away with it. Sheriff Garret was swearing in men. He didn't know me. Lucky none of the others did. And he swore me in."

"Then," Tex said thoughtfully, "you're a deputy. You got a legal right to hold Lane in your custody."

"And arrest Pat Donovan's murderer, when I find him," Starr added grimly.

The Texan looked at him admiringly. Black as the case was against the lad in there, he half believed with Starr that he was innocent, and prayed that he was.

"Any plans?" he asked.

"Not now," Starr said with a shrug. "I hoped Lane would tell me something, but he never will. There's two other people who knew what happened that night. I haven't been able to locate them in the months I've been searching. Now, with just two weeks . . . But" — his face was resolute in the sunrise — "folks can't live on this earth and not leave tracks. And with Lane dependin' on me . . ."

A loud whinny broke in. They turned. It was the sorrel, left to trail reins beside the dugout when they carried Lane in. A dead giveaway if, by some miracle of ill luck, the posse should return and decide to have a look in this pocket. It was too well known to them to be mistaken for an unused Loop Loop horse escaped from the little pasture down at the hut, where Quayle's and Florencio's mounts would be kept along with others from the remuda to serve as a blind.

"We'll have to turn him loose," said the Texan, "saddle and all. Then, if they see him, they'll think he's dropped his rider. He'll make for home as fast as he can kite."

He was rising to do this, when Starr caught his arm. "Wait!" he cried eagerly — no longer without a plan, if such a wild, fantastic idea could be dignified by the name. "That's not Lane's horse. He must belong to a friend . . . someone who's helped him. Maybe one of the very people I've got to find. He might lead me to them. I'm going to follow him!"

"By juniper," cried Tex, after the first startled gasp, "it might work at that! You can depend on a horse to light out for his home range, and there's a chance he might lead you right."

A chance was all Starr asked. Infused with this hope, he hurriedly saddled Pancho, then went into the dugout and ate the cold bite that Tex had set out for him. Alone in the room, he knelt over the unconscious form of his brother.

"You're holdin' out on me, Lane," he whispered in trembling tone, "but I'm goin' to save you in spite of yourself. When I come back, we'll take your mark off the old hat." All the unnatural steadiness of his young face breaking, he implored: "Be here then!"

Rising, he picked up the old sombrero with its fresh brand, the hat his father had worn to pay *his* father's debt. Until this debt was paid, he would wear it.

Out again in the dawn, now luminous, rosy, his good bye said to Florencio, he mounted Pancho and waited while Tex broke the snap in the sorrel's bridle, letting the bit fall free, so that the horse could eat and drink on the journey, but making it appear — should the posse pick him up — that it had been done by accident. Then Tex threw the reins over the saddle horn, and gave the animal a slap on the flank.

It moved away, but stopped within a few steps, looking back uncertainly. Tex threw a stone, frightening the horse into a run that carried it far down the sun-flushed swale, where it tossed up its head, sniffed the breeze, then swerved suddenly to the left, and struck off in a westerly direction.

With a warm handclasp and a husky — "So long." — to Tex, Starr Hallet rode after the sorrel. His one frail hope in all the world was that the sorrel might lead him to the nameless singer of a song heard over a starlit adobe wall, or a girl who was only a name — Rose of Lost Cañada.

The wildest goose chase ever man rode on! thought Tex, watching him recede in the rosy distance, gradually growing smaller and smaller, a tiny, toiling, ineffectual figure in the wild welter of dunes that rolled away like the waves of a storm-tossed sea. Pausing, a mere speck, Starr rose in his stirrups and waved back with the old sombrero.

Turning back to the dugout for a last look at Lane, ere leaving to take the cattle home, Tex was riveted in the doorway by the tableau in the room. Quayle was furiously pacing up and down, cursing his bargain. The old Mexican, his eyes slits, his lips set in a grim smile, one brown hand twitching at his shirt front where his knife was hidden, was poised between Quayle and that pallet on the earthen floor.

"A fool! That's what I've been!" Quayle raved. "Seven kinds, an' then some! A thousand in the hand's worth a mint on a hat. He won't come back! Or suppose he does? Suppose . . . he's got two weeks to do it in . . . he hatches up some scheme to clear his brother? He'll let me whistle! No, by thunder, I ain't waitin'. I'm turnin' him in!"

In one stride the Texan was across the floor.

"Listen, you!" he told Quayle in a dangerously quiet drawl. "You're not turning him in. You made your bargain, and you'll stick to it."

"Yeah!" was the wolfish snarl. "Who'll make me?"

"I will," said the Texan coolly.

"And me," said old Florencio.

"I'll be back the minute I deliver the cattle," Tex warned grimly, "and you'd better be here."

As surely as ever he knew it afterward, he knew right then that he shouldn't go, but failure to take the cows in would bring Loop Loop men to see what was wrong. They couldn't risk that.

"I'll be back as quick as God will let me," he promised Florencio, who followed him out. "Don't let him out of your sight. Watch him every minute."

"Like a hawk."

CHAPTER
SIX

"Lane Hallet"

In the Sandflow, that devil's pasture of dust and heat and glare, where nothing comes to flower but a modicum of spine-festering, sun-blasted things, where the sinister coiling diamondback stands out against white sand, flecked by the circling black shadow of the buzzard's wing, life's frustration is expressed by the ceaseless churn of mighty dunes, crawling before the fiery wind, seeking futilely surcease from their purgatory. In the Sandflow rode Starr Hallet, in the wake of a ranging horse that wandered hither and yon, pausing to crop this clump of brush, that tuft of grass, as if time were nothing.

Hither and yon, time everything to him, Starr followed the horse. For he knew that his brother's life might depend on the course this horse was taking. Starr knew, too, that, while a horse would be relied on to return to its home range, the sorrel's home range might not be the place Lane had ridden it from, and he would be thus led farther from the people he had to find. With ever-mounting despair, he realized that he had only two weeks to solve the murder and possessed no clue any sane man would follow.

Yet, doggedly, he clung to the trail over crumbling alkali flats, where Pancho sank to the fetlocks, and white dust came rolling up to plaster his wet, golden skin like alabaster, down arroyos choked with mesquite and prickly pear that caught at his chaps like a million talons holding him back, the dense chaparral swallowing the sorrel for hours together, up endless ridges, red with iron stain, black with pinon, and across high mesas, yellowed with low, curling buffalo grass, where sight of a fence would fill him with terror, lest the horse he was trailing heed the call of pastured horses and tarry there.

It was heartbreaking to follow that trail, hard to hold back far enough so the horse wouldn't suspect it was being followed and be diverted from whatever destination it had in mind, more difficult still to mark its course when dark came on, and trust to luck to pick it up in the morning. Many times it seemed to Starr that the quest was hopeless, that the horse was as lost as he was. Often it would depart from its original course, leading him miles to north or south, that seemingly led back to the Sandflow. But always, just as he decided this was a wild-goose chase and was on the verge of calling it off, the horse would resume its journey west.

Five days he followed the sorrel. Five days of the precious fourteen that numbered all of time to Starr! Five wasted days, he feared. Nine more, and Quayle would collect — either from the state or Starr. He had no illusions about the man. Quayle would play straight, only so long as it benefited himself to do it. Once convinced otherwise, he'd play into the sheriff's hands. Time was the very essence of their contract, and time was passing. Anything that reminded Starr of its passage was torture. The sun's crimson set meant a day gone. The rosy sunrise was yet another day on its way. Birds' matutinal songs, slanting shadows, the gathering amethyst of dusk — all, torturingly, pressed in on him, and always the cold fear lay on his heart that Lane had passed beyond his help. But when, for hours together, the sorrel forged steadily toward the higher ranges west, his heart would lift, and he was sure the solution lay in the purple distance. But where — to whom — was this trail taking him?

In the saddle, or broiling a rabbit or quail over his lonely campfire, or blanketed on the hard ground, stars blazing over him — he relived over and over the moment when he had stood under the wall, hearing that song. Constantly it rang in his mind. Would he recognize that voice in speech? Or would he meet the singer — perchance had already met him — and not know him? He could hear that song warning — who? Donovan? Lane? Hear that command from Donovan to halt! Who was he halting? Starr tried to separate fancy from fact. How many people were on the other side of that wall? Four — sure. Donovan, Lane, a woman, and the singer. But that queer cry, preceding the woman's scream? Had she uttered it, too? He didn't know. It hadn't sounded like a woman, nor yet like a man. It didn't sound — he thought with a shudder — like anything human. And the woman's cry — what had been in it? Surprise? Anger? The passion to murder? He

177

couldn't tell. But he knew what had been in that shot. Death, for Donovan! Death, almost certain, for Lane.

Then followed the hour when, the confusion over, he had gone back to search the scene. He had found Lane's gun — the .44 he always carried — thrown in the brush. Donovan had been slain with a .38. Undoubtedly it was the gun with which Lane had held the crowd at bay. Whose hand had he taken it from? For he must have taken it from someone, and discarded his own to make it appear that he had done the killing. Lane couldn't have done the killing! Wild he was, wild as the wild blood in him, but — not a killer.

By lonely campfires Starr would take off the old hat and read the record again, see what the Hallets had done, but find nothing like that! No record of a Hallet shooting a man like a coyote! He saw his I.O.U. due in a few days' time and that must be paid whatever the outcome, and wondered where the money was coming from. At no time in his life, till this last year, would it have been any trick to raise $2,000. But the collapse of the Zuñi Creek branch of the Valle chain had not only taken what money he had, but also the ranch that he and Lane had inherited from their father and had been running together. Yet he hadn't meant to deceive Quayle. It had seemed easy when he made the deal. He had a few horses he could sell, a few hundred dollars saved since the failure, and there was the $1,000 reward for finding the real murderer. Now — now he was sure of nothing, but that Lane was innocent, and he must find the guilty man. After that he'd find a way to cancel that brand.

Always he wondered who Lane was shielding — and why? Some enemy who held a club over him? Or perhaps a friend? Lane was loyal. He'd die for a pal. That singer? The girl . . . ? Here fancy became fact. He was sure — but had no proof of it — that the girl was Rose of Lost Cañada. Lane loved her. *Keep her out!* the boy's cry came back in all its fury of fear. *Keep her out . . . do you hear?* If Lane would die for a pal, what wouldn't he do for the woman he loved? Was Lane shielding her? Why was she hiding securely in that mysterious nowhere, letting him go to his death for Donovan's murder?

"Where's Lost Cañada?" he'd asked a thousand people this summer. Not one could tell him.

"On Mars," was the oft, joking assertion.

They were as vague about the girl. What was she like? Dark, fair, big, or little?

"Gee," one romantic waddy had countered help-lessly, "how can you describe the perfume of a flower . . . the shine of a star . . . electricity?"

Older, more prosaic men as utterly failed to describe her. But Starr knew what she was like. Beautiful — he had to concede that — but hard, cruel, unfeeling, like that Lorelei who sat on a rock, combing her hair, luring men to their doom. Because he was sure that Lane had gotten into this terrible trouble through her, and she hadn't opened her lips to save him, Starr's soul burned with a fierce hatred for Rose of Lost Cañada.

"If she's in this," he told Pancho, his tired eyes, under the battered old hat, black with brooding, "I'll show her no more mercy than she's showing Lane."

Mid-afternoon of the sixth day Starr rode out on a high promontory overlooking a grassy valley, thickly dotted with ranches and grazing cattle. Far off, at the valley's end, nestling in the shadow of a mighty, cloud-capped mountain range was a town. What valley, what town, Starr had no idea, but he knew those mountains, visible almost at the Sandflow, must be the Confusions, wildest of New Mexico's wild ranges, and he had the strangest conviction that he was nearing some definite milestone, if not — the thought struck sharply as pain — the end of the trail.

What would he find here? It was impossible for Lane to have hidden in a town all those months when the state had been ransacked for him. Wherever he had ridden from to steal back the old hat, it must have been some remote hide-out. Starr had hoped and prayed that it was Lost Cañada, and that the sorrel would take him there, where he might find the girl, and, through her, the singer who he had heard that night.

Sitting there in the saddle, watching the horse trot out in the valley below him, he still hoped and prayed. He tried to believe that the new interest and life the sorrel evinced was due merely to the presence of other horses ranging the valley and its eagerness for company. That in itself constituted a problem, for the horse would mix in with them, and loiter to graze at the cost of time increasingly precious, or it might be sighted by riders, who, seeing a saddled horse running loose, would catch it up to hold for the owner. This last fear was realized almost as soon as Starr rode out on the valley floor.

180

Trailing along, half a mile behind the sorrel, screened by the chaparral bordering a wide wash, he saw the horse suddenly start and swerve, saw, at the same instant, the cause — a cowboy, emerging from the brush in its path, and who, after one quick look, took after it, full-tilt, with swinging rope. With no ready explanation as to how he came to be in possession of *two* saddled horses, Starr pulled Pancho into the brush and, leaving him there, ran toward the scene of the chase, in terror lest the horse be lost, or turned definitely from its course.

Quickly overhauling the sorrel, the cowboy's rope snaked out, jerking it to a stop. Seeing a stranger hurrying up on foot, he turned and led the sorrel back to Starr, grinning happily, as one who has done another a favor.

"Figured he broke loose from somebody," he said, tossing Starr the reins, "so I picked him up. Might be hard to catch, if he got in with some of the wild stock in this valley."

"Thanks," said Starr shortly — almost curtly — in his fear.

Sensing Starr's displeasure, the waddy's grin faded. With a curious glance at the old sombrero and an abrupt — "So long." — he wheeled and was gone.

"Acted like I was tryin' to steal his hoss," he was telling his bunkmate a few moments later. "Acted . . . plumb hostile!"

"What for lookin' *hombre*, Pink?"

"Regular enough. Good hoss! Good outfit! But topped with a funny ol' Mex hat, plastered with brands."

"Brands!" His bunkmate gave a violent start. "Say, what color hoss was that you caught?"

"Blood sorrel, with a white forefoot. But what . . . ?"

"Why, you poor, plain, pitiful, blind idiot!" The bunkie was dancing on one foot. "I'll bet he didn't thank you a bit! I'll bet he acted plumb hostile. That's Lane Hallet! The *hombre* what killed the Lasco sheriff!"

"Gosh!" gasped Pink, and lunged for his horse. "The sheriff better know about this!"

CHAPTER
SEVEN

"The Wrong
Combination"

Unaware of the trouble piling up for him, Starr, riding
Pancho again, led the sorrel on until certain that he was
beyond the danger zone, then turned it loose, gave it a
scare, and galloped after, frantic lest any minute it be
picked up again. New hope surged through him when,
after half a dozen false starts in as many directions, the
horse suddenly swerved into a trail that would take it
above the town, straight through the valley, to the
colored heights beyond.

But a twisting mile on, just north of the settlement,
calamity struck again. Startled by a mighty rumble of
hoofs, Starr saw, cutting squarely across his trail, right
toward the sorrel that had stopped at the first
reverberations of this rumble, a large band of galloping
horses, hazed by half a dozen cowboys. Before his mind
fully grasped the danger, the plunging herd enveloped
the horse Starr had followed so far, sweeping it along in
their thunderous stampede toward the town.

Stunned by this catastrophe, not knowing what to
do, or where to turn — mercifully not knowing that

even then an armed posse was galloping out to capture
Pat Donovan's murderer — Starr watched the horses
disappear. His dark face set in resolution. The trail
couldn't end like this! Lane's one hope lay in that
horse. He'd follow the herd to town, claim the sorrel,
bring it back here, and free it again, nor did he
anticipate any particular danger in this. Unless, of
course, the real owner lived here, or someone who
knew the horse — knew who the real owner was — and
that was exactly what he was trying to find out himself.

Straightaway he spurred Pancho toward the town,
turning into the main highway so shortly where the
posse had just galloped over that the dust of their
passing had not settled yet. Starr had eyes only for the
dust funneling up from between the buildings beyond,
marking the route the galloping herd had gone.

The sun had dropped back of the towering hills. A
golden glow lay like a mighty searchlight on the town.
Swinging into the main street — narrow, crooked, for
the town had been built to no cut-and-dried plan, but
followed old trails that ran without rhyme or reason,
beginning or end — he rattled over a bridge, around a
bend, and saw, directly before him, a plaza, jammed
from curb to curb. Banners were flying; a band was
playing. Some sort of *fiesta* was going on.

"What's all the excitement, friend?" he reined over to
an old settler propped against a hitching rail.

Queerly the old-timer looked at him. "Thar usually is
excitement in Chuckaluck, stranger," he said dryly,
"when the roundup's on."

Starr asked: "Them rodeo horses just went past?"

"Sure war!"

"Where's the corrals?"

"At the track . . . straight out . . . a quarter mile." His old eyes dilated as they took in the sombrero, then they fell on Pancho and a baffled light clouded them. A red horse and a branded hat meant something, meant what that hastily organized posse had gone out to get. But a branded hat and a yellow horse didn't click. Something was wrong with the combination. While his mind still fumbled with it, Starr rode on.

Every eye turned to the hat, and, as Starr rode through the throng, a murmur rose and followed him. Men pointed him out, arguing that it must be Lane Hallet — nobody else would wear that hat. Still, they'd heard nothing about a buckskin, and, with the red horse firmly implanted in their minds, they made no move to stop Starr. Oblivious to all the commotion, Starr worked his way through the crowded square and rode steadily down the lane of flying banners and staring humanity, through the town, and out to the rodeo ground.

The day's activities here were over; the crowd was gone. As he came up, he saw men driving the horse herd into a pen near the bucking chute. Slowly approaching and wondering how best to explain his business to them, how he was to get the sorrel back, he was jerked to a standstill by the startled yell of a man climbing the corral for a better look.

"There's Lane Hallet's horse!" yelled the man — **Track Manager** said the badge on his checkered shirt. "No doubt about it. Pink Dawson ramped in an hour back. Said he'd met Hallet on the range! Said he caught the sorrel for him! Said Hallet . . ."

"If Pink caught him," a wrangler yelled back, "how did we come to rake him in?"

"Dunno . . . unless Hallet sensed the reception committee, an' took to the brush. Anyhow, I'm holdin' this here horse for the sheriff. Yank his saddle off, an' turn him in here with the rest."

Dazed, Starr could only stare blankly at horses and men. Nobody, miraculously, was looking at him. Suddenly instinct — for he was too upset for conscious thought — caused him to draw back around a vacant ticket box, where, slowly but surely, his numbed brain began to function.

That cowboy he met had thought he was Lane. A posse had gone out for him. How had he ever got through town without arrest? It must have been his very boldness, his disregard of everything but the horse. But for his following the sorrel into that by-trail, he'd be in jail right now, trying to prove his identity. It would take time — days, maybe — to do that. He dare not lose the time it would take. He didn't want to prove it. He wanted to draw the search as far as possible from that dugout. He gloried in the thought that the whole town of Chuckaluck would swear Lane Hallet was here, and that Sheriff Garret would hear it. But he despaired at the thought that the whole town of Chuckaluck would be after him, when it got its breath back.

It was up to him to get out of here quickly. But — his jaw set in lines of immutable purpose — he had to have that horse. There was only one way to get it. He must hide until dark, then slip into that corral and steal it!

So he decided, reckless as the most reckless Hallet, but reckless in decision only. Keenly alive to his danger, realizing that any moment word might reach here that Lane Hallet had ridden through the town, headed for the rodeo ground, Starr swung Pancho from the precarious shelter of the ticket box to the high grandstand. While the men still hung over the fence, excitedly discussing the sorrel, he eased away, careful to keep the grandstand between the corrals and him until a dip in the ground hid him from view.

Casting desperately about, then, for some place to hide, he saw that this slope ran down to the creek that wound through Chuckaluck and was widely belted with willow and mesquite. Camps of rodeo visitors were scattered along the near bank, but in the fading light no one would be apt to notice the old sombrero, or pay any attention to one rider among so many coming and going there.

Quickly he urged Pancho down the slope, and, riding wide of the tents, he splashed through the creek, where, clambering out on the bank opposite and breaking into a dense tangle of mesquite, he meant to wait the hour till dark. It was the hardest thing he'd ever done — kill time so terribly vital to Lane. Ages, he sat, eyes wary, his hard, lean body taut. With Pancho beside him, equally still and alert, he was ready for instant flight, should the cowboys organize to hunt him out, or the sheriff's posse come back and trail him here in the short time ere night fell.

One by one, over the river, campers drifted back to supper, their fires bright in the gathering gloom, the fragrance of cooking wafting to him. Plainly, over the ripple of water, their voices sounded as they came and went, shouting greetings from tent to tent, while down from the track echoed the shouts of men caring for stock, or practicing for tomorrow's events. Faintly, from Chuckaluck, came the sound of an orchestra tuning up. It was like Lasco, that night when he rode in to find Lane. That had been just another such celebration, Lane, just such a carefree, young cowpuncher, as most of these here, just a kid out for a good time. Yet since that night — hunted for murder — now, at death's door, his very life a pawn to Quayle.

Taut behind that darkening screen of leaf and water, Starr waited ages more. Was night ever so long coming before? He must have been crazy to take this course — pin all Lane's chances on a horse. There was no use going on. Quayle had turned Lane in. No! There was Florencio who had been his father's friend and, because of that friendship, would die for his son.

He tried to think of something, anything else, to stop these fears. That last nester he'd stopped with, pulling up stakes to leave his place — wiped out, he said, by the Valle bank crash. He recalled the home folks ruined by it; old Joe Willis, who'd shot himself, when his life's savings were swept away; Jim Hoyt's widow, cooking in a road camp to support herself and the children; Grandma Denton carted off to an institution. 'Oh, he'd rather be charged with murder than have what Jord Valle had to answer for. He'd never seen Valle himself.

Starr always had dealt with the Zuñi Creek branch, while Valle devoted his time to the main bank in Lasco. Nobody had seen him since last spring, when he got out one jump ahead of the grand jury indictment.

I'd sure like to meet him! His eyes burned under the old hat again. *And there's hundreds more with the same ambition!*

The river ran black with a silver sheen. Campfires had died down. Campers were leaving to join the revelers uptown. All noise at the track had faded away. There was only the rustle of leaves, the water's murmur, the occasional *clip-clop* of a distant rider.

"Reckon we took ourselves too serious," he told the listening horse. "Chuckaluck's sure not wasting its breath on us." As Pancho stamped an impatient hoof, he said: "Steady, boy. It won't be long now."

CHAPTER
EIGHT

"Rose of Lost Cañada"

Black as a pocket lay the Chuckaluck Rodeo track. Horses stamped in the corrals; a wild Brahma steer bellowed angrily. Behind the grandstand, the night's velvety black was pierced by the moving gleam of a yellow horse. Soft hoof beats neared and stopped; a faint thud followed as a dark form swung from its back.

"Quiet, boy, till I fetch the sorrel," the rider whispered softly.

Confident that the animal would not betray him by so much as a nicker, Starr took his rope from his saddle horn, and slipped stealthily around the grandstand. Pausing in its blacker shadow to look and listen, he saw, across the track, the dim outlines of the corral where they had penned the sorrel. Was it still there? Or — had the sheriff removed it to some unknown stable or corral? It *had* to be there! His luck couldn't be as bad as that. Crazed by the doubt, he started toward the corral to end it, but something held him back, a feeling all wasn't right, that danger lurked under this quiet. Cautious, he waited longer, but saw nothing amiss.

Naturally, I'd be nervous, he told himself. *First time I ever stole a horse.* Convinced it was this and nothing else, he crossed the track to the sorrel's pen and crouched under the gate to listen again. He heard nothing he couldn't account for, yet every instinct was shrieking *danger*. But with impatience driving him on, despite this warning, he swung the gate open, and slipped in.

Startled by his presence, the horses snorted and crowded against the far side of the corral. Starr waited for them to separate and circle back, as horses will. His heart pounded when he singled out the sorrel. Saddle and bridle had been stripped from it, but he had no trouble picking it out. A man couldn't watch a horse as he had that one and not be familiar with it.

Cutting it off from the rest as they circled past, he drove it into a corner of the fence. The lunging and snorting of the horses drowned other sounds that might have warned him even yet, and the task of getting a rope on the sorrel's neck kept him from noticing the shadowy figures appearing all around. Even as he led the sorrel to the gate, he saw nothing wrong. But as the gate swung, a man loomed before him with leveled gun. From the blackness behind, a chill voice crackled: "The game's up, Hallet!"

For Chuckaluck had found the combination and had wasted no breath hunting Lane Hallet. They figured he'd come back for the sorrel, and had laid here to trap him. But no game is up till the last card's played. Staking everything on that last card, Starr Hallet leaped to the sorrel's bare back and bolted. A man grabbed for the horse's head, but went down under its lunge of terror. Another was struck from its path. Straight on, a

191

solid line-up of men were yelling for Starr to stop, or they'd fire! He caught the glint of guns in their hands, but, throwing himself on the sorrel's neck, as small a target as possible, he spurred into that line, scattering them like leaves in a gale. A gun roared behind him. A bullet sang near! It only served to give wings to the terrified sorrel that, clearing the track almost in a bound, plunged through the gate and around the back of the grandstand to where Pancho waited.

Helpless to check its flight, with only a rope on its neck to control it, Starr threw himself to the ground, and pulled back on the rope. He slid along, his boot heels plowing up the earth, and dragged the choking horse to a stop. Quickly throwing a half-hitch about its nose, he led it back on a run, the few yards to where Pancho was hidden.

He was on the buckskin's back when the men who had cornered him — all mounted now — stormed from the gate, spreading out behind him to cut off retreat riverward. Giving Pancho his head and hanging like grim death to the sorrel's lead rope, Starr tore off in the only way open — straight up the road to Chuckaluck, hoping to give the pack the slip in the dark. But he hadn't one chance in a thousand of doing that!

Every citizen, every visitor in Chuckaluck, was out to win fame and fortune by taking Lane Hallet, and, as Starr raced up the street, men seemed to spring from the very ground ahead of him, yelling as madly as those pounding up behind, brandishing guns they were afraid to use in the dark, for the crowd was so thick a bullet from any quarter might hit an innocent bystander. A few blocks ahead was the brightly lighted plaza. It cleared magically before the turmoil; there a gun could be used with the certainty that the bullet would be stopped by the target it was meant for.

But one block from it, Starr swerved into a side street, galloping headlong into another group. Dodging into an alley, he eluded them. He raced along at breakneck speed, only to be brought up short by a wall, too high to jump, and with no visible way around. Whirling back, still dragging the frenzied sorrel, he plunged into the back yard of some citizen, overturning garbage cans, smashing down shrubbery, in his wild race to the street in front. Again he was turned back, for men were crowding into the block from both ends. Dashing back the way he had come, he found the exit blocked by a howling mob. Hoarse cries came.

"We got him!"

"That's one trap he can't spring!"

"Go get him, then!"

But it took more courage than they were yet able to muster, to invade a dark alley for a cold-blooded killer like Donovan's murderer. While they worked up their courage, Starr leaped the low fence of another yard. He jerked at the sorrel to make it follow, hoping by a desperate rush to break through. Then a voice froze him in his saddle, a voice that would have stopped him had all the men in Christendom been on his trail. The song that had rung in his heart since that night in April, the voice he'd listened for — prayed to hear — the rich, deep timbre of the voice, strange undertone to the barking of dogs and shouts of men, filled the alley.

**If I should die, and o'er oceans foam
Softly a white dove on a fair eve should come . . .**

Strangely it seemed to hold a message for him. His heart was crying that the trail ended here. The sorrel had brought him to the voice he'd heard over the wall. It never occurred to Starr that he could now free the sorrel and thus lessen his danger. His one thought was to find that singer.

But though his very heart seemed to stop as he listened, he couldn't tell just where the song was coming from. Somewhere near the alley's open end. Leaping back over the wall, he plunged toward it, lifting Pancho to a gallop in his fear that the song cease before he got there. He would have raced straight into that deadly fire — for now they had him singled out and would shoot to kill — had not a man suddenly sprung from the dark, grabbing his bridle, swinging on it, dragging Pancho down, wildly crying:

"Stop! For God's sake, Lane! It's me . . . Santone!"

But Starr scarcely heard him. The song was nearing an end. Madly he fought to shake off the restraining hand. Jerking Pancho back and forth, spurring him . . .

"Stop!" implored the man, featureless in the gloom, dark, somber, as the night and the situation. "They'll shoot you down like a dog!"

But Starr *couldn't* stop — the song was beginning again.

**The day I left my home for the rolling sea, I said
Mother dear, oh, pray to thy God for me . . .**

194

Abruptly it ceased then. A groan burst from Starr.

"The boss sent me here," explained Santone swiftly. "He's spotted the boys all through the mob to help you."

"The boss?" Starr echoed dully. "The boys? Who do you mean?"

Quickly the fellow stepped up, searching Starr's face in the dark. "Say, what the . . . ? *You* ain't Lane Hallet!"

"I didn't say I was!" cried Starr. "They think I'm Lane. And they've got to go on thinkin' it, till . . ."

"But that hat? The sorrel?"

"I'm Lane's brother."

The tumult was deafening. All Chuckaluck seemed concentrated around this block. Courage grew with numbers, had grown almost to the verge of rushing in here and dragging the fugitive to justice. There was a note in that roar that made Santone quake.

He said, and his tone was no longer that of a friend: "This is a pretty kettle of fish! I don't savvy it, but I've got to get you out of this jam. Come on!"

Still Starr held back. "There's a man out there I've got to see . . . that man who was singing! Do you know him?"

"I don't know nothin'!" was the freezing retort. "Only I'm gettin' out of here while the gettin's good." He moved toward the end of the alley. "Are you comin' or not?"

Starr whirled after him. This man had thought he was Lane, had taken grave risks to help him, had known the old sombrero and the sorrel. He couldn't let

195

this link between Lane and those blank months get away. He followed down the alley, to that high wall, where, groping along it, Santone suddenly stopped, fumbling in the tangle of vines covering it. Starr heard a rusty grating, as a gate was forced open. Almost immediately Santone was back, taking the sorrel, ordering Starr in a guarded whisper to follow.

"You seem to know your way around," Starr said, mighty glad that he did.

"I usually do!" There was something sinister in that. Santone seemed to realize it, for he added: "Played under this ol' wall when I was a kid."

He volunteered no other information, as they stumbled through the hidden gate, emerging in a vacant lot. There was no one in sight. But as they moved slowly along the wall, a wing of the mob swept around the corner and sighted them, for a shout went up. There was nothing to do but run for it.

Bounding to the sorrel's back, Santone led the flight across the lot, and into an alley, darker than the one he'd rescued Starr from, but not blind. For almost at once they were out of it, and into another, with those hoofs pounding after. On, around turn after turn, through yards, culverts, over rail-road tracks, doubling back and cutting corners, till Starr lost all sense of direction, all sense of everything, but that those hoofs were gaining. He must not be caught, locked up, while the days ran out, and the man he sought — one of the only two people on earth who could help his brother — left Chuckaluck! A sense of terror filled him, lest one of those bullets streaking the air hit its mark, and Lane's one chance die with him.

Wild with that fear, he was racing in the wake of the sorrel, along a high hedge, extending the full length of a twisting block, in what he guessed was the old Mexican quarter, when — so suddenly that Starr all but missed him — Santone drove the sorrel through an opening. Swinging Pancho after Santone, Starr plunged into a court, faintly illumined from an open door in the house beyond. He had a flashing glimpse of a low bench set against a wall of blossoming oleander.

As Santone leaped from the panting sorrel, a figure rose from the bench, and ran to meet them, crying, with relief unutterable: "Lane! Thank God, you're safe! I've been almost crazy, hearing them and . . ."

"It's not Lane! It's his brother," said Santone quickly silencing the other, then stepped away.

Starr was looking at her — the perfume of a flower, the shine of a star, electricity!

CHAPTER
NINE

"On Trial"

So he met her — unexpectedly, in that shadowy court, the mob thundering by, howling like wolves robbed of their prey. So he met her — and realized why men so miserably failed to describe her. How portray a girl whose charm lay in no particular grace of form or feature, but in some vital, electric quality that drew all? So that such lovely details, as a skin velvety white as the petals behind her, wide-spaced blue eyes that sparkled and flashed with inner fire, a slow, sweet, haunting wistful smile were noted by slow degrees, or missed altogether, in the stirring, colorful ensemble that was Rose of Lost Cañada!

The mere sight of her, poised against the tremulous green of that living wall — a bright rodeo scarf bound Gypsy style about the dark cloud of her hair, in flame silk blouse, fringed skirt, little riding boots, and all — quickened Starr's heart like mescal. But just for one beat. Instantly, over the picture she made there, was superimposed the one he had carried of her — beautiful, but hard, cruel. He told himself *this* was the real likeness. As her beauty hid all trace of the steel nerve and fiber she must possess to ride the worst outlaw horses that the West could produce, so it hid the heartlessness that could permit Lane blamelessly to suffer the consequences of murder, when a word from her could save him. She had hidden to keep from giving that word. He had kept track of all the rodeos since last April, and she had not appeared on a single bill.

Now, seeing her here, the very image of truth, hearing her thank God that Lane was safe, because she thought he was Lane, all the resentment concentrated in the summer of searching flamed up in Starr.

Swinging from the buckskin, he took a short, quick step, and bent over her. "You're Rose of Lost Cañada?" He knew that. He just wanted to hear her say it.

"Yes," she said anxiously. "But you . . . ? Is Lane with you? Is he in Chuckaluck?"

"No," his voice was harsh. "The festivities are all in my honor. Because I was riding Lane's horse, and wearing this hat."

She tried to lift her eyes to the old sombrero, but could not get them above the face in its shadow — so tired, worn, sorrowful — set in a look that fascinated her, a look she had never met in a man before. There was an animosity she could not fathom, a desperation that took no heed of her as a woman. Bravely she met it, insisting, and unconsciously fanning that flame.

"I don't understand. Where is Lane?"

"Dead . . . maybe!" It burst from Starr, in all his agony of fear and worry. "He was near it, when I left him six days ago . . . over in the Sandflow. Left him . . . shot up . . . charged with a murder he didn't commit.

That's why I'm here . . . to find the man who did do it."

It was as if he'd set off a bomb in the courtyard, stunning Santone and striking the girl in some vital spot, for she swayed, and her hand went out to the wall, clinging there for support.

"I bought two weeks of life for him," Starr went bitterly on. "*Two weeks* . . . if he can live to use them. Fourteen days. Six of them are gone. I've got eight days to find the guilty person, so I'm not standing on ceremony. In eight days, if I fail, Lane will be in custody. You know what that means."

She knew! She had been hearing that roar, was hearing it now, as the search turned back to that street. The note in it terrified her out of all thought of the news he'd brought. Steeling herself to hide her terror and meet the look so hostile to her, she asked: "What brought you here?"

"That sorrel." Starr pointed to it. "I turned him loose and followed him. He brought me to town. Then luck stepped in. I've been tryin' to find you."

Steadily she asked: "To find . . . me? Why?"

"Because," was his straight reply, "you were in Lasco the night Pat Donovan was shot. You were on the spot. And you've got to tell me what . . ."

Sinisterly Santone stepped between. "Hold on," he warned in deadly tone. "*She* ain't got to tell you nothin'."

But the girl caught his arm. "Please, Santone! I must talk to him."

The thunder of hoofs in the street shook the court, holding them speechless, taut, lest any instant the storm break through the opening. Voices howled in:

"Here's where we lost 'em! Last I seen they was streakin' . . ."

"There you go again! *They!* You was seein' double!"

"I tell you there was two! One on a buckskin, one on a sorrel!"

"Must 'a' been two other *hombres* then. There's only one of Lane Hallet."

Hoofs and voices rolled past.

"If you've got to talk," growled Santone, "go inside. I'll get the hosses under cover."

Starr followed the girl into the house with no premonition of what would befall him there. He had none of the apprehensive feeling that had warned him at the corral. He only felt, as he entered the small and dimly lighted room — bare, except for a faded Navajo rug on the cold stone floor, a littered table, and three handmade chairs of cane and leather — that it was not her home. There was in it no reflection of the personality stealing over him like a spell, so that he must continually remind himself that she was hard and cruel, and not, as she seemed, facing him over the narrow table, little and helpless. Well, many a fight was won by a false show of weakness. He must remember the helpless figure he'd left bleeding on the dirt floor of the old dugout and do what he had to do here.

And Lost Cañada Rose? What did she feel, facing Starr Hallet? Facing him, had he but known, in a desperation greater than his own, with more to

201

remember. She felt as if she were on trial and this tall, worn, dark-faced rider, standing before her, gray eyes implacable, was her accuser, as if the old hat, clutched in his grip — silver *conchas* sparkling, brands glaring, like eyes at her — was a witness, eagerly waiting to hear her perjure herself, then testify against her at the bar of justice.

It was her trial, and she opened it. "What have I got to tell you?" she asked quietly.

Starr wasted no second of the time so precious to him. "You've got to tell me," he said tensely, "who killed Donovan." Again he saw that living fear draining strength and color from her. Giving her no time to recover, he insisted: "You know! You were with Lane when it happened."

Her blue eyes rallied a fighting light that amazed him. "You've talked to Lane?"

"Yes."

"Then why come to me? Why didn't you ask him?"

"I did." Starr was as honest as if under oath. "I asked Lane. And he said . . ." He hesitated, uncertain whether or not to tell her this.

"He said . . . ?" she prompted, white as death.

"He said he did it."

Sharply she caught her breath. He prayed that she would deny it. He even leaned toward her, his face ablaze with eagerness to hear her speak the words that would clear his brother, but she didn't.

"You don't believe it?" she asked incredulously.

"Believe it?" flashed Starr with faith unshakable. "Believe Lane could kill a man like that? Not give him a chance to draw a gun? Believe *Lane* could do such a hellish thing?"

Her eyes fell from sheer weight of the horror in them.

"I know Lane" — all Starr's fanatical love for his brother was looking out of his gray eyes then. "He's shielding someone. It's not the first time. When he was just a little fellow at school, he was always taking the blame. He's got one creed . . . to be game. He'll die before he'll tell. But you know, and . . ."

"Why do you say that?" countered the girl. "How do you know I was there?"

He answered with absolute conviction: "I know! And I know others were there." That hit harder than anything yet. And he followed it up. "A man . . . singin' 'La Paloma'. Who was that?"

Her eyes, dark with nameless fear, flashed out to the shadowy court. Turning, Starr saw it was empty, silent. Even Santone had gone.

"Who was that man?" he demanded.

She stood, rigid in a terror that seemed crushing the very soul from her.

"No matter." He shrugged. "I'll find out. He's in Chuckaluck. And there was another . . ."

"No! No! That was all!"

The wild force of her cry checked Starr. After all, he wasn't sure that there had been another. Lest he was wrong, and she knew it, and insistence shake her belief in all that had gone before, he switched to a new tack.

"Whose gun did Lane take . . . hot from its murder work?" Her hands fluttered out in a mute appeal that tore his heart. But merciless, as he'd promised himself to be, he insisted: "Whose gun?"

"Speakin' o' guns," struck in a strange voice within a yard of his back, "here's one what'll do some killin' *pronto*, if you don't hark that talk."

Starr jerked about, his whole body tensing to the threat of an ancient gun, unerringly trained on him by the most singular personage he'd ever seen. One that compelled his wonder and awe, even in this instant of stark despair. A fierce-looking, little old man in shirt and trousers of deerskin, fringed at the seams and frayed everywhere, stood there. Gleaming hair, yellow-gray, brushed his shoulders. Gleaming eyes pierced from their deep recesses of jet-black brows. He might have stepped into that room straight out of a past generation, might have been one of the hell-roaring, old mountain men, familiar in the land in the wild days when the first Hallet was reversing the rule of that era by not keeping his sins under his hat, but branding them deeply on his sombrero.

Flanking this remarkable figure on either hand were two other men, as grim of visage, if not so spectacular, who, now, advanced on Starr. Deftly one — a cold-faced, wise-eyed stripling — removed Starr's gun and holster. The other — a loose-limbed, powerful fellow — producing a rope from somewhere, jerked his arms behind his back, and bound them there. Starr hadn't a doubt but it was the posse. Hiding his frenzy, he tried even yet to bluff them out.

"Arrest me," he said gamely, "and you'll be sorry for it! I've done nothin' against the law."

Coldly the fierce little man in fringed buckskin rejoined: "We ain't arrestin' you. Furthermore, we got no connection with the law, an' don't want any. We're friends o' this li'le white Rose" — indicating, with a vigorous sweep of his hair, the girl on the other side of the table — white now, in all truth, as one just convicted and sentenced to death! "Her friends" — a strange reverence softened his tone, even as his eyes flamed more fiercely on Starr — "aye, an' friends o' your brother."

Understanding burst on Starr without help by the sinister sight of Santone, entering then. Santone had brought these men — the boys he'd said were scattered all through the posse. While Starr had questioned the girl about the murder, Santone had brought them to make him prisoner.

"If you're friends of Lane," he voiced the natural thought, "why tie me up?"

"Knowed a steer once . . . ," drawled the old-timer with a seeming irrelevance, infuriating to Starr. Every eye turned to the speaker, while a deep hush fell. "Knowed a steer . . . over in the Panhandle. A ol' mossy-horn, what was a bad 'un to run. Clap o' thunder, an' he was gone. Takin' the whole herd with him. Too crazy scairt to know where he was takin' 'em, or care how many was kilt in consequence. Leadin' 'em over high bluffs, pilin' 'em in cañons, drownin' 'em in *rios*. Many hundreds o' cows dead, all because one fool steer lost his head!"

"Meaning," Starr was quick to get the point, "you're holdin' me so I won't get somebody else in trouble?"

Silence confirmed his interpretation.

"You can't do it!" he told them hotly. "No matter who I take over a bluff, or pile in a cañon, I'm goin' to find out who did that killin'!"

An ugly murmur broke out about him.

"There come a time when we had to do something, or be stampeded plumb outta the cattle game. Know what we done?" asked the old man, eyes gleaming over that gun.

Starr showed no interest.

"Why," said the terrible, little, old fellow, "we shot that steer."

CHAPTER
TEN

"A Fading Picture"

Indirect, veiled as the threat was, dispassionately spoken, it convinced Starr of the gravity of his position as nothing else could have done. For what he knew, or rather what they thought he knew about the murder, these men feared him. They wouldn't hesitate to make away with him if necessary to protect the girl, themselves, or whoever his knowledge might endanger. Who were they? Friends of the girl? Friends of his brother? Where had Lane known them? When? Last summer, or before? He knew very little of Lane's movements all the preceding fall and winter. When they lost the ranch, a year ago this September, Starr had gone to work for a neighboring stockman, and Lane had drifted around. After this girl, he'd heard folks say. In bad company. This company? Were they rodeo men? They didn't look like it. Ranchers? Townsmen? They didn't fall into any classification he could think of. Nor did they look criminal. But they *did* look desperate. Like men laboring under a terrific strain, and capable of shooting on slight provocation. Useless to resist them, had resistance been possible. But roped, as he was, at gun's point, one against four, it was foolhardy even to think of it.

Nevertheless, as he was hustled out into the court and realized that he was being taken away, losing all he had staked so much to win, he struggled, kicked, and fought, so that it took their combined strength to get him onto Pancho's back. Even then, with his feet tied down, he continued to threaten, until he heard the girl near him, giving an order to Santone. Then, even had they given him his freedom, he would have followed them, for Rose of Lost Cañada was going along.

They all mounted and closed around him. Someone picked up Pancho's reins, and he was led cautiously through that opening in the hedge, and back into the dark street — quiet now, for the search had gone on out of hearing. Reconnoitering at every turn, by a long and devious route they left town and headed straight for the high Confusions, bulking, dark, and mysterious, against the night.

'As they began a swift ascent of the slopes, the girl forged ahead. The moon had risen, its white light plainly etching her as she drooped wearily in the saddle, looking, somehow, up on her big black, very small and pitiful. But Starr didn't pity her. She had looked plenty pitiful back there — even as she was tricking him. A smart trick, that. Getting him into the house, and drawing him on, learning all he knew, and telling him nothing, while Santone brought these men.

He wondered what possible connection she could have with them. He wondered where they were taking him. In the hours and hours that he rode — racked by the movement of his horse, fetters galling ankles and wrists — through rocky defiles, black crags soaring overhead, he had plenty time to wonder. Across forested swells, through black pines, drawn up like regiments, they passed in somber silence. The night wind's murmur, an owl's dismal hoot, the far, quavering cry of a coyote, the jingle of riding gear were the only sounds. Of the few words that were spoken, none was addressed to Starr.

Before him on the steep trail, in single file, rode Rose and a youth they called Kid. Behind, pressing close on Pancho's heels, came the big fellow who had roped him — Steve, they had called him — and the fierce old codger he'd heard them aptly address as Parable. Santone was not here. For reasons that had necessitated a whispered conference at the start — having to do with the sorrel, Starr thought, for it had seemed to be the subject of the discussion, and had been left in the court — Santone had stayed behind in Chuckaluck.

So they rode the long night out. At sunup, high in the blue notch of a lofty summit, they halted for breakfast. Steve was breaking up dead limbs for a fire. Kid was taking provisions from a pack, while old Parable, braced against one of the scattering aspens, kept guard over the prisoner, who slumped on a weathered old log. He was gray with mental and physical torture, but, withal, acutely conscious of the girl, watching him from her horse a few paces off.

She had made no move to dismount, lacking the spirit to do it, but sat in her saddle, tired, pale, her whole bright figure dimmed by the sheepskin jacket Kid had made her wear against the night's chill. Her blue eyes fixed steadily on Starr, seemed to study him, measure her strength against him, and to despair of the estimate arrived at. Abruptly swinging the black, she rode up to Parable and, pointing to the ropes that bound Starr, asked: "Is that necessary?"

"Highly," the old fellow assured her.

Her red lips curved in a scornful smile. "With three guns here?"

The old-timer looked at her, at Starr, at the men about the crackling fire, then: "Knowed two fellers," he began. Tensely Starr listened to catch some hint of his fate. " 'Twas up in the Yellowstone an' they had a b'ar fer a pet. Built a strong cage fer it, an' treated it royal. But even after months has passed, the b'ar jist paces his cage an' gazes out wistful at the green grass an' flowers. Till one o' them fellers . . . a soft-hearted cuss . . . can't stand it no more, an' argues to give the b'ar some freedom. Keeps arguin' till his pardner gives in. So they freed the b'ar, an' watched him roll on the grass, an' otherwise have a time fer hisself. Allus farther an' farther off. Till finally he drops over a hill, an' they don't see him no more. Says the hard-hearted pardner . . . 'Didn't I tell you? We lost our b'ar!' But the other says . . . 'Never fear. He'll be back.' So they wait, whistle, an' yell. An' after a spell, sure enough, here comes their b'ar, lickety-split. But" — with ominous emphasis — "he ain't alone," declared Parable. "Thar's another b'ar right at his tail! A ferocious wild one, out fer his pelt. Fer as everyone knows, a wild b'ar has got

210

but one use for a tame 'un . . . that's to kill it! An' them b'ars come up so quick, the men don't have time to get in the cabin, up a tree, or a golblessed thing, but jump into the cage, an' slam the door. The latch was outside, an' they couldn't reach it. Consequence was, the b'ar they'd took pity on was at large to thrash it out an' enjoy his freedom, while they was locked in!"

Smiling a little at the roundabout way the old man had taken to point out the danger, Rose slipped to the ground and, going over to Starr, began loosening his bonds.

"I'll take the responsibility," she said quietly.

Parable made no move to stop her, but, as the ropes fell, he cast a terrible glance at Starr. "Know what them fellers done, when they got outta that pen?"

Starr thought he did, but he shook his head negatively.

"They was so mad," vowed the fierce little man, "they hunted up that pet b'ar and shot him!"

Having sent a nameless chill through Starr's heart, he stalked to a tree more strategically situated, and braced his back against it, tapping his gun significantly. Starr looked up at the girl, his eyes grateful, as one thanking an enemy for a humane act.

"The responsibility," he said frankly, rubbing his wrists and stretching his arms to take the ache out of them, "needn't rest heavy on you. I'm right where I want to be." With her — he meant, so as to finish what he had begun back there and now so nearly finished. No! He knew that she would die before she'd tell!

211

Dreading any renewal of the questioning, she turned from him and walked swiftly toward the fire. Then, suddenly, something stopped her, drew her back to Starr, some desire that was great enough to surmount her fear, and hold her there — uncertain, tremulous as the golden leaves of the aspens overhead — asking, with touching hesitancy: "Lane . . . Can you tell me about him? Will he . . . get well?"

"I don't know," Starr said slowly, unable to refuse that plea. "He's shot clean through the body. Not many men survive that . . . even with a doctor's care. Lane can't have a doctor. He can't have medicine. He's got to fight through on grit alone." His knuckles were white as he clenched the old hat in his hands. "I can't bear to think of his fightin' through that, only to be jerked up, and . . . ," he broke off shakily.

The girl was crying silently. He hadn't thought she cared. He had believed that, if she cared even a little, she would have gone to Lane's aid, even though it meant admitting some portion of guilt. But now she certainly acted as if she cared a lot. She was crying silently, in a way he couldn't bear. Relenting, in spite of his previous decision, he drew her down on the log beside him.

"I *ought* to be shot," he said tensely, "talking like that! I didn't mean to. This whole thing is driving me loco."

It was doing the same to her, but her sympathy was all for him. She lifted her wet face from her hands. "I know, Starr," she said gently.

Strangely her tears seemed to have washed away his conception of her. Rather they had dimmed it, for it was still there, but not so definite, and it was rapidly fading. He knew her concern for Lane was genuine, and, although it only deepened the mystery, it softened him. Hungry to talk about his brother, as well as make amends for the way he had gone with Sheriff Garret's men to the hut in the Sandflow, how he and Florencio had gotten Lane to the roof, while Quayle and the Texan talked to the posse, how Florencio had tolled the posse off, and of his bargain with Quayle. He concluded: "He was crazy to get the reward, but when I offered him double money if he'd hold Lane two weeks, he agreed." Holding out the old sombrero, he showed the latest brand. "My I.O.U. to pay Quayle two thousand dollars in seven days more," he explained.

One week was already gone, the other going. Time so torturingly pressed on him, that he had a mad impulse to seize the girl, make a break from this place, and somehow drag the truth from her. But he was restrained by sight of old Parable — his yellow-white hair gleaming in the sun — keeping a constant watch on them. Starr wanted to scream at the men muttering to each other over the fire, to quit dawdling there, and take him wherever it was they were taking him!

"In seven days more," bitterly he told the girl, "I've got to redeem Lane . . . like a watch I might have hocked." Then he explained the impossibility of his doing it, unless he found the real slayer — because of that bank failure!

She drew suddenly back. "You lost in that?"

"Everything but my shirt."

"Lane never told me."

Starr was sure of that. The kid had pride. He'd never tell his girl he was broke. He'd talk big to her, and go to any wild lengths to back that talk.

"I don't care about the money, but if anything happens to Lane, I won't forget I would have the two thousand dollars, but for Jord Valle crooking me out of it."

There was a light in her eyes that would stay with Starr till all the mysteries of life were over, but he hardly noticed it at the time. "Whatever happens, Jord Valle's to blame! We were getting along fine when the crash came. Lane had steadied down, was takin' an interest in ranch work. But the loss of everything seemed to do something to him . . . shake his faith in everyone and everything. He's not like other folks, never hits a balance."

"I know," Rose whispered again.

Of course, she knew! She probably knew Lane better than he did. A sweetheart usually knew a man better than his own family. But was she that? Just what was her regard for his brother? No doubt about Lane's!

"Now, he's helpless." Starr was putting her to the test. "If I don't show up with the money, Quayle will turn him over to a court that's already convicted him. That's why you must help. I know Lane didn't do that killing. I know your testimony will clear him." And, catching her arms in a painful grip: "You *will* help, won't you?"

214

Wildly she tore herself from him, crying heartbrokenly: "I can't! I can't! Oh, heaven help me!"

Breakfast, consisting merely of corn pone with weak coffee to wash it down, was brought to them. Had it been the nectar of the gods, Starr couldn't have tasted it. Why *couldn't* she help? Because she was afraid? Restrained by some fear greater than personal danger? He began to sense something back of all this, something bigger, blacker than murder, so black that the sacrifice of one man, perhaps of a dozen, meant nothing. His brain whirled with a thousand things he must ask her, but she gave him no chance to ask even one.

All through the meal, and afterward, while they rested, letting the horses graze, until the sun had passed its zenith, she avoided him. When the journey was resumed, she rode far in advance of all.

Bound again, guarded by the grim trio, Starr was taken deeper and deeper into the wild Confusions, through such a labyrinth of cañons and ridges that he doubted if he could ever find his way out again, even should some miracle free him. Until late in the afternoon they ascended a rocky gorge — up, up, till it seemed that their sweating horses must ram their heads against the very sky. At last he raised his tired eyes to a great, blue granite wall at the gorge's end that marked the end of the ascent and made out a rift in the wall, concealed by overlapping portals so closely spaced that one might ride within a hundred yards and never see it.

Passing through this gap, and down a short, twisting corridor of rock, they came unexpectedly out on a bench, overlooking a wild and eerie cañon that sent a thrill through all Starr's being. He felt no faintest surprise to hear, beside him, as they all pulled up — except Parable, who had ridden on for a better look — the girl's half sigh, half whisper: "Lost Cañada."

CHAPTER
ELEVEN

"No Dance"

Lost indeed, that cañon! Lost from creation's dawn. Lost in these high Confusions, as if it had been — as men, believing it to be a myth, jokingly said it was — on Mars itself! Lost and wild! The blue walls, soaring to fantastic heights, had fractured themselves in a thousand places, beaten their heads into a thousand pinnacles, rather than be stroked smooth by the tranquilizing hand of time. A wild stream roared through the cañon from end to end. Black piñons sprang from crevices all over the walls and clung there in defiance of all laws of gravity and nature, twisted out of semblance to their species elsewhere. Even the colors here were unlike other colors; they were more vivid, garish even, seemingly laid on with a lavish and furious brush. The sun shone fiercely on Lost Cañada. The wind, which had a hard time getting in and must swoop straight down, or writhe in through that corridor, howled and wailed like a lost soul.

Lost, but it had been found! Cabins under the northern rim showed that it had finally come to the knowledge and use of man. And it seemed to resent this, to resist with every atom of that wild spirit such

217

occupation. The very ground buckled under the cabins, as if spurning them. The stream frothed in their faces. Piñons shook distorted arms in wrath above. The frowning walls ever threatened to hurl down upon them the mass of boulders gathering since Genesis.

Yet in the girl's face, as Starr glanced at her, was relief, joy, as one who has reached sanctuary. "Lost Cañada," she said again.

His dark gaze turned toward those cabins. "And trail's end, I reckon."

A shade dimmed her brightness then. She said honestly: "It's been that for some, but others have found it a refuge in time of trouble."

"It's sure trail's end for Lane," he told her, "if I'm held here long." Adding as bitter afterthought: "Which must be why you brought me here."

Her eyes flashed up defensively. "I didn't bring you, Starr! I didn't want you here. Oh, if they could only see how much worse this is for everybody." Her hand came up in a gesture of absolute despair. "I wish to heaven you were a thousand miles from Lost Cañada."

With that she whirled the black and, spurring down the trail, passed Parable at a gallop. Starr stared after her, thunderstruck. If she didn't want him here, who did? A hundred fresh conjectures rose in his mind. But Kid's horse jolted Pancho into motion, and they began zigzagging down the trail, toward the cabins under the frowning rims.

The cabins, six, all identical, were built wall to wall, along the churning creek. Horses stamped among the cottonwoods before them. Four men came running from the cabins, men of the same cold cut as those with him, and as roughly dressed. Starr thought the Creator must have cast them from the cañon's dust, and breathed into their nostrils the wild spirit of this wild place. Every eye, it seemed to Starr, was frozen on the old sombrero. Not in the curiosity that hat always drew, but in some fierce gleam of pride or pleasure, such as might be occasioned by the return of a triumphant friend. The men seemed about to find expression in a wild cheer, but when their eyes fell on the wearer, lashed in the saddle, and they saw the stern faces of Kid, Steve, and Parable, they fell back in consternation. Silently they stood watching, as he was led to the farthest cabin, where Kid removed the ropes lashing his ankles, and ordered him down.

Starr didn't obey at once. His eyes were following the girl who represented Lane's one chance and must not be lost sight of. She hadn't stopped here, but was galloping up the hill toward a cabin at the cañon's end. A cabin larger than the rest, overlooking the whole place, and windowed like a lighthouse.

"Come back to earth!" Kid commanded, and his cold voice held a menace not there before.

Parable enforced the order with a sharp prod of his old revolver.

There was nothing to do but play their game and watch for a chance to play his own. Once his opportunity came, the rope wasn't made, the bullet molded, that could stop him.

Quietly he entered the cabin. Kid freed his arms and, at a nod from Parable, went out and closed the door.

219

The old-timer turned to Starr, who sank wearily into a chair at the table.

"*She* says," grimly he instructed his prisoner, "to give you the freedom of your pen. An' her word's law . . . as far as we can follow. But once outside this door, or too nigh it . . . say here!" — marking a deadline three planks in — "an' it's open season."

Parable dragged a bench to the door, and settled himself on it, as if he meant to stay forever. Starr looked about his pen — a single room, walled with logs of the tough, wild piñon that had bristled knots like armaments. Rough, whip-sawed slabs of piñon formed the floor and heavy door; windows were mere holes cut high at front and back, affording light and ventilation. They had no glass. Squares slashed from an old slicker served as a protection in inclement weather. There was no way out save by the door, and with a guard there — no escape.

The fiery sun blazed a red trail across the floor and shone on the youthful prisoner. He seemed not so hopeless as when he had entered the cabin. His face had lost much of the bitter intensity mirrored there since he had made his bargain with Quayle. Something about this cabin made it seem, not a prison, but a home. Although intangible, there was at once a consolation and goad to action here. Everything within this room, the very air, even the dust upon the floor, seemed to hold something inexpressibly familiar and dear. Everything seemed trying to tell him something. Those blankets on the bunk, wadded into a ball and kicked to the foot of it. The pillow doubled into a hard knot at its head. That soiled shirt on the floor. The tin cup on its side by the bucket, as if it had been thrown at the nail above, and missed its mark.

Why can't you learn to pick things up? a voice — his own voice — echoed in his ears. *When you go through a room, it's as if a cyclone had struck!*

A voice — Lane's voice — answering: *Aw, gee, who wants to waste their life tidying a house?*

Tears rose, blinding him. Rising, he fell to pacing the cabin. Up and down, up and down, hardly knowing what he was doing, but — exactly as he had forever been picking up after Lane at home — he hung the tin cup on the nail, picked the shirt up from the floor, pounded the pillow into shape. He was reaching for the blankets to straighten them, when realization flashed over him, and he swung around with an abruptness that brought Parable's gun within a breath of explosion.

Reckless of the gun, of the deadline, he went up to his jailer. "Lane's been here!" he cried. "He's been in this cabin!"

Parable just stared at him.

"Was he here all summer?" pleaded Starr. "Was this where he went from . . . to get the sombrero?"

Still the old man said nothing.

"Listen," Starr said desperately, "there's a lot here I can't savvy. Maybe it's none of my business, but Lane's my brother. It's my business to know about him."

Old Parable, his fierceness diminished some by this pleading, began: "Knowed a man . . ."

Wildly Starr cut in: "Don't tell it like that! I can't stand it! It's not fables I want, but facts. You know

221

somebody who did something, and you finally shot him. Now . . . go on from there."

Nothing could have insulted Parable more. He was proud of his allegorical style. So few men profit by experience, but he hoarded his like gems of the purest ray. He never made a serious move before he delved into the treasure house of his mind and dug up a glittering specimen — some way that he, or another man, had met a similar situation. He believed in telling what he knew, believed that it was his sacred duty to do it. Moreover, he had dipped into Scripture and found — as many a man has done — justification for his foible. Didn't it say there for a man to open his mouth in parable and utter "dark sayings"? Why, there'd even been a law in Israel, for men to arise and declare what they'd heard and known, that their children might not be "as their fathers had been, a stubborn and rebellious generation!" To have the very thing for which he was named and famed flouted like that offended him to the soul.

"Go on," pleaded Starr.

"I ain't inflictin' my talk on them as can't stand it," said Parable.

Appalled by what he'd done, Starr apologized earnestly. "Heaven knows I didn't mean it like that. I like your talk. It's just that I'm so crazy to know I can't wait. But tell it any way you like. You knew a man . . ."

But Parable sulked over his gun, and there was no getting a word out of him. Starr gave up trying. After all, he knew, as surely as if Parable had told him, that Lane had been here. He was on the right trail. The days weren't wasted, after all! It was from this wild hide-out that Lane had left to steal back the old hat. That's why these men had stared at it. They thought that he was Lane coming back. All summer, while the state was hunting his brother, while *he* was hunting him, Lane had been here in Lost Cañada, with these men, in daily association with the girl. She hadn't hidden from Lane, but *with* him. He wondered just who Rose was — and what? Her every look, act, intonation showed that whatever her life had been on the tracks, she'd had advantages far above it. These men here knew it, and treated her with profound respect, obeying her in everything that was compatible with their own mysterious affairs, as they had in giving him, plainly against their inclination, the freedom of his cabin. Yet he knew she was a rodeo rider, not that that was anything against her, rather all to her credit. But always the bare fact remained that she was there when Donovan was killed, and would tell him nothing.

He walked to the window, and looked up at the house on the hill. The girl's horse was gone. Not a living thing was visible. Every blind on the cabin was drawn. He had a wild desire to see behind them, an intuition that if he could get into that house he'd find the solution.

"Does Rose live here?" he asked Parable, narrowly watching him. "Is that her home? Has she got folks?"

"No matter, you won't be callin'," said the old man, and proved himself no prophet there.

Without taking his eyes from Starr, Parable opened the door in answer to a knock. It was Kid.

"My shift," he said.

Parable left, but Kid didn't come in. Through the tiny window in front, Starr saw him sitting just outside the door, gun in hand, and seemingly eager. Starr felt that of all the men he'd seen who might stand guard over him, this cold-faced, sharp-eyed stripling was the most dangerous — the most anxious for him to overstep that deadline, so he could proclaim open season.

Then, back on his bunk, thinking over all he'd learned up here, he forgot Kid, and all of them. The wind wailed about the cabin; gloom had crept in when Kid rapped on the door with the butt of his gun.

"Chuck's ready. Come along!"

Starr was escorted three cabins down and into a scene more bizarre than anything he had yet encountered in the cañon. A double row of men — all the men he'd seen here — sat around a rough board table, dressed up in a way wonderful to contemplate — dressed by no standards Starr had ever seen. Stiff, white dickey in a cowhide vest! Palm Beach coat over warped blue jeans! Even one full-dress suit — almost the first that Starr had seen. He couldn't see under the table, but knew by the smell of polish in the air that every boot was shined to mirror-like perfection. Steve sat, purple and miserable in a boiled shirt with a high, stiff collar. Next to Steve, barely recognizable, was old Parable, minus his buckskin, his yellow hair brushing the shoulders of a moldy, bottle-green, long-tailed coat that might have come out of the ark.

224

What in the world is going on here? Starr asked himself. *Is it customary to dress for dinner in Lost Cañada?*

Trying his best not to stare, Starr took the chair indicated to him near the head of the table, and was helped to the scanty fare — beans, bread, and dried venison. There was no butter for the bread, no trimmings of any kind. The food was in marked contrast to the festive dress. A deep gloom pervaded all. Silently, ravenously they ate, wasting no time. When finished, they got up and assembled near the door, rolling cigarettes and keeping a nervous eye on the clock. On the very second the hands pointed to eight, old Parable gravely opened the door, and they filed solemnly out.

Dumfoundedly, from the doorway, Starr watched them climb toward the big house on the hill. The blinds were up now, and lights blazed in every window.

"A dance?" he asked Kid, on guard beside him.

Kid's eyes fastened on him, blazing such wrath that Starr thought he was going to kill out of season, but he checked himself, savagely gritted: "No dance. Come on, get goin' back to your cabin!"

CHAPTER
TWELVE

"A Musical Interlude"

Long into the night, lying wakeful on his bunk, Starr wondered what that dress parade meant. What was going on up there? He felt it must fit into the puzzle somewhere, and he tried in every way to make it fit. Baffled, he drifted at last into troubled sleep. Every thought of it had vanished when he awoke in the wild dawn, conscious that another day had slipped from that calendar, and he was still a prisoner.

Two weeks! Quayle's words returned to him. *If you ain't here then, I'll turn him in!*

Six days left in which to pay Quayle. If he found the killer now, and were free to go, it would take some time to get back to the Sandflow. He had been six days just getting to Chuckaluck, but he had traveled slowly, with frequent long waits for the sorrel, rambling a mile out of the way for every mile forward. Riding hard, in a straight line, it wouldn't take long. But he wasn't free to go, and he had accomplished nothing. He had found the girl — yes — but she had refused to help. He was powerless to make her, powerless, now, to find the singer.

226

At breakfast, he found the men dressed in their usual attire, but stern, glum, obviously laboring under some tension that heightened his own.

Then he was back again in his cabin with nothing to do, hour after hour, but walk from one high window to another, and look out at the cañon ablaze with color and sun, watch Pancho — gold against the garishly green, grassy bank of the frothing stream, aloof from the other horses, lonesomely grazing — or pace his prison, to the wind's wild wail, thinking, in strain insupportable, of that lonely dugout, drifted over with sand. Strangely, he couldn't picture Lane there. Indelible as that last sight of his brother was, when he'd knelt over him, promising to come back and mark his brand off the old hat, begging the senseless boy to be there then, Starr couldn't see Lane as still in the dugout.

Hour on hour, he watched that house on the hill, feeling ever more strongly that the solution was there. But how to find it — with that guard at his door? Constantly he watched for the girl, not the least of this mystery to him. He now knew her habitation, but not her name. Rose — was all. And even that might not be true. *Rose* . . . , Starr thought, summoning up the picture she'd made in that flowery court in Chuckaluck. He hoped against hope that she'd come to see him, but the day dragged on, and she didn't come.

Night brought suppertime. Again the men were dressed in bizarre fashion; again, in solemn file, they mounted the hill. But what had struck Starr as ludicrous the night before seemed now — in the face of their deadly seriousness and dogged adherence to some purpose — somehow, pitiful! Again he went to bed, wondering what was happening up there. Again he woke to find another day gone. This couldn't go on. He must do something. But what?

All forenoon, locked up and conscious of a growing tension that the whole cañon seemed to share, he tried to plan some way out. A grim undertone to all his thoughts, that song, with its message of warning that he could not fathom, kept returning. Continually his mind flashed back to that moment of turmoil, when trapped in the alley, he had heard the song. A dozen times he re-fought his battle, on Pancho's back in the death-charged dark, to get to the singer. A dozen times he recalled Santone's grabbing his bridle, and heard him say: *The boss sent me!*

Who was the boss? — Parable? Or was he acting in the absence of the real leader? Boss — of what? He shouldn't have listened to Santone! He should have taken his chances on the mob — found his man — choked the truth out of him. But who was the man? Did he belong in Lost Cañada? Starr thought he did. He had been with the girl in Lasco, and he was in Chuckaluck when she was there. Was *he* the boss? If so, there was still a chance that he'd come, still a hope of getting the truth from him. But how find out? These men would never tell him.

Suddenly, in his desperation, a plan flashed to Starr, wild, fantastic, as his following the sorrel! It was a way to find out if the singer lived here, and if the song meant anything in particular to these men. He hadn't the voice that fellow had, but he could sing the tune. Yes, he would sing "La Paloma", and see what happened!

Acting instantly on his plan, he walked to the window and looked out. Kid was still on guard. One of the men was just riding away down the trail. Steve was on his way to the creek for a bucket of water. There was no one else in Starr's range of vision. Softly, humming a few bars to get the swing, Starr drew a long breath, then, in startling imitation of the tone and warning inflection that had so long haunted him, he began to sing:

If I should die, and o'er oceans foam . . .

The effect was electrical. So much happened all at once, Starr couldn't keep track of it. Kid sprang up, glanced wildly around, trying to locate the source of the sound. The man on horseback came back at a dead gallop. Steve dropped the bucket, and came on the run. Yelling men poured from the cabins. More loudly Starr sang:

Softly a white dove on a fair eve should come . . .

Frantically Kid pounded on the wall. "Shut up! Shut up in there!" Bursting in through the door, he madly flourished his gun at Starr. "Shut up, or I'll shut you up!"

In surprise that he didn't have to feign, Starr asked: "What's wrong?"

"That song!" Kid shrieked. "You can't sing it!"

"I don't claim to be any singer," Starr said with a grin, "but I didn't know I was as bad as that."

"I mean . . . ," Kid sputtered. Then a sharp voice behind bade him hold his tongue.

Old Parable pushed through the door, followed by the rest of Lost Cañada, wild-eyed, wildly excited.

What could it mean? Starr had hoped for some reaction, but nothing like this. It looked as though it might well be his swan song. They were pressing up with such savage ferocity, he feared for an instant they'd tear him limb from limb. That song meant something definite, something more than he had even dreamed.

Fiercely Parable demanded: "What you singin' *that* song fer?"

"Why not?" countered Starr. "I like it. It's an old favorite. Why not sing it as well as another?"

For a moment Parable was stumped for an answer. "But why sing at all?" he demanded. "I can't see where you got occasion to do any warblin'."

"I've got to do something!" hotly Starr told him. "I can't just sit here and twiddle my thumbs. I'd go loco!"

His answer satisfied the men, for their relief was apparent in the long, relieved breaths they drew.

Totally unimpressed, his fierce gaze unwavering, old Parable rejoined: "Thar's worse fates. Knowed a feller" — ominously he told Starr — "prospector up in the Salmon River country what didn't have enough to occupy him. He put in his surplus time apin' the dumb brutes around him. Got so he could outbray his burro,

230

quack a wild duck right down to his gun. Plenty wolves in them hills, so he gits to mimickin' them. Now wolves is too cute to be fooled by a human. But this *hombre* . . . a stubborn cuss . . . vows he won't leave off till he can call one right up to him. So he keeps on practicin'. He prospected by day, an' howled by night, but he don't get no place with them lobos.

"Howsomever" — grimly old Parable paused here, and none listened more intently than Starr — "his voice kept developin' volume, till it finally carries plumb outta the hills, an' into a valley where a sheepman is holdin' his band. Says the sheepman . . . 'That's a whoppin' big lobo, an' he'll be dinin' off mutton, less'n I do something about it.' So he shoulders his gun, an' goes on a wolf hunt. But he don't find no wolves, or airy tracks big enough to fit the howl he's heard. He's comin' in one night, about ready to give up, when he hears that howl right ahead o' him. Sneakin' up in the gloom, he sees a shadder movin' an', sure enough, the howl's emanatin' from it!" He paused. "Know what he done?"

"What?"

"Why" — transfixing Starr with a terrible look — "he ups with his gun an' blows hell outta that fool mimic!"

There was no telling how Parable intended to act in this familiar situation, for just then a commotion at the door jerked him around. The men were crowding back to make room for someone. Starr saw — as he had so hoped to see — Rose of Lost Cañada!

Rose stood there, breathless from her long run down the hill, blue eyes sweeping the room with eager expectancy. Her look changed quickly to blank bewilderment, and she whirled on Parable.

"It's nothin', Rose," the old man said. "Jist a musical outburst on the part o' our star boarder, but it give us a turn. He sure was murderin' that tune."

Ignoring his facetious attempts to dismiss the incident, ignoring him and all of them, she looked at Starr. Her eyes reflected fear, and that fear was for him.

"Come out," she said. "I want to talk to you."

Disapproval charged the air.

Kid stepped forward, his eyes glittering jealously. "He's a prisoner!"

"You can watch him outside, as well as here," she said quietly. "You can all watch him."

It was so true, that Parable, trying to select from numerous, brilliant instances proving irrefutably the danger of fraternizing with the enemy, desisted, and told Starr to go on.

CHAPTER
THIRTEEN

"Open Season"

Down by the frothing creek, in the checkered shade of the coloring cottonwoods — in full sight of the men nervously watching from the cabins, but just out of earshot of Kid, frenziedly watching, his hand on his gun, and fairly aching for an excuse to use it — the girl looked up at Starr, fear in her eyes still.

"It's dangerous to sing 'La Paloma' here," she said.

"So I notice." Soberly he smiled down at her.

"You did it deliberately!" she flashed accusingly. "It wasn't an accident."

"No," he admitted honestly. "I wanted to see if it meant anything to them, and it sure does."

A flash of the old terror leaped into her face. "Oh, it means so much . . ." Quickly she checked herself at his eager start. "Don't ask me, Starr! I can't tell you. But don't do it again. Promise you'll do nothing to arouse these men."

His heart quickened at her concern, but he couldn't promise. "I don't know what I'll do next, Rose. Only" — his jaw set — "I've got to do *something!* It's just five days till my I.O.U. is due to Quayle. If I don't meet it, he'll gladly give Lane up."

The desperation in his voice, in his dark face, and the very way his fingers clasped the old hat, terrified the girl. Thrilled her, too. She said softly: "You think a lot of your brother, don't you?"

"Yes," he said.

It was a simple statement, but there was in it, and in the look accompanying it, an utter devotion that, coupled with desperation, might lead to any mad thing. She alone could prevent it. She had only to tell him the next thing to happen here. *Should* she? Uncertainly she looked up at those men. They had thought it best to say nothing yet. Her eyes came back to Starr, and there was in them a resolution that filled him with a strange excitement. She said unexpectedly: "I'm trying to be your friend. You believe that, Starr?"

He said strainedly: "I hope so. I . . . think you are. But there are things . . ."

"You can't judge by appearances!" she broke in wildly. "Appearances were against Lane, but you believed in him! Appearances can be against other people! Jord Valle, for instance!" Her earnestness aroused a strange pang in his breast. "Do you think he can be possibly guilty of all he's charged with?" Giving him no time to answer, she asked: "Do I look like a girl who'd let a friend die, and not do everything in my power to help him?"

She looked like an angel out of heaven, in that white dress, her blue eyes looking so straight at him. "It's in your power to tell what happened that night," he said determinedly.

"It's not, Starr! There are some things a person *can't* do, things against human nature. I can't do what you ask. And I can't get them to free you. But I've done the next best thing!" Swiftly she leaned toward him. Dangerously Kid's finger twitched on the trigger up there. "Starr," she whispered eagerly, "Quayle won't give Lane up next week . . . or ever."

Blankly he asked: "What do you mean?"

"I've sent for Lane."

A lightning bolt from the blue sky overhead couldn't have stunned Starr more. "You . . . sent . . . ?"

"Santone, and the man who sang." Her eyes were starry in anticipation of the joy this would bring. "I sent them for Lane . . . before we ever left Chuckaluck."

Still he stared, unable to comprehend.

"You know now that Lane stayed here, Starr, that he left us to get the sombrero. We'd had no word from him after, till we went down to Chuckaluck. Then we heard he'd got the hat and shaken off pursuit, that he'd been seen here and there . . . each place nearer. We thought that he was working his way back to Lost Cañada. Then we heard he'd ridden through town, and that a trap was being laid for him. The men went to his help, but it was *you* they brought. You said Lane was in the Sandflow, so they went there."

His mind flashed to the Sandflow, to that wild welter of dunes he had traveled through. "They'll never find him!" he cried, and he told her about the dugout with only a door in sight.

"Santone will find him. He knows the Sandflow. He'd know where to find Lane . . . without even the shadow of that door."

Like he knew that gate in the alley wall, thought Starr.

"Lane will be here," Rose said happily, "as soon as he's able to travel. We'll get him well. He'll be safe in Lost Cañada."

Starr's face lost none of its desperation. "I've got to pay Quayle just the same."

"But if Lane's safe?"

"That makes no difference. I gave my word of honor to pay Quayle two thousand dollars in two weeks' time, and I've simply got to do it."

"But he'll be out of Quayle's power," protested the girl.

Starr silently raised the old sombrero.

"Oh, I know about that," the girl said. "Lane told me, when I was begging him not to go. He told me what that hat meant to a Hallet. All summer he'd worried about it. Afraid that he'd never get it back. He told me how your grandfather, dying, confessed to his sons that those brands were the record of old rustling, and begged them to sell his big Flying Dollar Ranch, and pay back what he'd stolen, so he could die clean, and how your uncle refused to use his half of the estate to repay them, how your father sacrificed everything to clear his father's honor. Oh, that was wonderful, Starr! But this is different. Can't you see that?"

"It's on the hat," he said doggedly, but he wasn't looking at Q2000 on the high crown — the only uncanceled brand — but with reverence at the Broken Bell, beside it, crossed by that black and wavering line. He pointed to it. "Did Lane tell you how that brand was marked out?"

"No," she said wonderingly.

"Few know outside the family. It's something that we don't tell everyone, but I'll tell you, Rose, and then you'll know why I've got to cancel Lane's brand."

She waited, white with prescience of what was to come. The wind moaned lowly, the mad stream seemed to pause in its rush, the blue walls above them to lean and listen, eager to hear a thing so sad that this Hallet could but touch on it.

"I'll leave Dad out," Starr told her, "except this . . . he was young, and he loved a girl . . . Connie Marsh, of the Broken Bell. He loved her so much . . . Well, Dad told me that he died twice, once when he learned what those brands on the hat meant and saw the Broken Bell there, and next, when our mother died. When he really *was* dying . . . it wasn't long after Mother went . . . he said . . . 'This isn't death, Starr, it's goin' to *her!*' That's how he loved her, but that brand had stood between. He could have paid it, and let the rest go. Nobody would ever have known. But for fear that he would do this, he left the Broken Bell to the last. When he had squared the others, his money was gone. It would be years, if ever, before he could possibly mark out that brand.

"In riding around . . . hunting up the other outfits branded on the hat . . . he lost all track of his brother, who had gone through his share of the Flying Dollar. Uncle Lane . . . in whatever gamblin' hell he was at the time . . . learned of a plot to blackmail Zain Marsh, father of his brother's sweetheart. He was asked to help. It woke him up. He followed that blackmailing snake to the lonely cabin where he was to meet his victim, determined to kill him before he brought old Zain to disgrace and ruin.

"He was young, Rose . . . no older than my brother Lane. Life must have been dear to him. He knew it was sure death to face that expert gunman, yet he did it. He was fatally shot, but his bullet, too, found its mark. In the one moment of life left to him, he heated his spur in a mesquite fire, and burned this line through the Broken Bell, believing, rightly, that any debt owed Zain Marsh by a Hallet was paid in full. By his death, he honored the last brand on the old sombrero, and cleared the way for Father to marry the girl who was . . . our mother. And that" — lifting his burning eyes to hers — "is what a debt on this hat means to a Hallet. Means to everyone who knows of it. Even to Quayle. For he accepted it as a guarantee, and it saved Lane that night." His eyes dropped back on the hat, burned black with the history of two generations of Hallets, with the third in the writing, and only God knowing what black thing might be recorded yet, ere the history was complete.

"My father sacrificed everything . . . love even . . . to square accounts. My uncle died for it. My brother risked his life to reclaim it. And" — his mouth set tightly — "I can't go back on it."

Rose of Lost Cañada, cowering there, praying for strength to meet this moment, however she failed thereafter, heard him say: "I've got to pay Quayle. And I can't do that unless I find Pat Donovan's murderer. If you can't testify for Lane, tell me who the killer is. Then I'll *know* that you are my friend, despite all appearances."

Stars shone above the cañon. The men had dressed and gone up the hill on their mysterious mission, and Starr Hallet paced his pen, more baffled, more desperate than before the meeting with Rose. She claimed to be his friend, tried to help him by bringing Lane here. But she could not realize that would neither alter his obligation to Quayle nor clear Lane of the terrible charge over him. When he had told her how she *could* help by naming the guilty man, she had turned from him, and gone up the hill, as if she were on her way to execution. He knew now she'd never tell. Could not! For some reason against human nature. The solution lay in that house up there, and he must get out — find that solution.

Again, as he had often done in his two days' imprisonment here, Starr drew that square of slicker over the window, lest the guard, Steve since supper, take a look in. Then he went painstakingly over the cabin, searching for some way of escape. The windows were too small to crawl through. The heavy roof was weighted with two feet of earth. The plank floor lay flatly on the ground. The log walls seemed to him strong as the very cañon's rims. Yet always his thought turned to them. Few structures fail to have at least one flaw somewhere; there must be one here.

Careful to make no sound, Starr worked free one of the poles of seasoned piñon that braced his bunk and, using it as a lever, began prying at the logs of the walls, testing the snugness with which each was notched in at the corners, standing on a chair to test the shorter timbers, graduated down to form the gable ends. Prying against the log directly above the joists — one hewed to fit the slope of the roof and form, as well, the upper sash of the window there — he felt it give. Ripping away the chink between it and the log below, he took a firmer purchase with his lever, prying with all his might. Slowly the log moved out. The sound of falling dirt and bark was drowned by the howling wind. Mad with exultation, he pried on that stout pole, moving the log, inch by inch, enlarging the window. He paused, to shore up the log above with chinks torn from the cracks. Then, exerting all his strength, he forced it another inch — another. There was space, now, to wriggle through.

Ready to go, he got down and crossed to the front window, to make sure that Steve was there. Seeing the dim outlines of that powerful figure keeping faithful vigil outside his door, he blew out the candle to make it appear that he was going to turn in. Stepping up on the chair again, he carefully pulled himself through the opening, and dropped lightly to the ground. He was over the deadline! Out where it was open season! But

Starr didn't think of that. He didn't think of anything that might come after. His one thought was to get to that house on the hill and find the solution he knew was there.

CHAPTER
FOURTEEN

"Light"

Every blind was up, every window open. Lights blazed from them. Yet no form moved within. No sound reached Starr of the company that he knew was assembled there. As he stealthily approached the side window, he caught a hum of voices — pitched low and with a funereal quality that slowed his step, sent a nameless chill through him. There, screened by the heavy shrubbery brushing the sill, he had to steel himself to look in, and see what was going on.

In the brightly lighted interior stood a long table piled high with papers, about which, painfully intent on some momentous business, were all the men he'd seen leave the cabins every night on the stroke of eight. At the head of the table, presiding over them, was a dead man, or so was Starr's first awful impression. For nowhere but in death had he seen such ghastly pallor, such absolute rigidity of limb and feature, such wide, staring, soulless vision. Yet even as the frightful thought froze in his mind, life leaped into those vacant eyes, a quivering soul looked out of them, and the man — merely the wasted shell of a once handsome and imposing figure — raised high a skeleton hand.

"Gentlemen" — his tone, lifeless but of an anguished wildness imaginable only in the tortured damned in the hereafter, struck some awful chord in Starr — "we can't survive another run. I'm depending on you, my directors, to meet this crisis. We *must* not fail. They entrusted their money to our care. 'Where is it?' they ask. 'Bad loans? Depreciated collateral? Bonds not worth their paper? What are they to us? We want our money! Robber! Thief!' " His voice, rising with every syllable, climaxed in a shriek in which no words were intelligible.

That wild and inarticulate shriek transported Starr back to that night in April. Again he stood in Lasco, hearing a voice — Donovan's — halting someone. That answering cry, that didn't sound like a woman, didn't sound like a man — didn't sound *human!* It was echoing here, ripping the black mystery wide open, letting light in.

But, recalling Starr to the scene in there, a voice said: "Sir!"

Old Parable got up in the bottle-green coat that might have come out of the ark. "Sir" — all his fierceness lost in a quavering formality more than pitiful — "knowed a feller once . . ."

"Facts," whispered a neighbor, plucking his sleeve. "Facts an' figures . . . that's what goes around this place."

Parable wasn't offended a bit. He even thanked the fellow for it. "Sir," he made a fresh start, "it ain't your . . . *our* fault. It's general conditions. The drought. The cattle market. We ain't the only ones caught! We held out longer'n some ...."

"Sleep," moaned the man, looking wildly around. "Where has sleep gone? Always" — shudder on shudder convulsed him — "the hate in the eyes. The finger of scorn. Always they march through my brain ... the hungry children, the broken men. Always they march ... and I cannot rest."

"Sir ... Jord, ol' pal," Parable pleaded pathetically, "try to savvy. That's all past. We're goin' to pay 'em back. It won't be long. We raised it all but twenty thousand and ...."

Through his shock, consciousness struck Starr of somebody near! Defensively he whirled about. Rose was standing there in the starlight, staring at him, death in her look. He stared back. His breath caught. His very heart stopped, expecting her to cry out — warn them that he was here. But she was as still, as motionless, as if she'd been the image of marble she looked in her white dress with her whiter face and stony expression.

Swiftly going to her, he took her arm, drew her away from that window, and around the building to the dark steps in front, hoarsely telling her: "That's Jord Valle. The man to blame for all this trouble. The man the whole country has been lookin' for."

"My father," whispered the girl in deep despair.

Jord Valle's daughter! Horribly clear, the mystery of her. That's where she had gotten the advantages that set her apart. That's why she was in Lost Cañada — hiding out with her father. That's why she couldn't tell. Why it was against human nature. Because Jord Valle was ...

"He was in Lasco that night." Starr's voice shook with horror. "I heard him . . . over the wall. It was him . . . *your father killed Donovan.*"

"No!" she cried piteously. "*Not* my father. He . . . died when his banks closed their doors, though his body still lives . . . suffers. Not my father, but the poor, crazed wreck that this trouble has made of him. But who'll believe that? There's not twelve men in the country who'll *want* to believe it . . . knowing it was Jord Valle. They'll hold him responsible, when . . . he doesn't even know what he's done." The strength that had upheld her so long suddenly snapped, and she sank down on the steps and dropped her head in her arms, sobbing as if her heart would break.

Starr sank beside her, mute, sick, stunned by this black horror that all these months, even as he had fought for his brother, she had been fighting for her father. He couldn't bear to think of her — anyone enduring such torture. He couldn't bear to think how *he* had tortured her — in that room in Chuckaluck! On the trail up! This very afternoon! He couldn't bear her torture here. He longed to take that shaking form in his arms and let her weep out this agony there, but he did not dare. He almost wished that the veil had not been lifted. His heart bled for her, trying, between sobs, to tell him: "It was . . . the only time he left the cañon." To go to Lasco, she meant. "There was an indictment against him. We knew he'd be arrested if he was recognized. But he . . . begged to go. We thought we could keep him out of sight. But the crowds . . . the excitement . . . We couldn't do anything with him, and were taking him away, when . . . He had a gun. We didn't know he carried one. And when Sheriff Donovan . . . who had been his friend . . . recognized him, and tried to stop him, he . . . Oh," she cried, chokingly, "I can't tell you, Starr! It's altogether too . . . terrible! Oh, why did it happen?"

But she went right on telling him, as if he were a friend she could trust — not a deputy sworn to take Donovan's murderer, *compelled* to take him to save his own brother!

"My one thought was to get him away. There was another man with us . . . a friend . . ."

"The man who sang?"

"Yes." Bravely she fought to go on. " 'La Paloma' is a signal song to these men in the cañon. That's why it was dangerous for you to sing it, why it caused such a commotion. And that man . . . I haven't the right to name him, Starr . . . was singing to signal to Lane in the hall that we were leaving." A shudder swept her, remembering. "When Dad . . . fired, I grabbed the gun from his hand, and this man pulled him away. Then Lane was there, snatched the gun from me, and pushed me after my father. I . . . I didn't know what I was doing, Starr."

Of course she didn't! He hadn't known what to do — had done nothing — when he saw his brother standing over the dead body of Pat Donovan with a gun gripped in his hand.

"Somehow," she said more steadily, "we got him away, and back to the cañon. And Lane came, and he . . . Oh, there's nobody like him. He insisted we let things ride as they were. He was in no danger here in the Cañada. There'd be some way out, he always said. But he did worry a lot about you, Starr, and about the hat of his. I've never left Dad since that night, except to go to the Chuckaluck Rodeo. I had to ride, to earn money for the things we needed here. I learned to ride on Dad's ranches when I was little. Then I was sent away to school. When I came back . . . after the failure . . . I'd changed so, that nobody knew that Rose of Lost Cañada was Jord Valle's daughter, except these men, and Lane . . . the only outsider they ever trusted, and who they worship for what he did for my father."

"Who are these men?" Starr asked. "Parable, and the rest of them?"

She did not answer at once. When she did, it was hesitantly, with the first sign of reservation. "Friends of my father," she told him. "From boyhood days, many of them. Dad has friends in strange places, Starr. In his young years, he was an adventurer . . . a soldier of fortune. He should never have been a banker. He hasn't the conservative nature. He's a plunger at heart. Always ready to stake his last cent on some wild scheme. Several years ago" — Rose was choosing her words carefully now — "he acquired huge mineral concessions in a small South American republic, then under a revolutionary government. But almost before the deal was completed, the old regime came back into power, exiling the leaders who'd granted the concessions, automatically canceling them. All Dad's private fortune was lost. But," she said quickly, "not the bank's money. He never put a cent of the bank's money into that. Yet"

— with a hopeless shrug — "it all amounted to the same thing. When the crash came, he had no reserve to tide him over. Strange as it may seem to you, Starr," — but it wasn't long strange to Starr — "these men were responsible for his loss down there, and blame themselves for his present trouble. When the grand jury indicted Dad, they rallied back from everywhere, and brought him here, so he'd be safe until feeling could cool. They built this house here on the bluff, so he could see how safe it was, see there were no depositors to accuse and threaten. He doesn't know them. He believes that they're his old directors and calls them out every night for a meeting. Painful as I know it is for them, they humor him, play the part as well as they can."

Starr blessed the whole wild-eyed lot — no matter what they did to him.

"But that," the girl's eyes shone, "is the least of what they've done. They've pooled their resources, raised money in a thousand ways, scrimped, saved . . . You've seen how they live here, hungry, almost . . . so that every cent can be turned in to the Valle banks. They've turned in so much that . . . while it's not generally known yet . . . they've reduced the loss to twenty thousand. But for that tragic Lasco trip, everything would have worked out. Now that . . ."

A sudden scrape of chairs within, a shuffle of feet, announced that the men were leaving.

Listening to her, Starr had lost all track of passing time, had utterly forgotten he was on forbidden ground. Rose was first to remember his danger. "They

248

mustn't see you, Starr! If they thought you knew . . . they'd kill to protect him."

Even as the door was opening, she guided him around the house and through a back door into the kitchen, closing it, just as the men turned the corner on their way down the trail.

Waiting, expecting to slip out the instant the coast was clear, Starr heard a strangled cry, and whirled to see Jord Valle there. He was shocked, as if he'd seen a dead man rise and stand. He'd have sworn that the man couldn't move from his chair, but he was standing, braced by the doorjamb, his dead eyes fixed on Starr in nameless fear, crying to the girl: "What have you done? Why did you bring him here?"

She said quickly: "It's Starr Hallet, Dad. Lane's brother! You remember Lane?"

But he cried awfully, dumfounding Starr by his accuracy: "He's a depositor! I know them all. Every bank . . . I know them! Starr Hallet . . . Zuñi Creek branch . . . five thousand!" Then, suddenly, the wildness subsided, and he lifted a trembling hand to his head. "Sleep," he said. "I must sleep. These names and figures . . . march through my brain."

Rose led Starr out then. It was a case of the blind leading the blind, for tears obscured their sight. Side by side, in the glimmering starlight, they stood on the high bluff overlooking the cañon, stood long in thought. Heaven only knew what Rose thought, her glistening eyes on the Hallets' old hat. Starr was thinking of all that he had not dared to think on the steps back there.

He'd found Pat Donovan's murderer, could clear his brother, demand the reward for capturing the guilty man, and pay Quayle. He was free to go, bring help, and take him. He could get started before Rose could spread the alarm. A 100-yard start on Pancho was freedom.

His eyes went to the grazing horses down by the creek, to Pancho — his pale coat like a star in the night — to the cabins, lights flaring up in them where the men would be getting ready for bed, not dreaming their prisoner was out of his pen. He envisioned Steve at his post — guarding nothing. It was all so simple, to run down there, whistle Pancho to him, and spring on his back, so simple, and yet . . . Slowly his eyes returned to Rose. Rose, who loved her father as he loved Lane, who would suffer as he couldn't possibly suffer — having faith in Lane's innocence to sustain him. Rose, who — short as the time he'd known her — he now knew he loved, as he would never love another woman, but who could never be anything to him, if only because his brother loved her, too. Her father was morally blameless of that crime, but, as she had said, there would be no extenuating circumstances where Jord Valle was concerned. Lane had insisted on taking the blame, and she had let him, hoping there'd be some way out. But there couldn't be. If he were to save his brother, he must do what he had set out to do.

In a tone that neither asked nor expected mercy, she said: "What will you do? It's in your hands now, Starr."

He was spared the answer, for, even as he groped for one, a sound broke in, wiping all thought of the question from his mind. A sound sweetly drifting down from that corridor — a voice of a deep, rich, musical timbre, filling the cañon with soft singing:

**The day that I left my home for the rolling sea,
I said, 'Mother dear, oh, pray to thy God
for me.' . . .**

"They've come!" cried Rose, as excited as he. "Maybe they've brought Lane!"

Starr started on the run, but she caught him and held him back.

"You can't go down there! Wait, here!"

Instantly she was flying down the trail, and he waited, hearing doors slam, men running, tenfold the excitement he had created by his poor imitation.

It seemed ages before he saw Rose coming back, coming with a slow and reluctant step that seemed to stab into his heart. He leaped to meet her, crying thickly: "Lane's . . . dead?"

"No," she said. "No, but he's gone from the Sandflow. They've brought Quayle."

251

CHAPTER
FIFTEEN

"The Man Who Sang"

They brought Quayle, the hard-eyed, disagreeable border drifter to that rough main cabin in Lost Cañada, where, bound and helpless, he cowered in their midst, dumb with terror. Everything about this cañon made his skin crawl. Nothing was natural, but queer — out of shape — like another planet. The wind howling like death's own dirge. These fierce, freakish natives — the men were still dressed in their bizarre, mismatched best — solemn as savages convened for some bloodthirsty rite.

Strong as was his fear of them, it was nothing to the terror inspired by the man who stood beside him, the man who had made him prisoner. For Quayle, who had drifted over many, many a border — even that great border which sets the hemispheres apart — had seen this man down there, in settings that made his presence in this wild place a thing incredible, grotesque. Rillito! A world figure. Leader of revolutions. Whose name was written in the records of turbulent governments with a black mark after it. And who looked the part. A tall, dark, iron-gray man of military bearing with a strange, haunted face, deeply set in lines of sadness, and the

252

volcanic eyes of the visionary, the romanticist, a man to love, to follow to the death — as legions of men had done, as these would do to a man! The proof of it lay in the affection that shone on every face, as he spoke to them, in a voice that, whether raised in impassioned appeal, merely conversational, or, as now, in rapier scorn, was music in every variation of tone.

"This, my friends" — indicating the prisoner with a scornful gesture — "is Quayle. The man from whom Starr Hallet bought two weeks of life for his brother. At a thousand per. *Bartered* for it, the night the all but dying boy sought safety in the Sandflow. But almost before Starr Hallet was out of sight, Quayle repented of his bargain and would have dealt with the law." Sharply Rillito threw up a hand to quell the uproar that was breaking out. "Two other men were there when the deal was struck, a Mexican and the man they call the Texan. Men who wouldn't traffic in human life. They undertook to see that Quayle lived up to his bargain. Oh, we had it all from his own tongue. It worked fast and free, when, by the grace of heaven and Santone's knowledge of that country, we found him in an old dugout in the Sandflow, found him locked in . . . by someone who'd gone to considerable pains to keep him there. He didn't know we were Lane's friends and told the whole story, even offered to share the blood money, if we'd help him find the boy. He'd do anything to get any part of it . . . which accounts for the shape we found him in. But I'll let him tell you about that."

Every eye centered on Quayle, but the quaking wretch was dumb, as he had been ever since reaching the top of the world and dropping into this pit, where anything could happen and nobody hear of it.

"Speak up!" ordered Rillito sternly. "Tell them what you told me."

"There's nothin' to tell," Quayle whined. "We was all livin' there. The Texan went back an' forth to the Loop Loop. An' this day I . . . I started to town, an' met him on the way. He drawed a gun on me, an' took me back. The greaser had skipped out with the kid while I was gone. So the Texan locked me in, an' went to look for 'em. You come before he got back."

"We left a note for the Texan," Rillito explained to his men, "telling him not to worry about Quayle, as he'd be taken care of. We didn't look any further for Lane, knowing he's free to travel and will work his way back here. Santone stayed in Chuckaluck to help him up. But" — turning on Quayle again, volcanic eyes erupting — "you've missed the point of your story. Tell them *why* you started to town."

Quayle refused to tell.

"He was going to Lasco" — Rillito was inexorable — "for Sheriff Garret, to turn Lane over to the law and collect the reward."

Hoarse, fierce cries, such as Quayle had never heard before, rang out. Hoarse, fierce breaths panted for his blood. "What if I did?" he cried with the courage of desperation. "I'd been gypped all around. His brother left me holdin' the sack. The greaser an' that Texan was backin' *him* up! Of course, I had to look out for Number One."

"Knowed a feller . . ." began Parable, and every word struck vibrations of terror on Quayle's raw nerves, "a hunter over in the Sierras. Hunted lions fer the bounty on 'em. Done right well at it, too. Folks about was pleased to have him operate, fer he was killin' off the lions what et their stock. But pretty soon he gits most of the big cats killed off in that section, an' has to hunt hard to find a pelt. Mighty discouraged one day, when he runs across a whoppin' big lion track right down in the valley. Says he . . . 'Here's a windfall. I don't even have to hunt this critter.' An' he sets off on its trail. He don't go far till he sights a yaller form slippin' through the grass. An' . . . *bang!* . . . he brings it down. *But*" — Quayle jumped a foot at the force with which Parable underscored the word — " 'bout that time a crowd comes rushin' on the scene. An' it turns out this ain't no wild lion he's shot, but a pet, one what's broke loose from a circus travelin' through. A valuable animile. An' the owners is plenty hostile. Which don't faze our hunter. He swears a lion's a lion, an' he'll collect on this one. He starts skinnin' it, not listenin' to them folks what can't bear the thought o' their pet bein' mutilated on top o' shot!" He paused, impaling the quivering captive on his piercing glance. "Know what happened?" asked Parable.

Quayle was literally unable to answer by word or sign, for his dull wits, sharpened by terror, had grasped the moral: Lane Hallet was a pet with these men. Quayle had tried to collect the bounty on him. Whatever that hunter's fate had been . . .

255

"Why" — Parable made that terribly plain — "the *hombre* what thought most o' that lion . . . trained him from a kitten . . . jist out with a pistol an' let daylight through that bounty collector!"

This trembling bounty collector hadn't a doubt they meant to do the same to him.

A knock at the door halted any action then. Rose rushed in, breathless, searching the room expectantly, and almost beside herself when she failed to see what she was looking for!

Swiftly Rillito went to her: "What is it, girl?"

"Dad," she told him. "He's not at the house. I thought he was here."

"He could hardly have made it this far," said the man anxiously. "But he may have started, and . . . We'd better look for him."

Leaving Quayle in Kid's custody, they all rushed out, scattering to cover the slope between the cabins and the house on the hill. They found Jord Valle staggering around in the dark not far from his home, more confused than they had ever seen him, frantically reiterating: "I must find him! He'll start a run!"

"Who?" they asked, humoring him.

"A depositor . . . Starr Hallet! He was just here. I was short with him! I must find him, and . . ."

"How does he know Starr Hallet's here?" a voice cut in. "Hallet ain't been out of that cabin except to eat."

Chancing to encounter the girl's gaze fixed on him with a strange look, old Parable gave a start. "Mebbe not," he yelled, "but are we sure he's there *now?*"

256

Before anyone could answer him, the old man was storming down the hill toward that end cabin. When he got close enough to see Steve at his post, he cried: "All quiet in there?"

"Not a peep," said Steve.

That did nothing to reassure Parable. Feverishly unbarring the door, he peered into the cabin. It was too dark to see anything. Scratching a match, he approached the bunk in the corner and by its feeble flare saw that it was empty. He lighted the candle on the table with a shaking hand.

"Lookin' for someone?" asked a cool voice across the room, and Starr Hallet turned back from the front window.

"No! Y . . . yes!" Weakly old Parable collapsed on the bench at the table. "I . . . I jist dropped in to see was you all right."

"In my usual health." Starr grinned, but it was an effort.

He had pulled that end log back into place and replaced the chinks, and there was nothing to show that it had ever been out, but he couldn't hide the guilt in his look. Keenly Parable eyed him for the cause of it. Starr was up and dressed, although the cabin had been dark an hour ago, and dark when he came in just now. A man didn't normally stand around that long in a dark room.

"You're up late," he hinted suspiciously.

"I couldn't sleep . . . with all the racket," Starr said easily. "What's goin' on, anyway? Who was that singin'?

Don't blame you for objectin' to my warblin', after hearin' that *hombre*."

But Parable wasn't a man one could question. He talked only when the spirit moved him, and other times a clam wasn't more close. Satisfied now that all was well here, he stalked to the door, stopping only to tell Starr: "They jist brung in that feller, Quayle. An' much as I hate to quarter a skunk on a white man, I'll have to bunk him with you."

Far from objecting to this arrangement, Starr was so pleased he could hardly feign the surprise expected of him. He hadn't dreamed of such a break. He had come back to the cabin — that was no longer a prison — in the hope of hearing something of Lane before he put into effect the decision he had made an hour ago on the bluff up there, a decision to ally himself with the Cañada men, Rose, and his brother. To wait — let things rest as they were — until Lane could be brought here, and something worked out. But not his debt to Quayle. That must be met on the day it was due, that debt of honor branded on the old sombrero. Whether Quayle had lived up to the letter of his bargain or not, he didn't know. He only knew that Lane would have faced the penalty for that crime, if Quayle hadn't accepted his I.O.U. that night. Even Rose had seen his position, and was going to help him, and she had promised to have Pancho saddled and waiting at the creek, as soon as this excitement was over and the lights all out. Quayle's being here would complicate his getting away, but on the other hand it would simplify things to see Quayle before he left to raise the money.

258

He didn't know how he could raise it, but neither had he known which way to turn that dawn at the dugout. A way had been shown him there. With the same faith that he had followed the sorrel, so would he follow the only course open to him here. Impatiently waiting for Quayle, he reached into his pocket for the checkbook he carried on the Zuñi National and opened it: $300 to his credit. Not much toward $2,000, but . . . strangely his mind flashed to a story, old as history — the widow's oil. A creditor had taken her sons as bondsmen for a debt she owed. A small cruse of oil was the only thing she had in the world to sell. When she went to the Prophet, he told her to go borrow vessels from all the neighbors and pour what oil she had into them. And she did. Poured, and kept pouring, and the oil didn't give out! And she sold it. Got money to square her debt and free her sons. This $300 was his cruse of oil. He'd pour from it, and maybe enough would come to pay his debt to Quayle.

CHAPTER
SIXTEEN

"An Unsigned Check"

Pale and shaken as one reprieved at the eleventh hour, Quayle was dragged into that end cabin only to be struck dumb again at seeing Starr here, a prisoner like himself. He was terrified at the thought of being locked up with Lane Hallet's brother! His fears subsided as Starr's face expressed only eagerness. Parable removed his bonds, warned him of the deadline and open season, and placed the cold-faced Kid on guard for this important shift. Starr fairly leaped at him, the instant they were alone, voicing the questions that were driving him crazy.

"Where is Lane? *How* is he? Is he getting well?"

"Well enough to skip out!" Quayle shot back with a venom meant to forestall further questioning. "Don't ask *me* where. I don't know. First time I turned my back, he skipped out with Florencio, leavin' me holdin' the bag . . . like you did!"

Thanking heaven that Lane had been able to escape, Starr retorted: "Nobody's left you holdin' the bag." Taking the old sombrero from the table, he pointed to that I.O.U. "The time's not up! Four days tomorrow till it's due."

"Think I'm puttin' faith in that? Think I'm crazy enough to believe I'll get two thousand just because it's marked on a hat? If you do, you're a bigger fool than I was to make the deal. How could you pay . . . say you was minded to . . . locked up in here?"

"I'm not stayin'," Starr coolly told him.

"You've stayed so far!" Quayle whirled back from his desperate appraisal of that prison. "An' if you couldn't get away from these other men, you got a fat chance . . . now Rillito's here."

"Rillito?" Starr echoed blankly. "Who's Rillito?"

"Who's Napoléon Bonaparte? You must know who Rillito is! Everybody does! He's a . . . world figure! Always raisin' hell in them little countries below the equator. Rilin' the people! Leadin' uprisin's!"

"You don't need to tell me about him!" Starr had read a lot about that soldier of fortune, and liked what he'd read. Rillito was always taking up for the underdog. "But what's he got to do with this?"

"How do I know? I don't even know what *this* is! But I know it was Rillito picked me up. That shows there's something mighty big in the wind. He ain't mixin' in no little games. Why, he ruled a government in South America till the ol' party come back in power an' booted him out."

Ruled a government! South America! It had been a South American government that Jord Valle got his concessions from. Rillito's government? Jord Valle had been a soldier of fortune, too, when he was young, made friends in strange places, made friends with Rillito, who had granted the concessions — for money

261

to run his country on maybe — but had been exiled. Parable and the rest were in on it. It all fit, but — Rillito — the man Rose hadn't the right to name. The man who sang! He'd come back to right the wrong he'd done Jord Valle. Just what a man like him would do. But just the same . . . "Rillito has nothing to do with me. You'll get your money!" Starr assured Quayle.

Quayle curled his lip. "How you goin' to pay it?"

"With a check," cried Starr, taking his first step in the plan he'd made up there. "I'm givin' you a check on the Zuñi National, dated next Friday . . . the day my I.O.U. is due. When the time comes, I'll have the money there to meet it."

"More hocus-pocus! A brand on a hat! Now a rubber check!"

"The money's not there now," admitted Starr honestly, "but it will be when it's due. That's all that need concern you. When I give you a check, and get the money in the bank to meet it on the day it's dated, I'll have done my part."

Quayle had no faith in the check, still less in his surviving to cash it. But he had an iron-ribbed faith in the fate to be meted out to him, as defined by old Parable, a fate the Cañada winds seemed to knell, howling like a banshee outside. The consuming desire of his cowardly soul was how to escape from this place — if escape were possible. "How you aimin' to get out of here?" he challenged Starr. "With a guard at the door?"

"When the time comes, I'll have help. My horse will be waitin' . . . saddled . . . at the creek."

Inside help! Escape *was* possible! A mountain rolled from Quayle. Fiercely he vowed: "If you go, I go!"

"Not with me," Starr vetoed coldly. "Neither of us would get away. We'd both be caught . . . shot maybe. And there's only one horse."

"Just a kind-hearted pal," sneered Quayle. "Just one horse, so you take it, an' leave me here!"

Hotly Starr's eyes flashed over the table. "Don't call *me* pal. I don't want anything to do with you, Quayle, but to pay what I owe. And" — his gray eyes burned on Quayle's hard ones — "to know where you are in case you've done something to Lane. I'm not satisfied with what you've told me about him. You've done something," grimly Starr accused him, "or they wouldn't have brought you here."

"How about yourself?" Quayle flashed. "They brought you, didn't they? What did *you* do?"

Plenty Starr knew. He'd gone ramming into that Chuckaluck courtyard, telling these men that he was out to get Donovan's murderer — a man they'd die to protect. If he hadn't been Lane's brother, he might have been shot, but he didn't tell Quayle that.

"No use in the pot callin' the kettle black," growled Quayle ingratiatingly. "We're both in a hole. It don't put me in any deeper, if you get out. But you ain't said how you're workin' that miracle."

"You'll know, anyhow, when I go." Fatally Starr pointed to that log in the back wall of the cabin. "It's loose. I can move it far enough to squirm through . . . where it spans the window."

"What's to prevent my squirmin' through after you?"

"I'll block it from the outside, when I go," was the even reply. "You won't be able to loosen it again before the men know I'm gone. Then you won't have a chance. But" — confident in his estimate of the man, an estimate formed back in the hut, where Quayle had inferred he'd see an innocent man hung for the reward — "you'll let me go an' keep quiet about it, for my gettin' safely away means money in your pocket."

But Quayle was sure he'd never collect that check. This was just a slick trick to keep him quiet in here while Starr Hallet crawled out of this prison and put the bars up again, leaving him to be slaughtered by Rillito's cut-throat gang! His hard eyes flashed a murderous gleam. One of them could leave this cabin. There was a horse for one, but that one would *not* be Starr Hallet. At the same time, it dawned on his heated brain that he needn't lose out all around. He had a good idea where Lane Hallet could be found. Rillito was sure he would come to Chuckaluck. Santone was waiting there to help him up. He knew where Santone stopped — at that house with the court where they'd had breakfast on the way in. He'd go to Chuckaluck, watch Santone, nab Lane Hallet, and collect *that* thousand. "I'll play your game," he said in a tone of sullen submission, shifting his eyes, lest they betray him. "When are you goin'?"

Stepping to the window, Starr looked out. Every cabin was dark. Only the gleaming tip of a cigarette showed that the most dangerous guard in Lost Cañada was on duty.

"Now," Starr said quietly, turning away from the window.

"Not till you write that check!" snarled Quayle with devilish cunning.

It was so characteristic of the greedy nature he'd shown when bargaining over Lane's senseless form, it would have dispelled Starr's last suspicion had he possessed one. All unsuspecting, he got out his checkbook, tore a blank from it, dug a stub of a pencil from his pocket, and, dropping on the bench at the table, filled in the date — four days from the morrow. He never noticed that Quayle had slipped behind him, breathing like a man after a hard run, until, the amount filled in, he was dropping his hand to sign it. Warned by a sudden movement behind, a shadow on the table, he jerked up, and met a blow that crushed all living consciousness from him. Utter and black oblivion submerged him.

CHAPTER
SEVENTEEN

"A Cry in the Night"

Dropping the chair that had been his weapon, Quayle leaped forward, caught Starr's body as it slid from the bench, and eased it carefully to the floor. Shaking like a leaf, great beads of perspiration rolling down his face, Quayle listened for any indication that the crash had carried beyond those walls. The only sound was the wind — the dirge-like wind.

Stretching forth a trembling hand, he picked up the old sombrero with its flashing *conchas* and glaring black brands. Casting his own hat aside, he put it on, congratulating himself that he had made a fair double for Starr Hallet on a dark night, and that this night was dark. Hallet had said he'd have help. Someone was waiting at the creek with the yellow horse. He wouldn't be recognized until he got the horse in his hands. If anyone tried to stop him after that, it would be their own hard luck. His gaze encountered the unsigned check that had fluttered to the floor. Savagely he ground it into the planks with his heel. He'd let Hallet trick him out of a thousand with this hat. No more fool plays like that. He'd turn Lane Hallet in, and collect from the state!

266

Cautiously he placed a chair under the high window in back, got up, and pushed the log out. Having been moved once, the log slipped easily and quietly, for the first move had dispelled all clogging dirt and bark. Without a backward glance at the crumpled figure lying so still in the light of the guttering candle, Quayle drew himself through the opening and dropped to the ground.

Crouching there, he listened again, then started on, skirting wide of the cabin and circling toward the creek where the horse would be waiting. Once on its back, he'd be safe. But he must go mighty slowly until he was on him. Moving carefully, he reached the creek and looked up and down. No horse was visible. *Probably being held farther upstream, where there would be less danger of arousing the men,* he thought, and headed that way, keeping to the brush, parting it ahead of him, stopping every few yards to look and listen, the wind rasping on his frayed nerves like a file.

It wasn't a strong wind. It didn't blow him back, or take his breath, or tear at his hat, or whip the leaves about, but it sounded like the voice of demons as it circled him with the awful howl. It frayed his nerves to breaking, as it followed him far upstream, where there was yet no sign of the horse waiting. He decided to try the other side then.

Reaching an opening in the twisted trees that bore so little resemblance to their species elsewhere, Quayle saw that the creek here widened out and foamed over a bed of boulders. He crossed, carefully testing each slippery rock ere trusting his weight to it. A sound

267

jerked him up, just as he was climbing out on the other bank. It was a step! A step right near! Motionless in the brush, he listened, but all was still. A rabbit likely. Or a bird startled up. Reassured, he started on.

Slipping along the high brink, where it overhung a deep pool formed by the dam of the rocks he'd crossed on, Quayle suddenly came face to face with a dead man. A ghastly figure, staring eyes fixed on the hat Quayle wore, its bony hands reached out toward him. "I've been looking for you!" The voice seemed to come from a tomb. "Time! You must give me . . ."

Quayle's nerves snapped like rotten threads at the strain. This awful apparition was between him and freedom. Quayle sprang.

Below the riffles where he had crossed, below the cabins in the fringing cottonwoods, Rose Valle — holding Pancho, saddled and ready — heard a strange cry, a cry that, whipped around by the swirling wind, seemed to come from no place in particular but to rebound from the granite rims and become forevermore a part of the wild wail. Frozen with nameless horror, she listened for some repetition of the sound, but none came. Sounds of running feet came nearer. A body crashed the brush toward her. She saw the old sombrero! Starr! She ran to meet him with Pancho, frantic lest Starr had been discovered, lest Kid had seen him leave the cabin and tried to stop him. Not until he plunged up to her, snatched the reins without a word of greeting, did she see that the distorted face beneath the sombrero was not Starr's, but that of the prisoner — Quayle!

Wildly, then, she jerked back the reins he was grabbing from her, screaming in a way to rouse every man in Lost Cañada. Still screaming, she clung to them, although he tried to tear them from her grip. Had she known what he'd just done up there, what he was leaving the cañon to do, she could not have made a braver fight. Supporting her in it, over her own cries, over Quayle's curses, she heard the slamming of doors, shouts, pounding footsteps.

Quayle, too, heard them. Still unable to wrest the lunging horse from the girl's grasp, he struck for the third and last time this night. As he bent over her fallen form to unclasp her fingers and take the reins from them, he saw that it was too late. Those steps and shouts had crossed the creek! If he got on that horse, he'd be stopped by a bullet!

In a frenzy of terror, he dodged into the cottonwoods, fleeing blindly he knew not where, except that it was away from the corridor where the search would center. Striking off for the black, frowning rims, he plucked courage from the thought that no one had seen him and that he could find his way over those walls and work back to civilization.

But he overlooked one factor. Kid! That keen-eyed, cold-faced stripling of Lost Cañada had been far in advance of the other men, and he saw the end of the struggle, saw the man in the old sombrero strike down the girl Kid so hopelessly worshiped. Thinking it was Starr Hallet, who he hated with a jealous hatred, feeling the urge to kill as he had never felt it, he followed Quayle's progress through the brush, sighted him in the rocks, and took up the trail. With dogged tenacity he followed over the walls, through the wild maze of cañons and ridges beyond, on and on, to the inevitable and frightful end.

CHAPTER
EIGHTEEN

"Right in my Hands!"

One! Two! Three! Four! The last day was torn from the calendar that had numbered all of them to Starr, the day when the debt marked on the old sombrero was due, a debt that was sacred to a Hallet and to be paid even at the cost of life itself. Would that last brand be canceled, as every other one had been? The set of this day's sun would tell, the set of this day's sun, now but an hour beyond the rising.

Brightly its rays shone on the jagged, blue-misted heights of the wild Confusions, so peaceful, so serene in their eternal, brooding calm. Impossible to believe they held anything less tranquil than the lazy stir of birds, the soft pad of furry paws, the ceaseless whisper in the serried ranks of pine. Impossible to believe that up there in a cañon — so lost in those wild peaks that few even believed in its existence — one man lay cold and still in death, that another man wandered in the welter of cañons, starving, exhausted, desperate, lost to reason — a man who had fled in terror from a shadow that had dogged his tracks four days and nights.

Far up in these tangled ridges such a thing was not credible. Yet here traveled one who had been told that the Confusions held the essence of these things. He traveled in a ramshackle buckboard, drawn by a ragged team of flea-bitten mustangs, and, as he lumbered over the rough trail, this one — an old Mexican, dressed in a long coat and slouch hat, as disreputable as his conveyance — kept a nervous and apprehensive watch. Constantly he urged the mustangs on toward those deceptively serene blue heights.

Leg-weary those horses were. Many and many a mile they had come, by trails far from human habitation. Swinging wide of the town of Chuckaluck, they followed an uncharted course through the foothills, and circled back to this trail, which he had been assured led to Lost Cañada. Pausing to rest the sweating team before the steep slope ahead, his quick ears caught the ring of hoofs behind, and, casting terrified eyes back, he saw, riding rapidly up the trail, a fierce-looking, little old fellow in frayed buckskin with long yellow-white hair that gleamed in the sun, and a stocky, grizzled man whose features were lost beneath the broad brim of his Stetson but on whose cowhide vest flashed the symbol of that far-reaching, all-powerful force — the law!

With despair heavy and cold as ice on his heart, the old man pulled his hat lower over his face, and hunched deeply into his collar, expecting a challenge, and wondering desperately how to meet it.

"¡Buenos dias!" greeted the officer, as they trotted by on the trail. "You're travelin' high, my friend."

"The good pine does not grow low, señor," rejoined the Mexican courteously, for all his fear.

272

"When I go to Glory," the big one said to his companion with a backward glance at the buckboard, "I'll find a Mexican hunting wood. Go where you will, there's always one ahead. But he comes far for the little he can carry in the buckboard."

Floating back on the clear morning air came the voice of the little one with the yellowish hair: "Knowed a feller . . ." Then they passed a bend out of sight and hearing.

Yet the Mexican sat like one turned to stone. There was an upheaval in the buckboard box behind, as the old tarpaulin, half filling it, was thrown back with an impatient hand, and a face raised from it — a boyish face, wasted and worn by suffering, but revealing the more markedly for this something willful, headlong, tameless.

"A close call, Florencio!" he said with a laugh.

Close! The old man shuddered. That one could make a joke when death brushed past him. But a gleam of pride and love, almost paternal, broke the frozen surface of his dark face, thawing his terror. He turned on the seat, fiercely scolding.

"*¡Madre Dios!* I told you we should not come! I told you we should go to my people who would keep you safe! But, no! You must come to this end-of-the-earth place . . . a journey that would tax the well. And you . . . not far past death's door. Even though there were no roads, you must come. We will make a road, you say? Well, we meet the very man I would hide you from going to your cañon! Now" — tightening rein — "we turn back to a hiding of my choosing!"

Determinedly he was swinging the team, but the boy stopped him, crying as determinedly: "We're goin' on!"

"On?" shrilled Florencio. "On . . . when that man is at the trail's end? Has that bullet got into your bloodstream and gone to your brain? Is it possible you do not know who passed us? I had one glimpse of him in the hut that night. And I tell you, that big fellow was Sheriff Garret!"

"Don't I know it?" cried Lane Hallet. "An' that isn't all. The other was old Parable. One of the men I told you about. Remember the old codger who goes all around Robin Hood's barn to tell you things?"

"A cañon man?" Florencio looked at him with puzzled eyes. "What does he do with the sheriff?"

"That's what we got to find out," Lane told him. "Something's wrong. Parable went clear to Lasco for him, and why is he takin' him to the cañon? This ain't even Garret's county. I don't savvy it. I told you we should have come through Chuckaluck and got a line on things."

"It was not safe," Florencio insisted again. "In town this outfit would draw notice."

"Well," the boy's mouth set willfully, "we've got to find out. There's only one thing to do . . . go back and see what's happened up there. Go to Santone's house. Bound to be somebody there who can tell . . ."

"Take you to Chuckaluck?" Florencio interrupted. "Ten thousand nos!"

"Leave me here! Dump me off anywhere! I'll wait, while you go back."

274

"Leave a sick man in this wild spot?" Florencio called on all his saints to witness that he would never do this. "A man who hasn't lifted a hand for himself . . . ?"

"I haven't had a chance to!" protested the boy wildly. "I could if I had to! Haven't I stood the trip you said would kill me? Got fat on it, too! It won't hurt me to lay over here. I know just the spot . . . where we always lay over when we come up. It's off the trail, and nobody passing can see. Whip up, Florencio! I'll tell you when to swing off. You can leave the outfit, and ride one of the horses back. Make the round trip by dark. Then we'll know what we're doing, and we won't be going it blind."

Conquered by that imperious spirit, as he always was, the old man drove on to the blue notch of a lofty summit, turning at Lane's direction off the trail to a grove of aspens scattered about a mountain spring — the very spot where the men had laid over when they brought Starr up. Pulling up beside the very log where Starr and Rose had had their talk, where her tears for Lane had dimmed that picture he carried of her and where he'd first seen, first thrilled to see, the beautiful, living reality, Florencio threw down the lines and, dropping the canvas out, lifted the boy to the ground.

While Lane watched impatiently, Florencio stretched the tarpaulin from the buckboard to the nearest tree, forming a shelter in which he piled the blankets that had cushioned the boy's long ride over the bumpy trail, anxiously protesting against leaving him the while and

275

giving him a hundred instructions on how to conduct himself in his absence.

"You must not stir!" That was the frequent injunction, delivered in a tone of prayer. "You get hungry, mebbe? Fine!" He set a covered basket on the grass. "Here is grouse and biscuit from breakfast right at hand. You want to drink? I fill this bucket and set it in the cool of the wagon. And so you will feel safe, I leave my gun, here on the wheel. Now, you do not stir, and anger that bullet in your side . . . which may be fatal!"

"If coddlin' can't kill me, nothin' will!" flashed the boy petulantly. Then instantly penitent, he caught the old man's hand in both his own. "Don't think I don't appreciate it, Florencio! I do! It's just that I never been bossed before. It doesn't come natural. I forget I'm not my own boss no more. But I'll never forget I wouldn't be here, if it wasn't for you. Now . . . go on! I'll be careful."

Comforted by this promise, Florencio dragged a saddle from under the buckboard seat, unhitched the horses, tied one to the wheel opposite the shelter, and saddled the other. Having done everything he could think of to insure the boy's comfort and safety, he reluctantly rode off on his arduous errand, armed with directions for finding Santone's house and a password that would let him in.

Lane watched him out of sight, his eyes dimmed with tears of real affection. He'd learned something of the faithfulness of Florencio's kind since the night when he had ridden into the Sandflow. Valiantly the old man had stood between Quayle and him the whole week in the dugout. On the morning that Quayle turned up missing and they knew he'd gone to fulfill his oft-repeated threat to get Sheriff Garret, old Florencio had carried Lane away from that place in his arms and hidden him in the dunes while he went to borrow this old rig from some Mexican friends who had then offered to take him in with them. But he'd persuaded Florencio to bring him to Lost Cañada, telling him only how secret it was and that he had friends there. Florencio had brought him all the way from the Sandflow, through many a call almost as close as that of a moment ago. If his own father had lived — his father, whose friend Florencio had been — he couldn't have done more for him, nor his own brother, Starr.

Lying there, alone in his shelter, Lane Hallet thought with tightening heart of his brother, wondered where he was and if he'd gone back to the Sandflow. This was the day that the debt was due on the old sombrero. What would Starr do about that? Would he feel duty bound to hunt up Quayle and pay it? Where would he get the money to do it? Maybe the debt didn't really exist now that Quayle had gone back on his bargain, but Starr wouldn't know that. And the brand was on the old hat! Lane — didn't want that mark on it! *His* mark — the mark of murder! He didn't care what the world thought of him, but he didn't want the old hat to go on for all time bearing that brand.

Looking up at the patch of blue sky, through the dancing leaves overhead, he wondered where the trail of that sorrel had led Starr. As far as Chuckaluck, he knew. Tex had told them that, when he brought the medicine out the night before they skipped. Tex said Chuckaluck thought Starr was Lane. The whole town had gone after him, but he'd gotten away, and nobody had heard of him since. Had the sorrel finally taken him to Lost Cañada? If so, what had happened up there?

Oh, why hadn't he told Starr everything? Made him see why he had to take the blame? Everything would have been all right, if he hadn't left the cañon! He had been so sure that he could get the hat. Too sure of himself — that's what he'd been! He couldn't let them hang Rose's poor, locoed father just because Lane had gone against everybody's advice and gotten into trouble. Rose! The thought of her went to his head like mescal, rather as at first wild love goes to the head of any young fellow! If Starr *was* in Lost Cañada, he'd have met Rose.

"There's nothin' I'd like better," the boy whispered. "I want Starr to know her. I want Rose to know my brother."

Wildly he wondered what was wrong in the cañon. Almighty wrong, or Parable wouldn't be taking the sheriff in! Could it be something connected with Starr? It seemed he couldn't wait till Florencio got back, wait the hours it would take to complete the trip! They couldn't go much farther in this old rattletrap. He had lied to Florencio when he told him they could make a road in.

"Could," — he grinned — "with a few ton of dynamite, an' a couple of years to do it in."

He hadn't dared tell Florencio that, or he'd never have come. They'd go as far as they could . . . He didn't know what they'd do then. Ride, if he could stick on. He grinned again in anticipation of the howl the old man would raise at that, but he'd show him! He could walk, if he had to! No reason why he had to stay flat the rest of his life, just because he had a bullet in him! Lots of men had bullets in them. Bullets didn't hurt. He didn't want to die with Tom Garret's sinker, but he didn't mind living with it.

Eager to see if his strength were equal to the ordeal before him, Lane crawled from shelter, and lay for a spell, telling himself it was just the altitude made his heart gallop like that. Painfully turning over, he tried to rise. He got to his knees, but everything began to swim and turn black, forcing him back. He must not give up. He had to climb on a horse soon! Reaching out to hook his hands about the trunk of an aspen, he slowly pulled himself to his feet, and, leaning back against the trunk, legs wobbling, black eyes triumphant, hands tightly gripping the bark to hold himself up, he boasted — "Made it!" — and bragged to the flea-bitten old mustang: "Florencio would raise Cain, but he'd be glad I made it. An' I'll make it there, all right! I'll see her! An' maybe I'll see . . ."

Catching the snap of a twig to the left of the horse, Lane turned that way. His galloping heart almost leaped out of his body as he saw, coming through the trees there — black brands and all — the old sombrero!

"Starr!" he cried joyously.

Then his eyes dropped from the hat to the face beneath it, widening in horror. Slowly, strength fading from him, his half-fainting form slipped down the trunk to the ground in the path of Quayle!

Bloody and torn from his blind flight through those wild ridges, terror glittered in Quayle's bloodshot eyes, terror of the shadow he'd fled from, although he'd shaken that shadow. Not once had he seen it today. And now he knew where he was! This campsite . . . He could find his way back!

His terror blazed into the horrible exultation that had shocked the Texan at the hut as he saw Lane Hallet! He didn't wonder how it came about. He didn't care! Greed alone survived in his disordered brain. And the blue notch rang to his greedy raving.

"Right in my hands! A thousand bucks!"

He sprang toward that aspen, as if the helpless form at the foot of it were a roll that he could pocket!

CHAPTER
NINETEEN

"Out of the Picture"

But, even as he sprang, the buckboard came within the range of his wandering vision and some gleam of sanity pierced his frenzied brain. A two-horse rig! One horse gone! The old Mexican had brought the kid here and rode off somewhere. Fearfully he glanced up the notch and down. There was no sign of Florencio. Nothing to stop him now! But the old man might come back any time and flash that knife on him. He must get the kid out of here — quick! Drawn by a sun glint on the wheel, his red eyes fell on the gun there, and he lunged for it. Nothing turned a blade like a bullet. Even a shadow wasn't immune to that.

Gun in hand, he lurched drunkenly up to Lane. "Get on that horse!" was his thick-tongued order.

In wide-eyed horror Lane stared up at him, realizing that he was in the hands of a madman.

"Get on that horse!" Quayle flourished the gun toward the mustang, raving with a daft laugh: "Pelts is scarce! I don't even have to hunt for this one! They don't want their *pet* mutilated none, but I ain't lissenin' to them!"

"Who?" Desperately the boy sought to distract him. "Who ain't you listenin' to?"

"Them cañon men. They picked me up, an' dropped me into that pit . . . where dead men walk." He quaked at the thought. "But I got out of it. The wind couldn't howl me back. I got out, but it sent a shadow."

Lost Cañada! Lane knew then that Rillito's men had gone to the dugout for him, found Quayle, taken him to the cañon, and now he'd escaped from them. What else had happened up there? In naked fear his black eyes flashed to the old sombrero.

"Where did you get Starr's hat?"

A demented gleam in Quayle's hard eyes was his only answer.

"Quayle," Lane started, "is Starr in there?"

"Get up! Rustle!"

But the boy didn't stir. He'd tried his strength, knew the size of it. He might make it to the cañon, would die to get there. But he'd rather die here than on the road back — just so Quayle could collect.

"I'm takin' you to Lasco to turn you in! For the last time, get up!"

"Are you crazy? You know I'd never live to get there."

Terrible the laugh that answered. "Dead or alive! Either way you're worth as much!"

Game to the core, the boy flashed back: "Then you'll take me dead, Quayle!"

Quayle raised the gun, but, as it rose, there was a movement in the trees over the buckboard before him. Glancing there, he saw the shadow he'd fled from. With a start of horror, he jerked the gun that way just as

Kid's hand flashed up, his gun crashing flame and smoke. Quayle staggered back, the old hat toppling to the ground, rolling to rest in the dead leaves of autumn. Slowly, grotesquely Quayle pitched face down, still clutching the gun he'd raised too late. His fingers, curved on the trigger, tensed in his last convulsive shudder. The gun roared. Then all was still.

Lying there, a horrified witness, Lane Hallet saw Kid go up to Quayle, kneel, and turn him over. Amazement overspread his cold features, amazement that he turned on Lane. "It's Quayle!" he said.

Lane nodded.

"The old hat . . ." Kid seemed stunned. "It fooled me. I thought that . . ."

"Kid, what happened?"

Slowly Kid got up. "They left me to watch him. He got away. I followed him four days. He went in circles, and I lost the trail a dozen times, but I couldn't give up. I had to get him . . . give him what he got. But I thought it was your brother. The old hat . . ."

"You thought it was Starr?" Then Starr was up there! "Why would you shoot Starr?"

"He . . . Quayle," corrected Kid tonelessly, "I thought it was Starr. The old hat fooled me. He hit . . . her!"

Quayle had hit Rose! "Was she hurt?" cried Lane.

Kid didn't know.

"Kid, is Starr all right?"

Kid didn't know that, either. "He was locked in with this one. I couldn't wait to find out anything. I took his trail."

What was the matter with Kid? He'd always been so straight to the point before. Now he stood picking at the bark on the tree, staring at the ground, hardly knowing what he was saying. Was it the shock of killing a man? No. Kid was always cool in a jam.

"Your brother . . . Starr . . . ," Kid said slowly, "he's sweet on her. And she . . . she tried to help him get away. She was holdin' his horse. But this one" — with a backward nod at the motionless form — "got away wearin' that hat. I don't savvy it."

Neither did Lane. Only that Starr had got to the cañon, met Rose Valle, and . . . "Kid," he broke in on the thought he couldn't stand yet, "why did Parable take the sheriff in?"

Kid turned a blank face on him.

"He just passed up an hour ago on the trail. What happened up there?"

But Kid didn't know. He could answer some of Lane's questions. He had taken up Quayle's trail, thinking he was Starr, and knew nothing of what had transpired in the cañon. He didn't seem to care. He wasn't so much like one who had no feeling, as one in whom all capacity for feeling had been burned out. Slowly his head turned. "I ain't goin' back," he told Lane. "When I leave you, it's . . . so long. I'm cuttin' my string. Your brother an' her . . . I can't stand to see them together. The way they look at each other . . . Lots of men have looked at her. *You* did. I didn't mind that. But she never looked at a man before. She's lookin' at him. An' I . . . I'm fadin'."

Coldly, unemotionally as he had followed that trail, had shot Quayle, Kid of Lost Cañada turned and strode out of the notch and forever out of the lives of those who had known him, leaving Lane alone with the dead man. Lane didn't mind that. He hardly knew it, hardly saw the prostrate figure with the dappling shadow and sun playing over it, or the old hat he had all but died to get back, lying beside it. Lots of men had looked at her. *He* had. But she — she was looking at Starr! He wished that bullet *would* have gone to his brain so he could fade out of the picture.

He hardly heard horses storming into the notch, Big Steve's paint and a yellow horse with a lithe young rider. But in an instant more the boy was sobbing for pain and joy in the arms of his brother!

CHAPTER
TWENTY

"Farewell"

Up the rocky gorge in the Confusions' wild heart, old
Parable led the Lasco sheriff. Up, up, till Tom Garret
thought he was going to Glory sure enough! Up to the
blue granite wall, through that hidden rift, down a
narrow, twining corridor, and, unexpectedly, out in
a wild, eerie cañon whose soaring pinnacles — garishly
blue in the blaze of noon — twisted growth, lashing
mad stream, cabins on the buckling ground, and the
many-windowed edifice, topping the hill at the end,
filled his heart with high apprehension. It was a feeling
that had grown on him ever since this queer old-timer
had burst into his office, babbling some wild
hodge-podge that he couldn't make head or tail of,
excepting that something mighty serious was afoot,
affecting half the people in the state, and he'd be
everlastingly sorry if he didn't come along and attend
to it.

So he'd come, night and day, unable to get anything
out of his guide on the way, except more crazy talk
about "fellers" he'd known here, there, and the other
place, till Garret's head was whirling, and every so
often the old man would swing around and spring

another one. All of which seemed to have some bearing on the case, but blessed if he could make any more out of them than he had of the first one. About a farmer in Arkansas — that one had been — who, hearing a commotion one night in his pigpen and the squeals of his prize shoat being carried away, rushed out, yelling — "Sick 'em!" — to his two dogs. And the greyhound — "fer as everyone knows a greyhoun' can't smell to no account" — took after the first thing in sight — the shadow of an owl flying over, and chased it till the moon went down, leaving him nothing to run! *But* the old foxhound — "an' everybody knows that breed runs by scent alone" — sniffed around till he got the trail, and nosed that shoat to the den of a painter. Garret got the impression he was the greyhound, chasing a shadow — or maybe the shoat. He wasn't sure which. He'd been a bull moose in the Selkirks, a blind mole in the Panhandle. Nervously looking at those cabins down there, he had a strong hunch he might be the goat, or maybe a lamb led to the slaughter. Risky business for a sheriff, letting himself be tolled away up here. He was hitching his holster where his gun would be handier, when the old fellow suddenly wheeled his horse around, and he knew by the signs he was about to bust out with another one.

But he was mistaken. Rack his brain as he did, Parable found nothing to fit this situation, and was forced to come flat out with it. "My advice is, Sheriff, to stick strickly to the business at hand. You're here to see certain things. Other times you'd best be blind."

Well, Garret wasn't one to poke his nose in what didn't concern him. Besides, he had no jurisdiction here. He didn't think anyone had, but the Almighty. He'd lived in these parts all his life and never even heard of such a community. He told Parable as much. The old man swung along the creek, leading the lawman down that zigzag trail past the cabins in the cottonwoods, and up the slope to the big house on the hill. Every blind was drawn, but grouped before it were several solemn-faced, wild-looking men, who made themselves scarce when the pair reined in.

Sticking strictly to the business at hand, Garret got down, and followed Parable up to the front door. That same nameless awe that had slowed Starr's step the night he'd come to see what was going on here filled Garret's being — an awe, sealed by the way Parable removed his hat before entering. It was not just the mannerliness with which one enters a home, but a ceremonious solemnity, as when the flag goes by, or before an altar. Taking off his Stetson in the same hushed manner, Garret went in.

After the fierce brilliance of the sun, it was a moment ere he could see anything, but he had an impression of a dark, soldierly figure, rising at his entrance and vanishing through a rear door. Surmising that this was one of the things he wasn't supposed to see, he looked no more. Gradually objects emerged through the gloom. He saw a big, bare room and at the far end on a dais of some kind stood a coffin — rudely made, from hand-sawed slabs of piñon. At the head of the coffin, looking up at him with touching appeal, her vividness undimmed by her pallor, or the simple dark dress she wore, stood the girl he'd seen make a championship ride at the Lasco Rodeo last summer, Rose of Lost Cañada, a girl who had haunted his mind because it was on that night that Pat had been shot. Pat had been with him that day at the track, and Pat had kept saying that she reminded him of someone, but couldn't figure who it had been. One always remembered the last words of a friend.

Parable raised a blind and motioned the sheriff toward the coffin. Slowly approaching, steeling himself for the shock he sensed coming, Garret looked down at the still face of Jord Valle. Jord Valle, in the sleep he'd prayed for. Sleep eternal.

Through his stunned wonder at finding in this unheard-of spot the man he'd hunted as assiduously as he had hunted Lane Hallet, the sheriff's trained eye was noticing things. That fleshless face. It looked like Valle had been sick a long time and suffered much before the passing. Frowningly he observed a blue-black bruise on the dead man's temple, then stooped to see it better.

"It wa'n't that," declared Parable, sticking to fact, as he must do even in the dead presence of his old friend. "Jord died . . . natural. Two full days after that blow was struck by a mangy coyote you'll hear more about. It might 'a' had somethin' to do with it . . . the straw that broke the camel's back . . . but what killed Jord was worry over the money folks lost in his banks. Fer months he lived only to pay it back. An' . . . you may not know it, but thar's money to pay everything but twenty thousand . . ."

"To pay all," quietly corrected the girl. "There's money now, Parable, to pay all." As he stared at her, speechless, she went to a corner desk, picked up a folded document, and, coming back, placed it in his hands. "It's a life-insurance policy," she said steadily, "for twenty thousand dollars . . . making enough to pay every depositor." She turned to Sheriff Garret. "It will go to the receivers as soon as we . . . tell Dad . . . good bye," she said tremulously.

"Are you takin' him down?" he asked, all sympathy.

She shook her head. Her blue eyes turned back to that peaceful face. She was desolate with grief for her father, but comforted by the thought that his suffering was over. "No," she said, "he'll rest better here. It's what he wanted. We're waiting for a friend who's been sent for. We wanted you to see Dad before we lay him to rest in Lost Cañada."

As by common consent, the two men moved toward the door, but paused there.

"That ain't all we brought you for," said Parable, and he told Sheriff Garret the true story of the Donovan murder. How Jord Valle, deranged by his trouble, had killed Pat Donovan. How Lane Hallet, his daughter's friend, had taken the blame. A greyhound, after all, chasing a shadow! He learned how Starr Hallet, a member of his own posse, had found his brother and hidden him on the roof.

290

"So that's how it was." Garret's brown cheek was stained by a blush. "Knew there was something funny somewhere."

Then Parable told how Starr had bartered for Lane's life with Quayle, and then, in following the sorrel's trail, had been eventually led to the solution up here. The foxhound that had found the painter — Jord Valle! All clear as day! Crazy — that talk? It had been sound all the way. But the old man had been flattering him. He hadn't been a greyhound. He'd been a loon.

"It's been the strangest situation I ever had to deal with," said the sheriff. "I believe it, of course, with three eyewitnesses . . . You'll all have to come in when it's handy, an' make a report, but it's just a matter of form. An' now," he told them, "when all business is disposed of here, I'll try to get hold of that fellow Quayle. I don't know just what he's guilty of. Murder, maybe. Assault and battery, anyway."

He left to find on the way down that, no matter what Quayle's crime had been, he'd paid the penalty for it. He assured the Hallet boys, who he met on their way back to the cañon, that he'd lost all professional interest in them.

Just as the sun hung on the western rim, Starr rode in with Lane. Steve remained at the notch till men could come from the cañon to take Quayle's body to Chuckaluck, and to guide Florencio up. The boy just made it, and that was all. Exhausted by the ordeal, he was taken immediately to his cabin, Parable looking after him, while Starr went up to tell Rose and Rillito what had happened.

When he left, she went out with him to where the trail dropped over the bluff, to look down toward the corridor for the friend they were waiting for.

"Dad would want him here of all people," she told Starr. "He loved him better than anyone . . . not excepting Rillito. Even Rillito hasn't done more for him. He gave Dad everything he owned in an effort to save the banks, and, though it seemed lost, he has never uttered a word of complaint. Dad's last wish was that he handle his affairs." Her eyes rose to Starr's, happy through all their tears. "Thank God," she said quiveringly, "the cloud lifted before he went. He knew the last dollar would be paid, and died happy knowing it."

Starr understood how she felt. He looked away — down the corridor. Two riders had appeared there. Santone and another man — the friend Rose was expecting. Something about him seemed vaguely familiar, but Starr gave it no thought then.

"Tell Lane," Rose said, as Starr turned to the trail, "I'll be down to see him later."

But Starr didn't tell Lane that when he got back, for the boy was asleep. Sitting beside him, he heard horses going by, but he didn't even raise his eyes to see who Santone had brought. Heavier things were on his heart. The drift of hopes and fears had stopped, but he was in the Sandflow yet — a dead waste, barren, sterile! Lane loved Rose Valle. And she — she had told him there was no one like Lane. He was glad! Her love would steady the boy. But it would be hard — going back to Zuñi Creek. Oh, the bank would pay out. He might get the old ranch back. But — he'd died once — when he learned he loved the girl beloved by his brother. He'd die again — when he left her.

Painfully he recalled every moment they'd spent together, even the ones when they fought each other — that had made him love her the more. Recalled, with shame intolerable, the thoughts he'd had of her before they met. He'd told her about that the morning after Quayle had knocked him out — before Jord Valle died of shock, before he'd left to hunt Quayle, and reclaim the old hat. She'd laughed at his idea of her being a Lorelei on a rock, combing her hair!

Rising, he went to the window, and looked up at the bluff. Men were carrying all that was earthly of Jord Valle out of the house. He watched the sad procession slowly move up to a knoll, where, under a twisted piñon, they were to lay Rose's father to rest in this cañon that had been his refuge. His heart was wrung at sight of her, on the arm of a man who looked from here startlingly familiar! And turning, he dropped back in the chair beside his brother.

A sound drifted in, mingling with the mourning wind, a deep, rich, musical tone, meltingly tender, with a note of farewell, a sound that brought tears to the eyes of Starr. That struck into Lane's deep slumber like a signal call! He jerked up, listening.

If I should die and o'er oceans foam,
Softly a white dove on a fair eve should come,

293

Open thy lattice, dearest, for it will be
My faithful soul that, yearning, flies back
to thee . . .

"It's Rillito," Starr said huskily, "tellin' Jord Valle good bye."

CHAPTER
TWENTY-ONE

"The Last Brand"

They were silent long after the last sad note died away. They'd had hours of talk this afternoon. Lane knew all that had happened to Starr. Starr knew all that had happened to Lane, but not one word had been spoken yet of the matter lying so heavy on each heart.

"Rillito," Lane said finally, "is one grand *hombre*."

"He sure is," Starr endorsed warmly. "I got to know him a little. Not as much as I'd like to. He sure thinks a lot of you."

The boy flushed with pleasure.

"How did you come to meet him, Lane?"

"Through Rose." Lane's eyes were eager. "He trusted me right off, Starr. He don't trust many people, but he let me come up here."

"I can't get the rest of the men just straight," said Starr. "How did they get in with Rillito?"

"Through Valle mostly. They took Kid in like they did me. But the rest have known Rillito a long time. He's been coming up here for years to see Jord Valle. Him and Valle were real pals . . . bummed all over the world together when they were young. These men were

295

in that South American deal, an' got exiled with Rillito, when he lost out down there."

"I can't see Parable in South America," said Starr with a smile.

"He's the exception." Lane grinned. "But he's known Rillito since the year one. And when they needed a place to hide, he brought them to this cañon, which he found years ago, prospecting. He built these cabins then. Was working a stringer. But it didn't pan out, and he forgot all about the place, till they needed it."

Silence fell again. Both men shrank from talking of the person nearest their hearts. The sun's last crimson was staining the rims. Its glow, coming in the western window, enveloped Starr, sitting there with something so hopeless in his face that Lane seized hard on his courage, and gamely struck out toward that topic.

"What are you going to do now, Starr? Go back to Zuñi Creek?"

"I reckon." Starr took hold of his courage, too, sensing it coming.

"Would you care," the boy asked slowly, "if I didn't go back?"

"Sure not, Lane," he said, prepared for it.

"Because," Lane said, punishing the pillow already doubled into a hard knot under his head, "Rillito's going back to South America. The shootin's over down there. He's been talking to me about going. And I thought, if you don't mind, I'd trail along."

Well, Lane's life was his own. But what was this? Did it mean he was taking Rose to South America?

"I'd hate to have you so far away," said Starr, "but if . . ."

"Oh, I'm not staying," Lane struck in. "I'll never want to stay away from you long again. I had a lot of things shot into me besides lead, Starr. When I get over . . . when I get this trip out of my system, I'm comin' home and stick to you like a burr! Nobody'll ever mean even half as much to me as my brother."

In the joy of that, Starr could bear the hurt. "You'll change your mind when you're married, Lane," he managed lightly.

"When I'm . . . *what?*" The boy jerked up.

"When" — every word scraped, Starr's throat was so dry — "when you're married to Rose Valle."

Prepared for that — having fought his battle — Lane's boyish laugh couldn't ring truer. The pain it cost, Starr never knew. "Where'd you ever get that idea?" The boy laughed carelessly. "Why she . . . she wouldn't look at me! A girl like her . . . ? Gee, I wouldn't have the nerve to even think of her, Starr, as anything but a . . . a sister."

Starr could only stare into the black eyes meeting his own unflinchingly. He was still staring, when the door opened, and a man came in. Rose Valle's friend! *His* friend! For Starr was looking into the grave, sun-bronzed face of the Texan!

"I might have known it was you, Tex!" cried Starr, wringing his hand. "Lane's told me what you did for him . . . packing out medicine, giving that dugout all the comforts of a hospital. I might have known you were the man Rose meant, after she told me what he had done for her father."

Smilingly Tex disparaged this. "It was nothing to speak of. Just some worthless Pecos River land, and a few mangy cattle. I'll get it back. Jord Valle died, as he lived . . . square with the world."

But Starr knew that the land hadn't been worthless, or the cattle few. He knew how far Tex must have dropped to punch cows for the Loop Loop. His eyes admiringly followed the man, bending now over Lane. "How's the sinker, boy?"

"Still holding me down." Lane grinned. "But I wouldn't part with it on a bet. It sort of . . . balances me right."

Tex laughed. But looking into that young face, which had so roused his interest that first night, with its imperious spirit reminding him of a high-bred colt with a loco streak that no handling could break, Tex saw it had changed. The spirit was still there, unbroken still, but strengthened, disciplined by the rough handling he had undergone. And he thought — as he'd thought, when he'd watched Starr Hallet ride away from the dugout — of a shaft of sand with the horseshoe on top. Lane Hallet was like that. The horseshoe that would anchor him firmly in every storm was that "sinker" he'd thought he had no need for!

᛫ Barring further talk or thought, Rose came then. And with her, Rillito, and all the men who hadn't seen Lane. Starr went out, dazedly trying to adjust his thoughts to what Lane had told him. Lane loved Rose like a sister! And in the light of this, Starr couldn't remember a thing to indicate that Rose had any feeling for his brother, other than the love she'd naturally have for anyone who had done what Lane had done for her.

Later he was standing by the creek, where he'd talked to Rose that afternoon under Kid's eager gun, when old Parable stepped up beside him. The old fellow seemed to want to say something, but couldn't get it out.

"Thar's times," Parable finally said diffidently, "when a *hombre* has to take desperate measures. Like when a man's in the quicksand. He sinks deeper an' deeper, grabbin' at everything he sees. Mebbe draggin' somebody in to sink with him. *But*" — with pleading emphasis — "that feller would hate like sin to have any hard feelin's . . . say they got out again."

Starr knew he was apologizing for what they'd done to him, and held out his hand. "No hard feelings, Parable."

Vastly relieved, and normal again, he began: "Knowed a feller . . . ," but a light footfall halted him, and he backed away. Rose stood where he had been.

Starr looked at her, realizing that he had a right to love her, to fight for her love — like any man. Something in her blue eyes, then, gave him the delirious hope — rightly, as was proved at no distant day — he would not lose.

Her eyes were on Starr's, but her thoughts were on the old sombrero in his hands, the silver *conchas* catching and holding the twilight's last gleam, as if it knew its day in the sun was almost over, that soon it would be laid away again, to gather dust, become a legend. "I was thinking, Starr," Rose said seriously, "of your I.O.U. I'm sorry about that. You'll never feel just right with an uncanceled brand on the old hat."

A strange expression came over Starr's face. "I've been waiting to tell you about it, Rose. You know how Quayle was holding a gun on Lane, when Kid shot him? Well" — his voice dropped and an awed note crept into it — "when he fell, his gun went off, and the bullet" — he lifted the hat — "went here."

No need to point to it — that jagged hole the bullet, fired by Quayle's dying hand, had burned through the high crown, completely obliterating that Q2000 — the last debt recorded on the old sombrero of many brands.

About the Author

Cherry Wilson enjoyed a successful career as a writer of Western stories for pulp magazines for twenty years, beginning in the mid 1920s. She was born in Pennsylvania, and moved with her family to the Pacific Northwest when she was sixteen. Having had some experience writing for newspapers, when her husband became ill, she was forced to earn a living by writing Western fiction. Over the course of her career she published over two hundred short stories, short novels, and serials. Five serials were published as hardcover novels, and six of her stories were brought to the screen. The majority of her work appeared in the highest paying of the Street & Smith publications, *Western Story Magazine*. Her stories were well regarded by both readers and editors, and quite often her work was singled out in letters to the editor, along with Max Brand's, as being some of the best to appear in *Western Story Magazine*. Her novels include *Stormy* (Chelsea House, 1929) filmed as *Stormy* (Universal, 1935) with Noah Beery, Jr., and Jean Rogers and *Empty Saddles* (Chelsea House, 1929) filmed as *Empty Saddles* (Universal, 1936) with Buck Jones and

Louise Brooks. *Thunder Brakes*, also published in 1929 by Chelsea House, the book publishing division of Street & Smith, was reprinted in 1997 in a hard cover edition in the Gunsmoke series from Chivers Press. However, much of her work has not been read in many years, having appeared originally only in magazines. A good example is "Ghost Town Trail" from *Western Story Magazine* (10/25/30) that has been collected in *The Morrow Anthology of Great Western Stories* (Morrow, 1997) edited by Jon Tuska and Vicki Piekarski. *Triangle Z Ranch* will be her next **Five Star Western**.